PRAISE FOR HENNING MANKELL

"Henning Mankell is an addictive writer."
—Los Angeles Times Book Review

"There's no one better. . . . His characters are his greatest invention." *—San Francisco Chronicle*

"Elegant and artful. . . . [Mankell] continues to understand, and probe, the underside of everyday living."
—The Washington Post

"Mankell's atmospherics . . . give you metaphysical goose bumps." *—Boston Herald*

"Mankell uses all his stories to address the most urgent problems of civilization." *—Newsday*

Henning Mankell

ITALIAN SHOES

Internationally bestselling novelist and playwright Henning
Mankell has received the German Tolerance Prize and the
U.K.'s Golden Dagger Award and has been nominated for
a Los Angeles Times Book Prize three times. His Kurt
Wallander mysteries have been published in thirty-three
countries and consistently top the bestseller lists in Europe.
He divides his time between Sweden and Maputo,
Mozambique, where he has worked as the director of Teatro
Avenida since 1985.

www.henningmankell.com

ITALIAN SHOES

Henning Mankell

TRANSLATED FROM THE SWEDISH BY
LAURIE THOMPSON

VINTAGE BOOKS
A Division of Random House, Inc.
New York

FIRST VINTAGE BOOKS EDITION, OCTOBER 2010

English translation copyright © 2009 by Laurie Thompson

Library of Congress Cataloging-in-Publication Data
Mankell, Henning, 1948–
[Italienska skor. English]
Italian shoes / by Henning Mankell ; translated from the Swedish by Laurie Thompson.
—1st Vintage Books ed.
p. cm.
ISBN 978-0-307-47224-3
1. Recluses—Fiction. 2. Surgeons—Malpractice—Fiction. 3. Psychological fiction.
I. Thompson, Laurie, 1938– II. Title.
PT9876.23.A49I8313 2010
839.73'74—dc22
2010022389

www.vintagebooks.com

Printed in the United States of America
10 9 8 7 6 5 4 3 2 1

When the shoe fits, you don't think about the foot.

Chuang Chou

There are two sorts of truth: trivialities, where the opposite is obviously impossible, and deep truths, which are characterised by their opposite also being a deep truth.

Niels Bohr

Love is a gentle hand which slowly pushes fate to one side.

Sigfrid Siwertz

CONTENTS

ICE

CHAPTER 1

I always feel more lonely when it's cold.

The cold outside my window reminds me of the cold emanating from my own body. I'm being attacked from two directions. But I'm constantly resisting. That's why I cut a hole in the ice every morning. If anyone were to stand with a telescope on the ice in the frozen bay and saw what I was doing, he would think that I was crazy and was about to arrange my own death. A naked man in the freezing cold, with an axe in his hand, opening up a hole in the ice?

I suppose, really, that I hope there will be somebody out there one of these days, a black shadow against all the white – somebody who sees me and wonders if he'd be able to stop me before it was too late. But it's not necessary to stop me because I have no intention of committing suicide.

Earlier in my life, in connection with the big catastrophe, my fury and despair were sometimes so overwhelming that I did consider doing away with myself. But I never actually tried. Cowardice has been a faithful companion throughout my life. Like now, I thought then that life is all about never losing your grip. Life is a flimsy branch over an abyss. I'm hanging on to it for as long as I have the strength. Eventually I shall fall, like everybody else, and I don't know what will lie in store. Is there somebody down there to catch me? Or will there be nothing but cold, harsh blackness rushing towards me?

The ice is here to stay.

It's a hard winter this year, at the beginning of the new millennium. This morning, when I woke up in the December darkness, I thought I could hear the ice singing. I don't know where I've got the idea from that ice can sing. Perhaps my grandfather, who was born here on this little island, told me about it when I was a small boy.

But I was woken up this morning, while it was still dark, by a sound.

It wasn't the cat or the dog. I have two pets who sleep more soundly than I do. My cat is old and stiff, and my dog is stone deaf in his right ear and can't hear much in his left. I can creep past him without him knowing.

But that noise?

I tried to get my bearings in the darkness. It was some time before I realised that it must be the ice moving, although it's a foot or more deep here in the bay. Last week, one day when I was more troubled than usual, I walked out towards the edge of the ice, where it meets the open sea, now stretching for a mile beyond the outermost skerry. That means that the ice here in the bay ought not to have been moving at all. But, in fact, it was rising and falling, creaking and singing.

I listened to this sound, and it occurred to me that my life has passed very fast. Now I'm here. A man aged sixty-six, financially independent, burdened with a memory that plagues me constantly. I grew up in desperate circumstances that are impossible to imagine nowadays in Sweden. My father was a browbeaten and overweight waiter, and my mother spent all her time trying to make ends meet. I succeeded in clambering out of that pit of poverty. As a child, I used to play out here in the archipelago every summer, and had no concept of time passing. In those days my grandfather and grandmother were still active, they hadn't yet aged to a point where they were unable to move and merely waited for death. He smelled of fish, and she had no teeth left. Although she was always kind to me, there was something frightening about her smile, the way her mouth opened to reveal a black hole.

It seems not so long ago since I was in the first act. Now the epilogue has already started.

The ice was singing out there in the darkness, and I wondered if I was about to suffer a heart attack. I got up and took my blood pressure. There was nothing wrong with me, the reading was 155/90, my pulse was normal at 64 beats per minute. I felt to see if I had a pain anywhere. My left leg ached slightly, but it always does and it's not something I worry about. But the sound of the ice out there was influencing my mood. Like an eerie choir made up of strange voices. I sat down in the kitchen and waited for dawn. The timbers of the cottage were creaking and squeaking. Either the cold was causing the timber to contract, or perhaps a mouse was scurrying along one of its secret passages.

*   *   *

4

The thermometer attached to the outside of the kitchen window indicated minus nineteen degrees Celsius.

I decide that today I shall do exactly what I do every other winter day. I put on my dressing gown, thrust my feet into a pair of cut-down wellington boots, collect my axe and walk down to the jetty. It doesn't take long to open up my hole in the ice – the area I usually chip away hasn't had time to freeze hard again. Then I undress and jump into the slushy water. It hurts, but when I clamber out, it feels as if the cold has been transformed into intensive heat.

Every day I jump down into my black hole in order to get the feeling that I'm still alive. Afterwards, it's as if my loneliness slowly fades away. One day, perhaps, I shall die of the shock from plunging into freezing cold water. As my feet reach the bottom I can stand up in the water; I shan't disappear under the ice. I shall remain standing there as the ice quickly freezes up again. That's where Jansson, the man who delivers post to the islands in the archipelago, will find me.

No matter how long he lives, he will never understand what happened.

But I don't worry about that. I've arranged my home out here on the little island I inherited as an impregnable fortress. When I climb the hill behind my house, I can see directly out to sea. There's nothing there but tiny islands and rocks, their low backs just about visible over the surface of the water, or the ice. If I look in the other direction, I can see the more substantial and less inhospitable islands of the inner archipelago. But nowhere is there any other dwelling to be seen.

Needless to say, this isn't how I'd envisaged it.

This house was going to be my summer cottage. Not my final redoubt. Every morning, when I've cut my hole in the ice or lowered myself down into the warm waters of summer, I am again amazed by what has happened to my life.

I made a mistake. And I refused to accept the consequences. If I'd known then what I know now, what would I have done? I'm not sure. But I know I wouldn't have needed to spend my life out here like a prisoner, on a deserted island at the edge of the open sea.

I should have followed my plan.

I made up my mind to become a doctor on my fifteenth birthday.

To my amazement my father had taken me out for a meal. He worked as a waiter, but in a stubborn attempt to preserve his dignity he worked only during the day, never in the evening. If he was instructed to work evenings, he would resign. I can still recall my mother's tears when he came home and announced that he had resigned again. But now, out of the blue, he was going to take me to a restaurant for a meal. I had heard my parents quarrelling about whether or not I should be given this 'present', and it ended with my mother locking herself away in the bedroom. That was normal when something went against her wishes. Those were especially difficult periods when she spent most of her time locked away in the bedroom. The room always smelled of lavender and tears. I always slept on the kitchen sofa, and my father would sigh deeply as he made his bed on a mattress on the floor.

In my life I have come across many people who weep. During my years as a doctor, I frequently met people who were dying, and others who had been forced to accept that a loved one was dying. But their tears never emitted a perfume reminiscent of my mother's. On the way to the restaurant, my father explained to me that she was oversensitive. I still can't recall what my response was. What could I say? My earliest memories are of my mother crying hour after hour lamenting the shortage of money, the poverty that undermined our lives. My father didn't seem to hear her weeping. If she was in a good mood when he came home, all was well. If she was in bed, surrounded by the scent of lavender, that was also good. My father used to devote his evenings to sorting out his large collection of tin soldiers, and reconstructing famous battles. Before I fell asleep, he would often lie down beside me on my bed, stroke my head, and express his regret at the fact that my mother was so sensitive that, unfortunately, it was not possible to present me with any brothers or sisters.

I grew up in a no-man's-land between tears and tin soldiers. And with a father who insisted that, as with an opera singer, a waiter required decent shoes if he was to be able to do his job properly.

It turned out in accordance with his wish. We went to the restaurant. A waiter came to take our order. My father asked all kinds of complicated and detailed questions about the veal he eventually ordered. I had plumped for herring. My summers spent in the archipelago had taught me to appreciate fish. The waiter left us in peace.

This was the first time I had ever drunk a glass of wine. I was intoxicated almost with the first sip. After the meal, my father smiled and asked me what career I intended to take up.

I didn't know. He'd invested a lot of money enabling me to stay on at school. The depressing atmosphere and shabbily dressed teachers patrolling the evil-smelling corridors had not inspired me to think about the future. It was a matter of surviving from day to day, preferably avoiding being exposed as one of those who hadn't done their homework, and not collecting a black mark. Each day was always very pressing, and it was impossible to envisage a horizon beyond the end of term. Even today, I can't remember a single occasion when I spoke to my classmates about the future.

'You're fifteen now,' my father said. 'It's time for you to think about what you're going to do in life. Are you interested in the culinary trade? When you've passed your exams you could earn enough washing dishes to fund a passage to America. It's a good idea to see the world. Just make sure that you have a decent pair of shoes.'

'I don't want to be a waiter.'

I was very firm about that. I wasn't sure if my father was disappointed or relieved. He took a sip of wine, stroked his nose, then asked if I had any definite plans for my life.

'No.'

'But you must have had a thought or two. What's your favourite subject?'

'Music.'

'Can you sing? That would be news to me.'

'No, I can't sing.'

'Have you learned to play an instrument, without my knowing?'

'No.'

'Then why do you like music best?'

'Because Ramberg, the music teacher, pays no attention to me.'

'What do you mean by that?'

'He's only interested in pupils who can sing. He doesn't even know the rest of us are there.'

'So your favourite subject is the one that you don't really attend, is that it?'

'Chemistry's good as well.'

My father was obviously surprised by this. For a brief moment he seemed to be searching through his memory for his own inadequate schooldays, and wondering if there had even been a subject called chemistry. As I looked at him, he seemed bewitched. He was transformed before my very eyes. Until now the only things about him that had changed over the years were his clothes, his shoes and the colour of his hair (which had become greyer and greyer). But now something unexpected was happening. He seemed to be afflicted by a sort of helplessness that I'd never noticed before. Although he'd often sat on the edge of my bed or swum with me out here in the bay, he was always distant. Now, when he was exhibiting his helplessness, he seemed to come much closer to me. I was stronger than the man sitting opposite me, on the other side of the white tablecloth, in a restaurant where an ensemble was playing music that nobody listened to, where cigarette smoke mixed with pungent perfumes, and the wine was ebbing away from his glass.

That was when I made up my mind what I would say. That was the very moment at which I discovered, or perhaps devised, my future. My father fixed me with his greyish-blue eyes. He seemed to have recovered from the feeling of helplessness that had overcome him. But I had seen it; and would never forget it.

'You say you think that chemistry is good. Why?'

'Because I'm going to be a doctor. So you have to know a bit about chemical substances. I want to do operations.'

He looked at me with obvious disgust.

'You mean you want to cut people up?'

'Yes.'

'But you can't be a doctor unless you stay on at school longer.'

'That's what I intend doing.'

'So that you can poke your fingers around people's insides?'

'I want to be a surgeon.'

I'd never thought about the possibility of becoming a doctor. I didn't faint at the sight of blood, or when I had an injection; but I'd never thought about life in hospital wards and operating theatres. As we walked home that April evening, my father a bit tipsy and me a fifteen-year-old suffering from his first taste of wine, I realised that I hadn't only answered my father's questions. I'd given myself something to live up to.

I was going to become a doctor. I was going to spend my life cutting into people's bodies.

CHAPTER 2

There was no post today.

There was no post yesterday either. But Jansson, the postman, does come to my island. He doesn't bring me junk mail. I've forbidden him to do so. Twelve years ago I told him not to bother making the journey if he was only bringing junk mail. I was tired of all the special offers on computers and knuckles of pork. I told him I didn't need it – people who were trying to control my life by pestering me with special offers. Life is not about cut prices, I tried to explain to him. Life is basically about something more important. I don't know what exactly but, nevertheless, one must *believe* that it is important, and that the hidden meaning is something more substantial than discount coupons and scratch cards.

We quarrelled. It was not the last time. I sometimes think it is our anger that binds us together. But he never came with junk mail after that. The last time he had a letter for me, it was a communication from the local council. That was over seven years ago, an autumn day with a fresh gale blowing from the north-east, and low tide. The letter informed me that I had been allocated a plot in the cemetery. Jansson claimed that all local residents had received a similar letter. It was a new service: all tax-paying residents should know the location of their eventual grave, in case they wished to go to the cemetery and find out who they would have as neighbours.

It was the only real letter I have received in the last twelve years, apart from dreary pension documents, tax forms and bank statements. Jansson always appears at around two in the afternoon. I suspect he has to come out this far in order to be able to claim full travel expenses from the Post Office for his boat or his hydrocopter. I've tried to ask him about that, but he never answers. It could even be that I'm the one who makes it practical for him to continue as postman. That the authorities would have cancelled deliveries altogether but for the fact that he heaves to at my jetty three times a week in the winter months, and five times a week in the summer.

Fifteen years ago there were about fifty permanent residents out here in the archipelago. There was a boat ferrying four youngsters to and from the village school. This year there are only seven of us left, and only one is under the age of sixty. That's Jansson. As the youngest, he is dependent on the rest of us keeping going, and insisting on living out here on the remote islands. Otherwise there'll be no job for him.

But that's irrelevant to me. I don't like Jansson. He's one of the most difficult patients I've ever had. He belongs to a group of extremely recalcitrant hypochondriacs. On one occasion a few years ago, when I'd examined his throat and checked his blood pressure, he suddenly said he thought he had a brain tumour that was affecting his eyesight. I said I didn't have time to listen to his imaginings. But he insisted. Something was happening inside his brain. I asked him why he thought that. Did he have headaches? Did he have dizzy spells? Any other symptoms? He didn't give up until I'd dragged him into the boathouse, where it was darker, and shone my special torch into his pupils, and told him that everything seemed to be normal.

I'm convinced that Jansson is basically as sound as a bell. His father is ninety-seven and lives in a care home, but his mind is clear. Jansson and his father fell out in 1970, and then Jansson stopped helping his father to fish for eels and went to work at a sawmill in Småland instead. I've never understood why he chose a sawmill. Naturally, I can understand his failing to put up with his tyrannical father any longer. But a sawmill? I really have no idea. However, since that trouble in 1970, they've not spoken to each other. Jansson didn't return from Småland until his father was so old that he'd been taken into a home.

Jansson has an older sister called Linnea who lives on the mainland. She was married and used to run a cafe in the summer – but then her husband died. He collapsed on the hill down to the Co-op, whereupon she closed the cafe and found Jesus. She acts as messenger between father and son.

Jansson's mother died many years ago. I met her once. She was already on her way into the shadows of senility, and was convinced I was her father, who had died in the 1920s. It was a horrible experience.

I wouldn't have reacted so strongly now, but I was different in those days.

I don't really know anything more about Jansson, apart from the fact that his first name is Ture and he's a postman. I don't know him, and he doesn't know me. But whenever he sails round the headland, I'm generally standing on the jetty, waiting for him. I stand there wondering why, but I know I'll never get an answer.

It's like waiting for God, or for Godot; but instead, it's Jansson who comes.

I sit down at the kitchen table and open the logbook I've been keeping for the past twelve years. I have nothing to say, and there's nobody who might one day be interested in anything I write. But I write even so. Every day, all the year round, just a few lines. About the weather, the number of birds in the trees outside my window, my health. Nothing else. If I want, I can look up a particular date ten years ago and establish that there was a blue tit or an oystercatcher on the jetty when I went down there to wait for Jansson.

I keep a diary of a life that has lost its way.

The morning had passed.

It was time to pull my fur hat down over my ears, venture out into the bitter cold, stand on the jetty and wait for the arrival of Jansson. He must be frozen stiff in his hydrocopter when the weather's as cold as this. I sometimes think I can detect a whiff of strong drink when he clambers on to the jetty. I don't blame him.

When I stood up from the kitchen table, the animals came to life. The cat was the first to the door, the dog a long way behind. I let them out, put on an old, moth-eaten fur coat that belonged to my grandfather, wrapped a scarf round my neck and reached for the thick fur hat with earflaps that dated back to military service during the Second World War. Then I set off for the jetty. It really was extremely cold. There was still not a sound to be heard. No birds, not even Jansson's hydrocopter.

I could just picture him. He always looked as if he were driving an old-fashioned tram in the days when the driver had to stand outside at the mercy of the elements. His winter clothes were almost beyond description. Coats, overcoats, the ragged remains of a fur coat, even an old dressing gown, layer upon layer, on days as cold as this. I would ask him why he didn't buy one of those special winter overalls I'd seen in a shop on the mainland. He'd say he didn't trust them. The real reason was that he was too mean. He wore a fur hat similar to mine. His face was covered by a balaclava that made him look like a bank robber, and he wore an old pair of motorcycle goggles.

I often asked him if it wasn't the Post Office's responsibility to equip him with warm winter clothing. He mumbled something incomprehensible. Jansson wanted as little to do with the Post Office as possible, despite the fact that they were his employers.

There was a seagull frozen into the ice next to the jetty. Its wings were folded, its stiff legs sticking up straight out of the ice. Its eyes were like two glittering crystals. I released it and laid it on a stone on the shore. As I did so, I heard the sound of the hydrocopter's engine. I didn't need to check my watch, Jansson was on time. His previous stop would have been at Vesselsö. An old lady by the name of Asta Karolina Åkerblom lives there. She is eighty-eight years of age, has severe pains in her arms, but stubbornly refuses to move away from the island on which she was born. Jansson tells me her eyesight is poor, but even so she still knits jumpers and socks for her many grandchildren scattered all over the country. I wondered what the jumpers looked like. Is it really possible to knit and follow various patterns if one is half blind?

The hydrocopter came into view as it rounded the headland reaching out towards Lindsholmen. It is a remarkable sight as the insect-like vessel approaches and you can make out the muffled-up man at the wheel. Jansson switched off the engine, the big propeller fell silent, and he glided in towards the jetty, pulling off his goggles and balaclava. His face was red and sweaty.

'I've got toothache,' he said as he hauled himself up on to the jetty with considerable difficulty.

'What am I supposed to do about that?'

'You're a doctor, aren't you?'

'I'm not a dentist.'

The pain is down here to the left.'

Jansson opened his mouth wide, as if he'd just caught sight of something horrific behind my back. My own teeth are in relatively good shape. I don't normally need to visit the dentist more than once a year.

'I can't do anything. You need to see a dentist.'

'You could take a look at least.'

Jansson was not going to give up. I went into the boathouse and fetched a torch and a spatula.

'Open your mouth!'

'It is open.'

'Open wider.'

'I can't.'

'I can't see a thing. Turn your face this way!'

I shone the torch into Jansson's mouth, and poked his tongue out of the way. His teeth were yellow and covered in tartar. He had a lot of fillings. But his gums seemed healthy, and I couldn't see any holes.

'I can't see anything wrong.'

'But it hurts.'

'You'll have to go to a dentist. Take a painkiller!'

'I've run out.'

I produced a pack of painkillers from my medicine chest. He put it in his pocket. As usual, it never occurred to him to ask what he owed me. Neither for the consultation nor the painkillers. He takes my generosity for granted. That's probably why I dislike him. It's not easy when your closest friend is somebody you dislike.

'I've got a parcel for you. It's a present from the Post Office.'

'Since when have they started giving away presents?'

'It's a Christmas present. Everybody's getting a parcel from the Post Office.'

'Why?'

'I don't know.'

'I don't want it.'

Jansson dug down into one of his sacks and handed over a thin little packet. A label wished me *A Merry Christmas from the Chief Executive Officer of the Post Office.*

'It's free. Throw it away if you don't want it.'

'You're not going to convince me that anybody gets anything free from the Post Office.'

'I'm not trying to convince you of anything at all. Everybody gets the same parcel. And it's free.'

Jansson's intractability sometimes gets the better of me. I didn't have the strength to stand in the bitter cold and argue with him. I ripped open the parcel. It contained two reflectors and a message: *Be careful on the roads! Christmas greetings from the Post Office.*

'What the hell do I need reflectors for? There are no cars here, and I'm the only pedestrian.'

'One of these days you might get fed up with living out here. Then you might find a couple of reflectors useful. Can you give me a glass of water? I need to take a tablet.'

I have never allowed Jansson to set foot in my house, and I had no intention of doing do now.

'I'll give you a mug and you can melt some snow by placing it next to the engine.'

I went back into the boathouse and found the cap of an old Thermos flask that doubled as a mug, filled it with snow and handed it over. Jansson added one of his tablets. While the snow melted next to the hot engine, we stood and waited in silence. He emptied the mug.

'I'll be back on Friday. Then it's the Christmas holidays.'

'I know.'

'How are you going to celebrate Christmas?'

'I'm not going to celebrate Christmas.'

Jansson gestured towards my red house. I was afraid that all the clothes he was wearing might make him fall over, like a defeated knight wearing armour that was far too heavy for him.

'You ought to hang some fairy lights around your house. It would liven things up.'

'No thank you. I prefer it to be dark.'

'Why can't you make your surroundings a bit more pleasant?'

'This is exactly how I want it.'

I turned my back on him and started walking up the slope towards the house. I threw the reflectors into the snow. As I reached the wood-shed, I heard the roar as the hydrocopter engine sprang into life. It sounded like an animal in extreme pain. The dog was sitting on the steps, waiting for me. He could think himself lucky that he's deaf. The cat was lurking around the apple tree, eyeing the waxwings pecking at the bacon rind I'd hung up.

* * *

I sometimes miss not having anybody to talk to. Banter with Jansson can't really be called conversation. Just gossip. Local gossip. He goes on about things I have no interest in. He asks me to diagnose his imagined illnesses. My jetty and boathouse have become a sort of private clinic for just him. Over the years I have transferred into the boathouse – in among the old fishing nets and other equipment – blood pressure cuffs and instruments for removing earwax. My stethoscope hangs from a wooden hook together with a decoy eider my grandfather made a very long time ago. I have a special drawer in which I keep medicines that Jansson might well need. The bench on the jetty, where my grandfather used to sit and smoke his pipe after gutting the flounders he'd caught, is now used as an examination couch when Jansson needs to lie down. As blizzards raged, I have kneaded his abdomen when he suspected he had stomach cancer, and I have examined his legs when he was convinced he was suffering from some insidious muscle problem. I have often thought about the fact that my hands, once used in complicated operations, are now used exclusively to frisk Jansson's enviably healthy body.

But conversation? No.

Every day I examine my own boat which has been beached. It's now three years since I took it out of the water in order to make it seaworthy again. But I never got round to it. It's a splendid old clinker-built wooden boat that is now being destroyed by a combination of weather and neglect. That shouldn't be allowed to happen. This spring I shall get down to sorting it out.

But I wonder if I really will.

I went back indoors and returned to my jigsaw puzzle. The theme is one of Rembrandt's paintings, *Night Watch*. I won it a long time ago in a raffle organised by the hospital in Luleå in the far north of Sweden, where I was a newly appointed surgeon who concealed his insecurity behind a large dose of self-satisfaction. As the painting is dark, the puzzle is very difficult to solve; I only managed to place one single piece today. I prepared the evening meal and listened to the radio as I ate. The thermometer was now showing minus twenty-one degrees. The sky was cloudless, and the forecast was that it would become even colder before dawn. It looked as if records for low temperatures were about to be broken. Had it ever been as cold as this here? During one of the war years, perhaps? I decided to ask Jansson about that – he usually knows about such things.

Something was nagging at me.

I tried lying down on the bed and reading. A book about how the potato came to Sweden. I had read it several times before. Presumably because it didn't raise any questions. I could turn page after page and know that I wasn't going to be faced with something unpleasant and unexpected. I switched off the light at midnight. My two animals had already gone to sleep. The wooden walls crackled and creaked.

I tried to come to a decision. Should I continue to man the defences of my island fortress? Or should I accept defeat, and try to make something of the life that was left to me?

I could not decide. I stared out into the darkness, and suspected that my life would continue as it had done hitherto. There would be no significant change.

It was the winter solstice. The longest night and the shortest day. Looking back, it would become clear to me that it had a significance I had never suspected.

It had been an ordinary day. It had been very cold, and in the snow around my frozen-in jetty were a couple of reflectors from the Post Office, and a dead seagull.

CHAPTER 3

Christmas came and went. New Year came and went.

On 3 January a snowstorm blew in over the archipelago from the Gulf of Finland. I stood on the hill behind my house, watching the black clouds piling up on the horizon. Almost two feet of snow fell in eleven hours, and I was obliged to climb out of the kitchen window in order to shovel snow away from the front door.

When the snowstorm drifted away, I noted in my logbook: 'Waxwings vanished. The bacon rind deserted. Minus six degrees Celsius.'

Fifty-eight letters and three full stops. Why did I do it?

It was time for me to open up the hole in the ice and take a dip. The wind cut into my body as I trudged down to the jetty. I hacked away the thin covering of ice and stepped into the water. The cold felt like burning.

Just as I had clambered out and was about to return to the house, the wind fell momentarily. Something made me feel afraid and I held my breath. I turned round.

There was somebody standing out on the ice.

A black figure, a silhouette, outlined against all the white. The sun was only just over the horizon. I squinted in the glare, and tried to make out who it was. It was a woman. It looked as if she was leaning on a bicycle. Then I saw that it was in fact a wheeled walker, a Zimmer frame with wheels. I was shuddering with cold. Whoever it was, I couldn't just stand here by my hole in the ice, naked. I hurried up to the house, and wondered if I'd had a vision.

I dressed and walked up the hill with my binoculars.

I hadn't been imagining things.

The woman was still there. Her hands were resting on the handles of the walker. She had a handbag over one arm, and had wrapped a scarf round her fur hat, which was pulled down over her forehead. I had difficulty in making out her face through the binoculars. Where had she come from? Who was she?

I tried to think. Unless she was lost, it must be me she'd come to visit. There is nobody else here but me.

I hoped she had lost her way. I didn't want any visitors.

She was still standing there motionless, her hands on the walker's handles. I began to feel increasingly uncomfortable. There was something familiar about that woman out there on the ice.

How had she managed to make her way over here, through a snowstorm, pushing a Zimmer frame? It was three nautical miles to the mainland. It seemed incredible that she could have walked that far without freezing to death.

I stood watching her through the binoculars for over ten minutes. Just as I was about to put them away, she slowly turned her head and looked in my direction.

It was one of those moments in life when time doesn't merely stand still, it ceases to exist.

The binoculars brought her closer towards me, and I saw that it was Harriet.

Although it was in spring almost forty years ago that I last saw her, I knew it was her. Harriet Hörnfeldt, whom I had loved more than any other woman.

I had been a doctor for a few years, to my waiter father's endless surprise and my mother's almost fanatical pride. I had managed to break out of poverty. I was living in Stockholm then, the spring of 1966 was outstandingly beautiful and the city seemed to be bubbling over with life. Something was happening, my generation had burst through the floodgates, torn open the doors of society and demanded change. Harriet and I used to walk through Stockholm as dusk fell.

Harriet was a few years older than I was, and had never had any ambition to continue her studies. She worked as an assistant in a shoe shop. She said she loved me, and I said I loved her, and every time I went home with her to her little bedsit in Hornsgatan, we made love on a sofa bed that constantly threatened to fall to pieces.

Our love was like a raging fire, it would be fair to say. And yet I let her down. I had been given a scholarship by the Karolinska Institute to do postgraduate work in the USA. On 23 May I would be leaving for Arkansas, and would be away for a year. Or at least, that's what

I told Harriet. In fact, the flight was due to leave for New York via Amsterdam on the 22nd.

I didn't even say goodbye to her. I simply disappeared.

During my year in the USA I made no attempt to contact her. I knew nothing about her life, nor did I want to know. I sometimes woke up out of dreams in which she committed suicide. I had a guilty conscience, but always managed to silence it.

She gradually faded away from my consciousness.

I returned to Sweden and started work at a hospital in the north, in Luleå. Other women entered my life. Sometimes, especially when I was on my own and had drunk too much, I would wonder what had become of her. Then I would call directory enquiries and ask about Harriet Kristina Hörnfeldt. But I always hung up before the operator had tracked her down. I didn't dare to meet Harriet again. I didn't dare to discover what had happened.

Now she was standing out there on the ice, with a wheeled walker.

It was exactly thirty-seven years since I had vanished without explanation. I was sixty-six years old. Which meant she must be sixty-nine, going on seventy. I wanted to run into the house and slam the door shut behind me. And then, when I eventually stepped outside again, she would have gone. She would no longer exist. Whatever it was she wanted, she would have been a mirage. I would have simply not seen her standing out there on the ice.

Minutes passed.

My heart was racing. The bacon rind hanging in the tree outside the window was still deserted. The birds had not yet returned after the storm.

When I raised my binoculars again, I saw that she was lying on her back, her arms outstretched. I dropped the binoculars and rushed down to the ice, falling over several times in the deep snow, to where she lay. I checked that her heart was beating, and when I leaned over close to her face, I could just about feel her breathing.

I wouldn't have the strength to carry her to the house. I fetched the wheelbarrow from behind the boathouse. I was drenched in sweat by the time I had eased her into the barrow. She hadn't been as heavy as that in the days when we were close. Or was it me who no longer had the strength? Harriet lay doubled up in the wheelbarrow, a grotesque figure who had not yet opened her eyes.

When I came to the shore, the wheelbarrow became stuck. I briefly considered pulling her up to the house with the aid of a rope, but I rejected the idea – too undignified. I fetched a spade from the boat-house and cleared the snow from the path. Sweat was dripping off me. All the time I kept checking on Harriet. She was still unconscious. I felt her pulse again. It was fast. I shovelled away for all I was worth.

I eventually succeeded in getting her to the house. The cat was sitting on the bench under the window, and had been watching the whole process. I placed some planks over the steps up to the door, opened it, then ran with the barrow as fast as I could. At the third attempt, I managed to get Harriet and the wheelbarrow into the hall. The dog was lying under the kitchen table, watching. I chased him out, closed the door and lifted Harriet on to the kitchen sofa. I was so sweaty and out of breath that I was forced to sit down and rest before beginning to examine her.

I took her blood pressure. It was low, but not worryingly so. I removed her shoes and felt her feet. They were cold, but not frozen. Nor did her lips suggest that she was dehydrated. Her pulse fell slowly until it was 66 beats per minute.

I was just going to place a cushion under her head when she opened her eyes.

'Your breath smells something awful,' she said.

Those were her first words after all those years. I had found her on the ice, struggled like crazy to get her into my house, and the first thing she said was that I had bad breath. My immediate impulse was to throw her out again. I hadn't invited her, I didn't know what she wanted, but I could feel my guilt rising to the surface. Had she come to call me to account?

I didn't know. But what other reason could there be?

I realised that I was afraid. It was as if I'd been caught in a trap.

CHAPTER 4

Harriet looked slowly round the room.

'Where am I?'

'In my kitchen. I saw you out there on the ice. You'd fallen over. I brought you in here. How are you?'

'I'm fine. But I'm tired.'

'Would you like some water?'

She nodded. I fetched a glass. She shook her head when I made to help, and sat up of her own accord. I observed her face and decided that she hadn't really changed all that much. She had grown older, but not different.

'I must have fainted.'

'Are you in pain? Do you often faint?'

'It happens.'

'What does your doctor say about that?'

'The doctor doesn't say anything, because I haven't asked him.'

'Your blood pressure's normal.'

'I've never had problems with my blood pressure.'

She watched a crow clinging on to the bacon rind outside the window. Then she looked at me, her eyes clear and bright.

'I'd be telling a lie if I said I was sorry to disturb you.'

'You're not disturbing me.'

'Of course I am. I've simply turned up here unannounced. But that doesn't bother me.'

She sat more upright. I could see that she was in fact in pain.

'How did you get here?' I asked.

'Why don't you ask how I found you? I knew about this island, where you spent your summers, and I knew it was off the east coast. It wasn't easy to track you down, but I managed it in the end. I phoned the Post Office, because I realised they must know where somebody called Fredrik Welin lived.'

I began to remember something. Early in the morning I'd dreamed about an earthquake. I'd been surrounded by extremely loud noise, but suddenly everything was silent again. The noise hadn't woken me up, but I'd opened my eyes when silence returned. I must have been awake for a couple of minutes, listening for sounds outside in the darkness.

Everything had been as normal. And I went back to sleep.

I now realised that the noise I'd heard in my dream had been Jansson's hydrocopter. He was the one who had brought her here, and left her on the ice.

'I wanted to arrive early. It was like travelling in an infernal machine. He was very nice. But expensive.'

'What did he charge you?'

'Three hundred for me and two hundred for the walker.'

'But that's scandalous!'

'Is there anybody else out here with a hydrocopter?'

'I'll see to it that you get half of that back.'

She pointed at her glass.

I refilled it with water. The crow had flown away from the bacon rind. I stood up and said I would go and fetch her walker. There were large pools of water all over the floor from my boots. The dog appeared from somewhere behind the house, and accompanied me down to the shore.

I tried to think clearly.

After close to forty years, Harriet had reappeared from the past. The protective wall I'd erected out here on the island had proved to be inadequate. It had been breached by a Trojan Horse in the form of Jansson's hydrocopter. He had rammed his way through the wall – and charged a lot of money for doing so.

I walked out on to the ice.

A north-easterly breeze was blowing. A flight of birds could just be made out in the far distance. The rocks and skerries were all white. It was one of those days characterised by the mysterious stillness one experiences only when the sea has iced over. The sun was low in the sky. The walker was frozen fast in the ice. I carefully worked it loose, then started wheeling it towards land. The dog was limping along behind me. I would soon have to have him put down. Him and the cat. They were both old, and their ancient bodies were causing them a lot of pain.

When we came to the shore, I went to the boathouse and fetched a threadbare blanket that I laid out on Grandfather's bench. I couldn't go back to the house until I'd decided what to do. There was only one possible reason for Harriet being here. She was going to take me to task. After all these years, she wanted to know why I had left her. What could I say? Life had moved on, that was the way things turned out. Bearing in mind what had happened to me, Harriet ought to be grateful that I had vanished out of her life.

It was cold, sitting there on the bench. I was about to get up when I heard noises in the distance. Voices and the sound of engines travel a long way over water and ice. I realised that it was Jansson. There wouldn't be any post today, but he was busy running his illegal taxi service, no doubt. I walked back to the house. The cat was sitting on the steps, waiting to go in. But I shut her out.

Before entering the kitchen, I examined my face in the mirror hanging in the hall. A hollow-eyed, unshaven face. Hair uncombed, lips squeezed together, deep-set eyes. Not exactly pretty. Unlike Harriet, who looked much the same as she had always done, I had changed with the passing years. I flatter myself that I looked pretty good when I was young. I certainly attracted a lot of interest from the girls in those days. Until the events that put an end to my career as a surgeon, I was very particular about what I looked like and how I dressed. It was when I moved out here to the island that deterioration set in. For several years, I removed the three mirrors that had been hanging in the house. I didn't want to see myself. Six months could pass without my going to the mainland for a haircut.

I stroked my hair with my fingers, and went into the kitchen.

The sofa was bare. Harriet wasn't there. The door to the living room was ajar, but the room was empty. The only thing in there was the gigantic anthill. Then I heard the toilet flushing. Harriet returned to the kitchen, and sat down on the sofa again.

Once again, I could see from the way she moved that she was in pain but I couldn't work out where.

She had sat down on the sofa so that the light from the window fell over her face. She seemed to look just the same as she'd done when we used to wander around Stockholm in the spring evenings, when I was planning to flee without taking leave of her. The closer the day came, the more often I would assure her that I loved her. I was afraid that she would see through me, and discover my carefully planned treachery. But she believed me.

She was staring out of the window.

'There's a crow on the lump of meat hanging in your tree.'

'Bacon rind,' I said. 'Not a lump of meat. The small birds vanished when the gale blew up, before it became storm force and brought the blizzard with it. They always hide away when there's a strong wind. I don't know where they go.'

She turned to face me.

'You look terrible. Are you ill?'

'I look like I always look. If you'd come tomorrow afternoon, I'd have been clean-shaven.'

'I don't recognise you.'

'You're the same as ever.'

'Why do you have an anthill in your living room?'

The question was direct, without hesitation.

'If you hadn't opened the door, you wouldn't have seen it.'

'I didn't mean to go snooping around your house. I was looking for the bathroom.'

Harriet transfixed me with her clear eyes.

'I have a question to ask you,' she said. 'Obviously, I ought to have been in touch before coming. But I didn't want to risk you vanishing again.'

'I have nowhere to run away to.'

'Everybody has somewhere. But I want you to be here. I want to talk to you.'

'So I understand.'

'You understand nothing at all. But I need to stay here for a few days, and I have difficulty in walking up and down stairs. May I sleep on this sofa?'

Harriet wasn't going to reproach me. So I was prepared to agree to anything. I told her that of course she could sleep on my sofa, if that's what she wanted. As an alternative I had a collapsible camp bed that

I could set up in the living room. Assuming she had no objection to sleeping in the same room as an anthill. She said she didn't. I fetched the camp bed and erected it as far away from the anthill as possible. In the middle of the room was a table with a white cloth, and next to it was the anthill. It was almost as high as the table. Part of the cloth hanging down over the edge had been swallowed up by the anthill.

I made the bed, and supplied an extra pillow as I remembered that Harriet always liked to have her head comparatively high when she slept.

But not only then.

Also when she made love. I soon learned that she liked to have several pillows underneath the back of her head. Had I ever asked her why that was so important? I couldn't remember.

I laid out the quilt, then looked out through the half-open door. Harriet was watching me. I switched on the two radiators, checked that they were warming up, and went into the kitchen. Harriet seemed to be recovering her strength. But she was hollow-eyed. Her face was constantly on the alert, ready to parry pain that could strike at any moment.

'I'll have a lie-down for a while,' she said, and stood up.

I opened the door for her. I'd closed it again even before she'd lain down. I felt a sudden urge to lock the door and throw the key away. One day Harriet would have been swallowed up by my anthill.

I put on a jacket and went out.

It was a fine day. The gusts of wind were becoming less violent. I listened for Jansson's hydrocopter. Was that a chainsaw I could hear in the distance? Perhaps getting fuel for a fire?

I walked down to the jetty and into the boathouse. A rowing boat was hanging there, suspended from ropes and pulleys, reminiscent of a gigantic fish that had been beached. There was a smell of tar in the boathouse. It was ages since I'd stopped using tar on the boats and fishing equipment out here in the archipelago, but I still have a few tins that I open now and then, just for the smell. It gives me a sense of tranquility – more than anything else is capable of.

I tried to recall the details of our farewell that wasn't a proper farewell, that spring evening thirty-seven years ago. We'd walked over Strömbron Bridge, strolled along the quay at Skeppsbro, and then continued to

Slussen. What had we spoken about? Harriet had talked about her day in the shoe shop. She loved telling me about her customers. She could even turn a pair of galoshes and a tin of shoe polish for old leather boots into an adventure. Memories of events and conversations came back to me. It was as if an archive that had been closed for ever had suddenly been opened up.

I sat on the bench on the jetty for a while before returning to the house. I peeped into the living room. Harriet was asleep, and had curled up like a little child. I felt a lump in my throat. That's how she had always slept. I walked up the hill behind the house and gazed out over the white bay. It felt as if it was only now that I realised what I'd done on that occasion so long ago. I'd never dared to ask myself how Harriet had reacted to what had happened. When had it dawned on her that I would never be coming back? I had extreme difficulty in imagining the pain she must have felt when she knew that I had abandoned her.

When I got back to the house, Harriet had woken up. She was sitting on the kitchen sofa, waiting for me. My ancient cat was lying on her knee.

'Did you get some sleep?' I asked. 'Did the ants leave you in peace?'

'I like the smell of the anthill.'

'If the cat is pestering you we can throw her out.'

'Do you think I look as if I'm being pestered?'

I asked if she was hungry, and began preparing a meal. I had a hare in the freezer that Jansson had shot. But it would take too long to thaw out. Harriet sat on the sofa, watching me. I fried some cutlets and boiled some potatoes. We spoke hardly at all, and I was so nervous that I burned my hand on the frying pan. Why didn't she say anything? Why had she come?

We ate in silence. I cleared the table and made coffee. My grandfather and grandmother always used to boil their coffee grains and water in a saucepan – there was no such thing as filter coffee in those days. I make my coffee like they used to do, and always count to seventeen once it starts boiling. Then it turns out exactly as I like it. I took out a couple of cups, put some cat food in a dish, and sat down on my chair. It was dark outside already. All the time, I was waiting for Harriet to explain why she had come. I asked if she wanted a refill. She slid her cup forward. The dog started scratching at the door. I let him in, gave him some food, then shut him in the hall with the walker.

'Did you ever think we would meet again?'

'I don't know.'

'I asked what you thought.'

'I don't know what I thought.'

'You are just as evasive now as you were in those days.'

She withdrew into herself. She always used to do that when she'd been hurt, I remembered that clearly. I felt an urge to stretch out my hand over the table and touch her. Did she feel an urge to touch me? It was as if nearly forty years of silence had started to bounce back and forth between us. An ant crawled over the tablecloth. Had it come from the anthill in the living room, or had it been unable to find its way back to the nest I suspect was inside the south wall of the house?

I stood up and said I was going to let the dog out. Her face was in shadow. It was a clear, starry night, dead calm. Whenever I see a sky like that, I wish I could write music. I walked down to the jetty again – I'd lost count of the number of times I'd done so already today. The dog ran out on to the ice in the light from the boathouse, and stopped where Harriet had been lying. The situation was unreal. A door had opened into the life I had more or less considered to be over, and the beautiful woman I had once loved but deceived had come back. In those days, when I used to meet her when she'd finished work in the shoe shop in Hamngatan, she used to be wheeling a bicycle. Now she supported herself on a wheeled walker. I felt lost. The dog returned, and we walked up to the house.

I paused at the back and looked in through the kitchen window. Harriet was still sitting at the kitchen table. It was a while before I realised that she was crying. I waited until she'd dried her eyes. Only then did I go in. The dog had to stay in the hall.

'I need some sleep,' said Harriet. 'I'm tired out. I'll tell you tomorrow why I've come.'

She didn't wait for me to respond, but stood up, said goodnight and eyed me briefly up and down. Then she closed the door. I went to the room where I keep my television set, but I didn't switch it on. Meeting

Harriet had tired me out. Naturally, I was afraid of all the accusations I knew would come. What could I say? Nothing.

I fell asleep in the armchair.

It was midnight when I was woken up by a stiff neck. I went to the kitchen and listened outside Harriet's door. Not a sound. And no strip of light under the door. I cleared up in the kitchen, took a loaf and a baguette out of the freezer, let the dog and the cat in, and went to bed. But I couldn't sleep. The door that had shut out everything I thought was in the past was banging; swinging back and forth. It was as if the time we had spent together was using the wind to force its way in.

I put on my dressing gown and went back down to the kitchen. The animals were asleep. It was minus seven degrees outside. Harriet's handbag was on the kitchen sofa. I put it on the table and opened it. It contained a hairbrush and comb, her purse and a pair of gloves, a bunch of keys, a mobile phone and two bottles of medicine. I read the labels; it was clear that they were painkillers and antidepressants. Prescribed by a Dr Arvidsson in Stockholm. I began to feel uneasy, and I continued searching through her handbag. Down at the very bottom was an address book. It was worn and well thumbed, full of telephone numbers. When I looked up the letter 'W', I saw to my surprise that my Stockholm telephone number from the middle of the 1960s was there.

It had not even been crossed out.

Had she kept the address book all those years? I was about to put it back when I noticed a piece of paper tucked into the cover. I unfolded it and read it.

After doing so, I went to stand outside the front door. The dog sat by my side.

I still didn't know why Harriet had come to my island.

But I had found in her handbag a letter informing her that she was seriously ill and did not have much longer to live.

CHAPTER 5

The wind came and went during the night.

I slept badly and lay listening to the gale. Squalls coming from the north-west – I could feel the draught through the wall. That was what I would note down in my logbook the following day. But I wondered if I would record the fact that Harriet had come to visit me.

She was lying on a camp bed directly underneath where I was. Inside my head, I kept going through the letter I'd found in her handbag, time and time again. She had stomach cancer, and it had spread. Cytotoxic drugs had only slowed things down a little, operations were out of the question. She had a hospital appointment with her consultant on 12 February.

I still had enough of the medical practitioner in me to be able to read the writing on the wall. Harriet was going to die. The treatment she had received so far would not cure her, and might not even prolong her life. She was passing into the terminal and palliative phase, to use the medical terms.

No cure, but no unnecessary suffering.

As I lay there in the darkness, the same thought kept coming to me, over and over again: it was Harriet who was going to die, not me. Although it was I who had committed the cardinal sin of deserting her, she was the one afflicted. I don't believe in God. Apart from a short period in the early stages of my training as a doctor, I have barely been affected by religious considerations. I have never had discussions with representatives of the other world. No inner voices urging me to kneel. But now I was lying awake and feeling grateful for not being the one under threat. I barely slept for many hours. I got up twice for a pee and to listen outside Harriet's door. Both she and the ants seemed to be asleep.

I got up at six o'clock.

When I went down to the kitchen, I saw to my surprise that she had already had breakfast. Or at least, she had drunk coffee. She had warmed up the dregs from the previous evening. The dog and the cat were out – she must have let them out. I opened the front door. There had been a light snowfall during the night. Tracks made by the paws of a dog and a cat were visible. And footprints.

Harriet had gone out.

I tried to see through the darkness. Dawn was still a distant prospect. Were any sounds to be heard? The wind came and went in squally gusts. All three sets of tracks led in the same direction: towards the back of the house. I didn't need to look far. There is an old wooden bench in among the apple trees. My grandmother used to sit there. She would knit, straining her short-sighted eyes, or would simply sit with her hands clasped in her lap, listening to the sounds of the sea, which was never silent when not frozen over. But it wasn't my grandmother's ghostly figure sitting there now. Harriet had lit a candle that was standing on the ground, sheltered from the wind by a stone. The dog was lying at her feet. She looked the same as when I had first seen her the previous day: hat pulled over her ears, a scarf wrapped round her face. I sat down next to her on the bench. It was below freezing, but as the overnight wind had faded away, it didn't feel particularly cold.

'It's beautiful here,' she said.

'It's dark. You can't see anything. And you can't even hear the sea, as it's frozen over.'

'I had a dream that the anthill was growing and surrounding my bed.'

'I can move your bed to the kitchen if you'd prefer that.'

The dog stood up and wandered off. It was moving cautiously, as dogs do when they are deaf and hence afraid. I asked Harriet if she'd noticed that the dog was deaf. She hadn't. The cat came flouncing up. She took a good look at us, then withdrew into the darkness. The thought I'd had many times before came to me yet again: nobody understands the way cats behave. Did I understand the way I behaved? Did Harriet understand the way she behaved?

'You're naturally wondering why I've come here,' she said.

The candle flickered without going out.

'It is unexpected.'

'Did you ever think you would see me again? Did you ever want to?'

I didn't answer. When a person has abandoned another without explaining why, there isn't really anything to say. There is no abandonment that can be excused or explained. I had abandoned Harriet. So I said nothing. I merely sat there, watching the dancing candle flame, and waited.

'I haven't come here to put you in the dock. I've come to beg you to keep your promise.'

I understood immediately what she meant.

The forest pool.

Where I went swimming as a child, the summer when I celebrated my tenth birthday, and my father and I paid a visit to the area in the north of Sweden where he was born. I'd promised her a visit to that forest pool when I returned from my year in America. We would go there and swim together in the dark water under the bright night sky. I'd thought of it as a beautiful ceremony – the black water, the light summer sky when it never gets dark, the great northern divers calling in the distance, the pool said by the locals to be bottomless. We would go swimming there, and after that, nothing would ever part us.

'Perhaps you've forgotten the promise you made me?'

'I remember very well what I said.'

'I want you to take me there.'

'It's winter. The pool will be frozen.'

I thought about the hole in the ice that I made every morning. Would I be able to chop away at a frozen forest pool in the far north of Sweden? Where the ice is as hard as granite?

'I want to see the pool. Even if it is covered in snow and ice. So that I know it's true.'

'It is true. The pool exists.'

'You never said what it's called.'

'It's too small to have a name. This country is full of small lakes without names. There's hardly a single city street or country lane without a name, but lakes and pools without names are plentiful in the forests.'

'I want you to keep your promise.'

She stood up with difficulty. The candle fell over and went out with a fizzing noise. It was completely dark all around us. The light from the kitchen window didn't reach this far. Even so, I could see that she had brought her walking aid with her. When I held out my hand to assist her, she waved it away.

'I don't want help. I want you to keep your promise.'

When Harriet and her green wheeled walker came to where the light illuminated the snow, it seemed to me that she was walking down a moonlit street. When we were together almost forty years ago, we'd somewhat childishly pretended that we were moon worshippers. Did she remember that? I watched her side-on as she worked her way through the snow-covered stones and rocks. I found it hard to believe that she was dying. A person approaching the ultimate border. A different world or a different kind of darkness would take over. She parked the walker at the foot of the three steps and held on hard to the rail as she struggled up to the front door. As she opened it, the cat scampered between her legs and into the house. She went to her room. I listened with my ear pressed against the closed door. I could hear the faint clinking noise from a bottle. Medicine from her bag. The cat miaowed and rubbed herself against my legs. I gave her something to eat, and sat down at the kitchen table.

It was still dark outside.

I tried to read the temperature on the thermometer attached to the outside of the window frame, but the glass containing the mercury column had misted over. The door opened, and Harriet came in. She had brushed her hair and changed into a new jumper. It was lavender blue. I was reminded of my mother and her lavender-scented tears. But Harriet wasn't crying. She smiled as she sat down on the kitchen sofa.

'I'd never have believed that you would become a person who lived with a dog and a cat and an anthill.'

'Life seldom turns out the way you thought it would.'

'I'm not going to ask you about how your life turned out. But I do want you to keep your promise.'

'I don't think I could even find my way back to the forest pool.'

'I'm quite sure you could. Nobody had a sense of direction and distance anywhere near as good as yours.'

I couldn't challenge Harriet's claim. I can always find my way through even the most complicated maze of streets. And I never get lost in the countryside.

'I suppose I might be able to find it if I think hard enough. It's just that I don't understand why.'

'Because it's the most beautiful promise I've ever been given in my life.'

'The most beautiful?'

'The only genuinely beautiful one.'

Those were her very words. The only genuinely beautiful promise. It was as if she'd started off a large orchestra playing inside my head, such was the power of her speech.

'We're always being made promises,' she said. 'You make them yourself and you listen to others giving theirs. Politicians are always going on about providing a better quality of life for people as they get older, and a health service in which nobody ever gets bedsores. Banks promise you high interest rates, some food promises to make you lose weight if you eat it, and body creams guarantee old age with fewer wrinkles. Life is quite simply a matter of cruising along in your own little boat through a constantly changing but never-ending stream of promises. And how many do we remember? We forget the ones we would like to remember, and we remember the ones we'd prefer to forget. Broken promises are like shadows dancing around in the twilight. The older I become, the more clearly I see them. The most beautiful promise I've ever been given in my life was the one you made to take me to that forest pool. I want to see it, and dream that I'm swimming in it, before it's too late.'

I would take her. The only thing I might be able to avoid was setting off in the middle of winter. But perhaps she didn't dare wait until the spring, because of her illness?

I thought that perhaps I should tell her I knew she was mortally ill. But I didn't.

'Do you understand what I mean when I talk about all the promises that accompany one's journey through life?'

'I've tried to avoid being taken in. One is so easily fooled.'

She stretched out her hand and placed it over mine.

'There was a time when I knew you. We walked along the streets of Stockholm. In my memory, it's always spring when we're out walking there. The person I had by my side then is not the same person that you are now. He could have become anything at all – apart from a solitary man on a little island on the edge of the open sea.'

Her hand was still lying on top of mine. I didn't touch it.

'Do you recall any darkness?' she asked.

'No. It was always light.'

'I don't know what happened.'

'Nor do I.'

She squeezed my hand.

'You don't need to lie to me. Of course you know. You caused me endless pain. I don't think I've got over it even now. Do you want to know what it felt like?'

I didn't answer. She took away her hand and leaned back on the sofa.

'All I want is for you to keep your promise. You must leave this island for a few days. Then you can come back here, and I'll never bother you again.'

'It's not possible,' I said. 'It's too far. My car isn't up to it.'

'All I want is for you to show me how to get there.'

It was obvious she wasn't going to give up.

It was starting to get light. The night was over.

'I married,' she said out of the blue. 'What about you?'

'I divorced.'

'So you got married as well? Who to?'

'You don't know them.'

'Them?'

'I was married twice. My first wife was called Birgit, and she was a nurse. After two years we had no more to say to each other. And she wanted to retrain as a mining engineer. What did I care for stones and gravel and mine shafts? My second wife was called Rose-Marie, and was an antiques dealer. You can't imagine how often I left the operating theatre after a long day and accompanied her to some auction sale or other, and then had to ferry home an old cupboard from some peasant's kitchen. I lost count of how many tables and chairs I had to soak in lye in an old bathtub in order to get rid of the paint. That lasted for four years.'

'Have you any children?'

I shook my head. Once upon a time, ages ago, I had imagined that when I grew old, I would have children to lighten the darkness of my old age. It was too late now – I'm a bit like my boat, out of the water and covered by a tarpaulin.

I looked at Harriet.

'Do you have any children?'

She eyed me for a long time before answering.

'I have a daughter.'

It struck me that she could have been my child, had I not abandoned her.

'She's called Louise,' said Harriet.

'That's a lovely name,' I said.

I stood up and made coffee. Morning was now in full swing. I waited until the water started to boil, counted to seventeen, and then let it brew. I took two cups from the cupboard, and sliced up the loaf of bread that had thawed by now. We were a couple of OAPs sitting down to coffee in the middle of January. We were one of the thousands of coffee mornings that take place every day in this country of ours. I wondered if any of the others were taking place in circumstances anything remotely like the one in my kitchen.

After drinking her coffee, Harriet withdrew into her anthill room and closed the door.

For the first time in many years I skipped my winter bath. I hesitated for some considerable time, and was about to get undressed and fetch the axe when I changed my mind. There would be no more winter baths for me until I had taken Harriet to the forest pool.

Instead of my dressing gown I put on a jacket and walked down to the jetty. There had been an unexpected change of weather: a thaw had set in, and the snow stuck to my boots.

I had a few hours to myself. The sun broke through the clouds, and melting snow and ice began dripping from the boathouse roof. I went inside, fetched one of my tins of tar and opened it. The smell calmed me down. I almost fell asleep in the pale sunlight.

I thought back to the time when Harriet and I were together. I felt that nowadays I belonged to an epoch that no longer existed. I lived in a strangely barren landscape for those who were left over, who had lost their footing in their own time and were unable to live with the innovations of the new age. My mind wandered. When Harriet and I were together, everybody smoked. All the time, and everywhere. The whole of my youth was filled with ashtrays. I can still recall the chain-smoking doctors and professors who trained me to become a person with the right to wear a white coat. In those days, the postman who delivered mail to the skerries was Hjalmar Hedelius. In winter he would skate from island to island. His rucksack must have been incredibly heavy, and that was before the modern obsession with junk mail.

My rambling thoughts were broken by the sound of an approaching hydrocopter.

Jansson had already been to the widow Mrs Åkerblom, and was now heading for me at full speed, bringing all his aches and pains. The toothache that had been pestering him before Christmas had gone away. The last time he moored by my jetty, he had asked me to examine a few brown moles that had formed on the back of his left hand. I calmed him down by assuring him that they were normal developments as a man grew older. He would outlive all the rest of us on the islands. When we pensioners have gone, Jansson will still be chugging along in his old converted fishing boat, or rushing around in his hydrocopter. Unless he's been made redundant, of course. Which will almost certainly be his fate.

Jansson glided up to the jetty, switched off the engine and began wriggling out of all his coats and hats. He was red in the face, his hair was standing on end.

'A Happy New Year to you,' he said when he was standing on the jetty.

'Thank you.'

'Winter is still very much with us.'

'It certainly is.'

'I've been having a few problems with my stomach since New Year's Eve. I've been finding it hard to go to the toilet. Constipation, as they say.'

'Eat some prunes.'

'Could it be a symptom of something else?'

'No.'

Jansson had difficulty in concealing his curiosity. He kept glancing up at my house.

'How did you celebrate New Year?'

'I don't celebrate New Year.'

'I actually bought some rockets this year. Haven't done that for years. Unfortunately one shot in through the door of the woodshed.'

'I'm usually fast asleep by midnight. I see no reason why I should change that habit simply because it's the last day of the year.'

Jansson was dying to ask about Harriet. No doubt she hadn't told him who she was, just that she wanted to visit me.

'Have you any post for me?'

Jansson looked at me in astonishment. I'd never asked him that before.

'No, nothing,' he said. 'There never is much in the way of post at this time of year.'

The conversation and consultation were over. Jansson took one last look at the house, then clambered down into his hydrocopter. I started walking away. As he switched the engine on, I put my hands over my ears. I turned and watched him disappear in a cloud of snow round the headland generally known as Antonsson's Point, after the skipper of a cargo boat who'd had a drop too much to drink and ran aground while on the way to beach his craft for the winter.

Harriet was sitting at the kitchen table when I went in.

I could see that she had been making herself up. In any case, she was less pale than she had been before. It struck me again how good-looking she was, and what an idiot I'd been to ditch her.

I sat down at the table.

'I shall take you to the forest pool,' I said. 'I'll keep my promise. It'll take two days to get there in my old car. We'll have to spend one night in an hotel. And I should say that I'm not sure I'll be able to find my way there. Up in those parts, the logging tracks keep changing, according to where the felling is taking place. And even if I can find the right track, it's by no means sure that it will be passable. I might need to find somebody with a plough attachment for his tractor who can open up the road for us. It will take at least four days altogether. Where do you want me to take you, when it's all over?'

'You can just leave me at the side of the road.'

'At the side of the road? With your walker?'

'I managed to get here, didn't I?'

There was an edge in her voice, and I didn't want to persist. If she preferred to be left at the side of the road, I wasn't going to argue.

'We can set off tomorrow,' I said. 'Jansson can take you and your walker to the mainland.'

'What about you?'

'I'll walk over the ice.'

I got up, as it had dawned on me that there was an awful lot for me to do. First of all I needed to make a catflap in the front door, and make sure that my dog could use the kennel that had been abandoned for many years. I would have to provide them with enough food to last them for a week. Needless to say, they would eat everything as soon as they could. Saving for the future was not a concept with which they were familiar. But they'd be able to manage without food for a few days.

I spent the day fixing a catflap in the front door and trying to teach the cat to use it. The kennel was in a worse state than I thought. I nailed some felt on to the roof to keep out the snow and rain, and laid out a couple of old blankets for the dog to lie on. I'd barely finished doing that before he had lain down inside it.

I phoned Jansson that evening. I'd never rung him before.

'Ture Jansson, postman.'

It sounded as if he were reciting a noble rank.

'Fredrik here. I hope I'm not disturbing you.'

'Not at all. You don't often ring.'

'I have never rung you. I wonder if you could do a taxi run tomorrow?'

'A lady with a wheeled walker?'

'As you charged her such a disgraceful amount when you brought her here, I take it for granted that there will be no charge tomorrow. If you don't go along with that, I shall naturally report you for running an illegal taxi business out here in the archipelago.'

I could hear Jansson's intake of breath at the other end of the line.

'What time?' he asked eventually.

'You won't have any post to deliver tomorrow. Can you be here for ten?'

Harriet spent most of the day lying down and resting while I made all the preparations for the journey. I wondered if she'd be able to cope with the strain. But that wasn't really my problem. I was only going to do my duty, nothing else. I thawed the hare steak and put it in the oven for dinner. My grandmother had placed a handwritten recipe for preparing a hare steak inside a cookery book. I had followed her instructions before with some success, and this time was no exception. When we sat down at the kitchen table, I noticed that Harriet's eyes had glazed over again. I realised that the clinking noise I'd heard coming from her room was not from medicine bottles, but from bottles of alcohol. Harriet kept retiring to her room in order to knock back the booze. As I started to chew the hare steak, it occurred to me that the journey to the frozen forest lake might turn out to be even more problematic than I had first thought.

The hare was good. But Harriet poked around rather than eating much. I knew that cancer patients are often afflicted by a chronic lack of appetite.

We rounded off the meal with coffee. I gave the remains of the steak to the dog and the cat. They can generally share food without resorting to scratching and fighting. I sometimes imagine them as an old couple, something like my grandmother and grandfather.

I told her that Jansson would be coming to collect her the next day, handed over my car keys and explained what the car looked like and where it was parked. She could sit in it and wait while I walked ashore over the ice.

She took the keys and put them in her handbag. Then, without warning, she asked me if I'd ever missed her during all those years.

'Yes,' I told her, 'I have missed you. But missing something only makes me depressed. It makes me afraid.'

She didn't ask anything more, but disappeared into her room again; and when she came back, her eyes were even more glassy than before. We didn't speak much to each other at all that evening. I think we were both worried about spoiling the journey we were going to make together. Besides, we had always found it easy to be silent in each other's company.

We watched a film about some people who ate themselves to death. We made no comment when it was over, but I'm sure we shared the same opinion.

It was a very bad film.

I slept fitfully that night.

I spent hours thinking about all the things that could go wrong on the journey. Had Harriet told me the whole truth? I was wondering more and more if what she really wanted was something else, if there was another reason why she had tracked me down after all those years.

Before I finally managed to go to sleep, I had made up my mind to be careful. I couldn't know what was in store, of course. All I wanted was to be prepared.

Uneasiness was persisting, whispering its silent warnings.

CHAPTER 6

It was a clear, calm morning when we set off.

Jansson arrived on time. He lifted the walker on board, and then we helped Harriet to squeeze in behind his broad back. I didn't mention my intention of going away as well. The next time he came, and found that I wasn't waiting for him on the jetty, he would walk up to the house. Perhaps he might think I was lying dead inside? And so I had written a note and pinned it to the front door: 'I'm not dead.'

The hydrocopter vanished behind the headland. I had fixed a pair of old hunting clamps to my boots, so that I wouldn't keep slipping on the ice.

My rucksack weighed nine kilos. I had checked the weight on my grandmother's old bathroom scales. I walked quickly, but avoided working up a sweat. I always feel afraid when I have to walk on ice covering deep water. It's nerve-racking. Just off the easternmost headland of my island is a deep depression known as the Clay Pit, which at one point is fifty-six metres deep.

I squinted in the dazzling sunlight, reflected off the ice. I could see some people on skates in the distance, heading for the outermost skerries. Otherwise, nothing – the archipelago in winter is like a desert. An empty world with occasional caravans of ice skaters. And now and then, a nomad like me.

When I came to the mainland at the old fishing village whose little harbour is hardly ever used nowadays, Harriet was sitting in my car, waiting for me. I collapsed the walker and packed it away in the boot, then sat down behind the wheel.

'Thank you,' said Harriet. 'Thank you for this.'

She stroked my arm briefly. I started the engine, and we set off on our long journey northwards.

* * *

The journey began badly.

We'd barely gone a mile when an elk suddenly strode into the middle of the road. It was as if it had been waiting in the wings, to make a dramatic entrance as we approached. I slammed on the brakes and narrowly missed crashing into its massive body. The car skidded and we became stuck in a snowdrift at the side of the road. It all happened in a flash. I had screamed out loudly, but there hadn't been a sound from Harriet. We sat there in silence. The elk had bounded away into the dense forest.

'I wasn't speeding at all,' I said in a lame and totally unnecessary attempt to excuse myself. As if it had been my fault that an elk had been lurking around at the side of the road, and chosen that moment to take a closer look at us.

'It's OK,' said Harriet.

I looked at her. Perhaps there's no need to be frightened of elks that appear from nowhere when you're shortly going to die?

The car was well and truly stuck. I fetched a spade from the boot, cleared the snow away from around the front wheels, broke off some fir branches and laid them on the road behind the wheels. I then reversed out of the drift with a sudden spurt, and we were able to continue our journey.

After another six or seven miles, I could feel the car starting to pull to the left. I pulled over and got out. We had a puncture in a front tyre. It occurred to me that the journey could hardly have started any worse than this. It is not a pleasant experience, kneeling down in snow and ice, messing about with nuts and bolts and handling dirty tyres. I have not been deserted by the surgeon's demand for cleanliness during an operation.

I was soaking in sweat by the time I'd finished changing the tyre. I was also angry. I would never be able to find the pool. Harriet would collapse, and no doubt a relative or friend would turn up and accuse me of acting irresponsibly, undertaking such a long journey with somebody that ill.

We set off again.

The road was slippery, the snow piled up at the sides of the road very high. We met a couple of lorries, and passed an old Volvo Amazon parked on the hard shoulder: a man was just getting out with his dog. Harriet said nothing. She was gazing out through the passenger window.

I started thinking about the journey to the pool I'd made with my father a long time ago. He had just been sacked again for refusing to work evenings at the restaurant that had employed him. We drove north out of Stockholm and spent the night in a cheap hotel just outside Gävle. I have a vague memory of it having been called Furuvik, but I may be mistaken. We shared a room; it was in July, very stuffy, one of the hottest summers of the late forties.

As my father had been working at one of Stockholm's leading restaurants, he had been earning good money. It was a period when my mother cried unusually little. One day, my father came home with a new hat for her. On that occasion she cried tears of happiness. That very same day he had served the director of one of Sweden's biggest banks, who was very drunk even though it was an early lunch, and he had given my father far too big a tip.

As I understood it, being given too large a tip was just as degrading for my father as being given too little, or even no tip at all. Nevertheless, he had converted the tip into a red hat for my mother.

She didn't want to come with us when my father suggested that we should go on a trip to Norrland and enjoy a few days' holiday before he needed to start looking for work again.

We had an old car. No doubt my father had started saving up for it at a very early age. Early in the morning, we clambered into that selfsame car and left Stockholm, taking the main road to Uppsala.

We spent the night at that hotel I think might have been called Furuvik. I remember waking up shortly before dawn and seeing my father standing naked in front of the window, gazing out through the thin curtain. He looked as if he'd been petrified in the middle of a thought. For what seemed like an eternity but was probably just a brief moment, I was scared to death and convinced that he was about to desert me. It was as though only a shell were standing there in front of me, nothing else. Inside the skin a large vacuum. I don't know how long he stood there immobile, but I clearly recall my breathless fear that he was going to abandon me. In the end he turned round, glanced at me as I lay there with the covers pulled up to my chin and my eyes half closed. He went back to bed, and it was not until I was sure he was asleep that I turned over and lay with my head pressed up against the wall, and went back to sleep.

We reached our destination the following day.

The pool was not large. The water was completely black. On the opposite side to where we were standing, cliffs towered up; but either side was dense forest. There was no shore as such, no transition between water and forest. It was as if the water and the trees were locked together in a trial of strength, with neither being able to cast the other to one side.

My father tapped me on the shoulder.

'Let's go for a swim,' he said.

'I don't have any swimming trunks with me.'

He looked at me in amusement.

'Who do you think does? Who do you think's going to see us? Dangerous forest goblins hiding in among the trees?'

He started to undress. I observed his large body surreptitiously, and felt embarrassed. He had an enormous belly that bulged out and wobbled when he removed his underpants. I followed suit, nervously aware of my own nakedness. My father waded out and then flopped down into the water. His body seemed to be surging forward like a gigantic whale, causing chaos in every part of the pool. The mirror-like surface was shattered in his wake. I waded out and felt the chill of the water. For some reason I had expected the water to be the same temperature as the air. It was so hot in among the trees that steam was rising. But the water was cold. I took a quick dip, then hurried to get out.

My father swam round and round with powerful strokes and kicks that created cascades of icy water. And he sang. I don't recall what he sang, but it was more a bellow of delight, a fizzing cataract of black water that transmogrified into my father's headstrong singing.

As I sat in the car with Harriet by my side, it occurred to me that there was nothing else in my life that I could recall in such vivid detail as the time at the pool with my father. Although it had happened fifty-five years ago, I could see the whole of my life summed up in that image: my father swimming alone and naked in the forest pool. Me, standing naked among the trees, watching him. Two people belonging together, but already quite different.

That's the way life is: one person swims, another watches.

I started to reassess returning to the pool. It was now more than a matter of keeping a promise I'd made to Harriet. I would also have the pleasure of seeing again something I never thought I would.

We travelled through a winter wonderland.

Freezing fog hovered over the white fields. Smoke was rising from the chimneys. Small icicles were hanging down from the thousands of dishes pointing their metallic eyes towards distant satellites.

After a few hours, I stopped at a petrol station. I needed to top up the windscreen washer fluid, and we also had to eat. Harriet headed for the grill bar attached to the petrol station. I watched how cautiously she moved, one painful step at a time. By the time I got there, she had already sat down and started eating. The day's special was smoked sausage. I ordered a fish fillet from the main menu. Harriet and I were just about the only diners. A lorry driver was sitting at a corner table, half asleep over a cup of coffee. I could read from the logo on his jacket that his job was to 'Keep Sweden Going'.

What are we doing? I wondered. Harriet and I, on our journey northwards? Are we keeping our country going? Or are we peripheral, of no significance?

Harriet chewed away at her smoked sausage. I observed her wrinkled hands, and thought about how they had once upon a time caressed my body and filled me with a sense of well-being that I had hardly ever found again later in life.

The lorry driver stood up and left the cafe.

A girl with a heavily made-up face and a dirty apron served me my fish. Somewhere in the background I could hear the faint sound of a radio. I could gather that it was the news, but I had no idea what was being said. Earlier in my life I was the kind of person who was always eager to discover the latest news. I would read, listen and watch. The world demanded my presence. One day two little girls drowned in the Göta Canal, another day a president was assassinated. I always needed to know. During my years of increasing isolation on my grandparents' island, that habit had gradually deserted me. I never read the newspapers, and watched the television news only every other day at most.

Harriet left most of the food on her plate untouched. I fetched her a cup of coffee. Snowflakes had begun to drift down outside the window. The cafe was still empty. Harriet took her walker and disappeared into the toilet. When she came back, her eyes were glazed. It worried me without my being able to explain why. I could hardly blame her for trying to deaden the pain. Nor could I very well take responsibility for her secret drinking.

It was as if Harriet had read my thoughts. She suddenly asked me what I was thinking about.

'About Rome,' I said evasively. I don't know why. I once attended a conference for surgeons in Rome that had been exhausting and badly organised. I skipped the last two days and instead explored the Villa Borghese. I moved out of the big five-star hotel where the conference delegates were staying, and moved to Dinesens' Guest House where Karen Blixen once used to be a regular guest. I flew from Rome convinced that I would never return.

'Is that all?'

'That's all. I wasn't thinking about anything else.'

But that wasn't true. I had in fact returned to Rome two years later. The major catastrophe had taken place, and I rushed away from Stockholm in a frenzy in order to find peace and quiet. I remember dashing to Arlanda airport without a ticket. The next flights to southern Europe were to Madrid and Rome. I chose Rome because the travelling time was shorter.

I spent a week wandering round the streets, my mind full of the great injustice that had stricken me. I drank far too much, occasionally got into bad company, and was mugged on my last evening. I returned to Sweden severely beaten up, with my nose looking like a blood-soaked dumpling. A doctor at the Southern Hospital straightened it out and gave me some painkillers. After that, Rome was the last place on earth I ever wanted to visit again.

'I've been to Rome,' said Harriet. 'My whole life has revolved around shoes. What I thought was just a coincidence when I was young, working in a shoe shop because my father had once worked as a foreman at Oscaria in Örebro, turned out to be something that would affect the whole of my life. All I've ever done, really, is wake up morning after morning and think about shoes. I once went to Rome and stayed there for a month as an apprentice to an old master craftsman who made

45

shoes for the richest feet in the world. He devoted as much care to each pair as Stradivari did to his violins. He used to believe feet had personalities of their own. An opera singer – I can no longer remember her name – had spiteful feet that never took their shoes seriously or showed them any respect. On the other hand, a Hungarian businessman had feet that displayed tenderness towards their shoes. I learned something from that old man about both shoes and art. Selling shoes was never the same again after that.'

We set off again.

I had started to think about where we should spend the night. It wasn't dark yet, but I preferred not to drive in bad light. My sight had deteriorated in recent years.

The winter landscape's uniformity gave it a special kind of beauty. We were travelling through country where practically nothing happened. Though now as we passed over the brow of a hill we both noticed a dog sitting by the side of the road. I braked in case it suddenly darted out in front of the car. When we'd passed it, Harriet remarked that it had a collar. I could see in the rear-view mirror that it had started following the car. When I slowed again, it caught up with us.

'It's following us,' I said.

'I think it's been abandoned.'

'Why do you think that?'

'Dogs that run after cars usually bark. But this one isn't barking.'

She was right. I pulled up on the hard shoulder. The dog sat down, its tongue hanging out of its mouth. When I reached out, it didn't move. I took hold of its collar, and saw that it had a disc with a telephone number. Harriet took out her mobile phone and dialled the number. She handed the phone to me. Nobody answered.

'There's nobody there.'

'If we drive off, the dog may run after us until it drops dead.'

Harriet took the phone and called directory enquiries.

'The owner is Sara Larsson, who lives at Högtunet Farm in Rödjebyn. Do we have a map?'

'Not a sufficiently large-scale one.'

'We can't just leave the dog on the road.'

I got out and opened the back door. The dog immediately jumped in and curled up. A lonely dog, I thought. No different from a lonely person.

After five or six miles we came to a little village with a general store. I went in and asked about Högtunet Farm. The shop assistant was young and wearing a baseball cap back to front. He drew a map for me.

'We've found a dog,' I said.

'Sara Larsson has a spaniel,' said the shop assistant. 'Perhaps it's run away?'

I returned to the car, gave Harriet the hand-drawn map and drove back the way we'd come. All the time the dog lay curled up on the back seat. But I could see that it was alert. Harriet guided me into a side road hidden between banks of snow carved by the snowplough. It was disorientating entering this white corridor, all sense of direction lost. The road meandered along between fir trees heavily laden with snow. Though the road had been ploughed nothing had been through since last snowfall.

'Look – animal tracks in the snow,' said Harriet. 'They're leading back towards the main road.'

The dog had sat up on the back seat, its ears cocked, staring out through the windscreen. It kept shuddering, perhaps feeling cold. We drove over an old stone bridge. Ramshackle wooden fencing was just visible by the side of the road. The forest opened up. On a hillock ahead of us was a house that hadn't seen a coat of paint for many years. There was also an outhouse and a partially collapsed barn. I stopped and let the dog out. It ran to the front door, scratched at it, then sat down to wait. I noticed that no smoke was coming from the chimney and the outside light over the front door was not on. I didn't like what I saw.

'Just like a painting,' said Harriet, 'left behind by the artist on nature's easel.'

I got out of the car and lifted out the walker. Harriet shook her head, and stayed in the car. I stood in front of the house, listening. The dog was still sitting there motionless, staring at the door. A rusty old plough stuck out of the snow like the remains of a shipwreck. Everything seemed to be abandoned. I could see no tracks in the snow apart from those made by the dog. I was feeling more and more uneasy. I walked up to the house and knocked on the door. The dog stood up.

'Who's going to open it?' I whispered. 'Who are you waiting for? Why were you sitting out there on the main road?'

I knocked again, then tried the handle. The door wasn't locked. The dog ran in between my legs. It smelled stuffy inside the house – not unaired, but as if time had stood still and begun emitting a scent of doom. The dog had run into what I assumed was the kitchen, and not returned. I shouted, but there was no answer. On the left was a room with old-fashioned furniture and a clock with a pendulum swinging silently behind the glass. On the right was a staircase leading to the upper floor. I went to where the dog had gone and stopped abruptly in the doorway.

An old woman was lying prone on the floor of grey linoleum. It was obvious that she was dead. Nevertheless, I did what one ought to do in the circumstance: knelt down and felt for a pulse in her neck, her wrist and in one temple. It wasn't really necessary as the body was cold and rigor mortis had already set in. I assumed it was Sara Larsson lying there. It was cold in the kitchen as one of the windows was half open. That was no doubt the way the dog had taken in order to get out and try to fetch help. I stood up and looked around. Everything was neat and tidy in the kitchen. In all probability, Sara Larsson had died of natural causes. Her heart had stopped beating; perhaps a blood vessel had burst in her brain. I estimated her age at somewhere between eighty and ninety. She had thick white hair tied in a knot at the back of her head. I carefully turned the body over. The dog was watching everything I did with great interest. When the body was lying on its back, the dog sniffed at her face. I seemed to be looking at a painting different from the one Harriet had seen. I was looking at a depiction of loneliness beyond description. The dead woman had a beautiful face. There is a special kind of beauty that manifests itself only in the faces of really old women. Their furrowed skin contains all the marks and memories imprinted by a life lived. Old women whose bodies the earth is crying out to embrace.

I thought about my old father, shortly before he died. He had cancer that had spread all over his body. By the side of his deathbed was a pair of immaculately polished shoes. But he said nothing. He was so

48

afraid of death that he had been struck dumb. And wasted away to such an extent that he was unrecognisable. The earth was crying out to embrace him as well.

I went out to Harriet, who had got out of the car and was leaning on her walker. She accompanied me back to the house, and held tightly on to my arm as she walked up the steps. The dog was still sitting in the kitchen.

'She's lying on the floor,' I said. 'She's dead and stiff and her face has turned yellow. You don't need to see her.'

'I'm not afraid of death. What I think is horrific is the fact that I shall have to be dead for so long.'

Have to be dead for so long.

Later, I would remember those words spoken by Harriet as we stood in the dark hallway just before entering the kitchen where the old woman was lying on the floor.

We stood in silence. Then I scanned the house, looking for evidence of a relative I could contact. There had once been a man in the house, that much was obvious from the photographs hanging on the walls. But now she was alone with her dog. When I came downstairs again, Harriet had placed a handkerchief over Sara Larsson's face. She'd had great difficulty in bending down. The dog was lying in its basket, watching us attentively.

I telephoned the police. It took me some time to explain exactly where I was.

We went out on to the porch to wait, both subdued. We said nothing, but I noticed that we were trying to stand as close together as possible. Then we saw headlights slicing through the forest, and a police car drew up outside. The officers who got out of it were very young. One of them, a woman with long fair hair tied in a ponytail behind her cap, seemed to be no more than twenty or twenty-one at most. Their names were Anna and Evert. They went into the kitchen. Harriet remained on the porch, but I followed them.

'What will happen to the dog?' I asked.

'We'll take it with us.'

'And then what?'

'I suppose it will have to sleep in the cells with the drunks until we can establish if there is some relative or other who can take care of it.

49

Otherwise it will have to go to a dogs' home. If the worst comes to the worst, it will be put down.'

There was a constant scraping sound coming from the radio receivers attached to their belts. The young woman made a note of my name and telephone number.

She said there was no need for us to stay there any longer. I squatted down in front of the basket and stroked the spaniel's head. Did she have a name? What would happen to her now?

We drove through the gathering dusk. The headlights illuminated signs with unfamiliar names.

Everything is silent travelling in a car through a winter landscape. Summer or spring are never silent. But winter is mute.

We came to a crossroads. I stopped. We needed somewhere to stay; a sign indicated the Foxholes Inn five miles off.

The inn turned out to be a mansion-like building with two wings, situated in extensive grounds. A lot of cars were parked outside the main building.

I left Harriet in the car and entered the brightly lit lobby, where an elderly man, who gave the impression of being in another world, sat playing an old piano. He came down to earth when he heard me come in, and stood up. I asked if he had any rooms for the night.

'We're full,' he said. 'We have a large party celebrating the return of a relative from America.'

'Have you any rooms at all?'

He studied a ledger.

'We have one.'

'I need two.'

'We have one large, double room with a view of the lake. On the first floor, very quiet. It was booked, but somebody in the big party fell ill. It's the only room we have available.'

'Is it a double bed, or a twin?'

'It's a very comfortable double bed. Nobody has ever complained about it being difficult to get to sleep there. One of Sweden's elderly princes, now dead, slept in that bed many times without trouble. Although I'm a monarchist, I have to admit that royal guests can sometimes be demanding.'

'Can you divide the bed?'

'Only by sawing it in half.'

I went out to Harriet and explained the situation. One room, a double bed. If she preferred, we could drive on and try to find somewhere else.

'Do they serve food?' Harriet asked. 'I can sleep anywhere.'

I went back in. I recognised the tune the man at the piano was churning out, something that had been popular when I was a young man. Harriet would certainly be able to name it.

I asked if they served an evening meal.

'We have a wine-tasting dinner that I can thoroughly recommend.'

'Is that all?'

'Isn't that good enough?'

His response sounded very disapproving.

'We'll take the room,' I said. 'We'll take the room, and look forward to the wine-tasting dinner.'

I went out again and helped Harriet out of her seat. I could see that she was still in pain. We walked slowly through the snow, up the ramp for wheelchairs, and entered the warmth. The man was back at the piano.

'"Non ho l'età",' said Harriet. 'We used to dance to that. Do you remember who sung it? Gigliola Cinquetti. She won the Eurovision Song Contest in 1963 or 1964.'

I remembered. Or at least I thought I did. After all those solitary years on my grandparents' island, I no longer relied on my memory.

'I'll sign us in later,' I said. 'Let's take a look at our room first.'

The man collected a key and escorted us down a long corridor that led to a single door with a number inlaid in the dark wood. We were to occupy room number 3. He unlocked the door and switched on the light. It was a large room, very attractive. But the double bed was smaller than I'd expected.

'The dining room closes in an hour.'

He left us alone. Harriet flopped down on to the bed. The whole situation suddenly seemed to me totally unreal. What had I got myself into? Was I going to share a bed with Harriet after all these years? Why had she agreed to go along with it?

'I can find a sofa to sleep on,' I said.

'It makes no difference to me,' said Harriet. 'I've never been afraid of you. Have you been afraid of me? Scared that I'd stick an axe into your skull while you were asleep? I need to be left alone for a while. I'd like to eat in half an hour. And you don't need to worry – I can pay for myself.'

I went out to the piano player and signed the register. From the part of the dining room sealed off by a sliding door came the buzz of conversation of the party welcoming their relative home from America. I went into one of the lounges and sat down to wait. It had been a long day. I was restless. Days on the island always passed by slowly. Now I had the feeling I was under attack and felt defenceless.

Through the open door I saw Harriet emerging from the corridor with her walker. It looked as if she was standing at the wheel of some strange vessel. She was moving unsteadily. Had she been drinking again? We went into the dining room. Most of the tables were vacant. A friendly waitress with a swollen and bandaged leg gave us a corner table. Just as my father had taught me to do, I checked to see if the waitress was wearing decent shoes. She was, although they could have done with polishing. Unlike earlier in the day, Harriet was hungry. I wasn't. But I made up for that by drinking greedily the wine served by a thin youth with a freckled face. Harriet asked questions about the wine, but I said nothing, merely drank up whatever was put before me. They were mainly Australian wines, with some from South Africa. But so what? All I wanted just now was to get tipsy.

We toasted each other, and I noticed that Harriet became quite drunk almost immediately. I wasn't the only one drinking too much. When was the last time I'd been so drunk that I had difficulty in controlling my movements? Very occasionally, when depression got the better of me, I would sit at the kitchen table and drink myself silly, then kick the cat and dog out, and crash out fully clothed on top of the bed. It hardly ever happened during the winter. Perhaps on a light spring evening or early in the autumn I would have an attack of angst, and would bring out the bottles.

The dining room closed. We were the last diners. We had eaten and drunk, and as if by tacit agreement had mentioned nothing about our lives, nor where we were heading. Even Sara Larsson and her dog were

52

not discussed. I charged the meal to our room despite Harriet's protests. Then we stumbled off. Somehow or other Harriet seemed to manage with her walker in a controlled manner, I had no idea how she managed it. I unlocked the door of our room, and said I would go for an evening walk before going to bed. It wasn't true, of course. But I didn't want to embarrass Harriet by being present when she went to bed. I suppose I was just as keen not to embarrass myself.

I sat down in a reading room. It was lined with shelves of old books and magazines. The man at the piano had disappeared, and the large party had dispersed. Sleep came without warning, as if it had ambushed me. When I woke up, I didn't know where I was. I could see from the clock that I'd been asleep for nearly an hour. I stood up, staggered slightly as a result of all the wine I'd drunk, and went back to our room. Harriet was asleep. She had left the light on at my side of the bed. I undressed quietly, had a wash in the bathroom and crept down into bed. I tried to hear if she really was asleep, or just pretending. She was lying on her side. I felt tempted to stroke her back. She was wearing a light blue nightdress. I switched off the light and listened to her breathing in the darkness. I felt very uneasy inside. And there was something else that I had been missing for a very long time. A feeling of not being alone. As simple as that. Loneliness had been banished, just for a moment.

I must have fallen asleep. I was woken up by Harriet screaming. Half asleep, I managed to switch on the bedside light, She was sitting upright in bed, screaming from deep despair and pain. When I tried to touch her shoulder, she hit me – hard, and in the face.

My nose spurted blood.

We got no more sleep that night.

CHAPTER 7

Dawn rose over the white lake like grey smoke.

I stood at the window, thinking about how I recalled seeing my father doing the same. I'm not as fat as he was, even though I've acquired a bit of a pot belly. But who could see me? Only Harriet, who had plumped up the pillow behind her back.

You could say I was a half-naked man in a winter landscape.

I thought about going down to the frozen lake and creating my hole in the ice. I missed the pain involved in exposing myself to the freezing cold water. But I knew I wouldn't do it. I would stay in our room, together with Harriet. We would get dressed, have breakfast and continue our journey.

I was intrigued by Harriet's dream, which had woken her up screaming. What she said about it seemed extremely muddled. She could only remember fragments. Somebody had nailed her down, intent on ripping her to pieces because she had refused to let go of her body. She had resisted: she had been in a room – or perhaps it was outside – surrounded by people, none of whose faces she recognised. Their voices had sounded like cries from threatening birds.

And that's when she woke up. When I tried to calm her down, or perhaps rather to calm myself down, she had still been in the border-land between dream and consciousness, and was defending herself against whatever had pinned her down. The punch she gave me was in the heavyweight class. Its effect reminded me of the pain I'd felt when I was beaten up and mugged in Rome.

But this time my nose wasn't broken.

I stuffed rolled-up toilet paper into my nostrils, wrapped a hand-kerchief soaked in cold water round the back of my neck, and after a while, the nosebleed petered out. Harriet knocked on the bathroom door and asked if she could be of assistance. I wanted to be left in peace, so I told her 'no'. When I eventually came out of the bathroom with two wads of paper in my nose, she had gone back to bed. She had taken off her nightdress and hung it over the bedstead. She looked me in the eye.

'I didn't mean to hit you.'

'Of course you didn't. You were dreaming.'

I sat down on one of the chairs by the big window looking out over the lake. It was still dark outside. I could hear a dog barking in the distance. Individual barks, like broken-off sentences. Or like the way you speak when nobody's listening.

I watched her as she continued to recount her dream, and it seemed to me that she was just the same as when I had known and loved her. I wondered what exactly it was that made me think so. I eventually realised that it was her voice, which hadn't changed at all over the years. I recalled telling her many times that she would always be able to get a job as a telephone operator. She had the most beautiful telephone voice I had ever heard.

'An enemy cavalry company was hiding in the forest,' she said. 'They suddenly burst into the open and attacked before I had chance to defend myself. But it's all over now. Besides, I know that certain nightmares never return. They lose all their strength and don't exist any more.'

'I know that you're seriously ill,' I said.

I hadn't planned to say that at all. The words simply tumbled out of my mouth. Harriet looked at me in surprise.

'There was a letter in your handbag,' I said. 'I was looking for some explanation for why you had fallen down on the ice. I found the letter, and read it.'

'Why didn't you say you knew?'

'I was ashamed of having rooted around in your handbag. I would be furious if somebody did that to me.'

'You've always been an interfering nosy parker. You were always like that.'

'That's not true.'

'Oh yes it is. Neither of us have the strength to lie any more. It's a fact, isn't it?'

I blushed. I've always rummaged around other people's property. I've even been known to steam open letters, and reseal them afterwards. My mother had a collection of letters from her younger days in which she opened her heart to a friend of hers. Shortly before she died she had tied a ribbon round them and asked for them to be burned. I did so – but read them first. I used to read my girlfriends' diaries and raid their drawers; I've been known to ransack fellow doctors' desks. And there have been patients whose wallets I have comprehensively investigated. I never stole any money. I was after something different. Secrets. People's weakness. Knowledge of things nobody knew that I knew about.

The only person who ever found me out was Harriet.

It happened at her mother's house. I had been left alone for a few minutes, and had started to work my way through their bureau when Harriet entered the room silently and wondered what on earth I was doing. She had already noticed that I used to go through her handbag. It was one of the most embarrassing moments of my life. I can no longer remember what I said. We never spoke about it again. I never touched her belongings after that. But I continued digging into the lives of other friends and colleagues. Now she had reminded me of the kind of person I am.

She smoothed down the covers and beckoned me to sit next to her. The thought that she was naked underneath the sheets suddenly excited me. I sat down and put my hand on her arm. She had a pattern formed by birthmarks near her shoulder. I recognised them all. Everything's the same, I thought. Such a long time has passed, but we are still the same as we were at the beginning.

'I didn't want to tell you,' she said. 'You might think that was why I tracked you down. Looking for help where there is no help possible.'

'Nothing is ever hopeless.'

'Neither you nor I believe in miracles. If they happen, they happen. But believing in them, expecting them – that's nothing more than wasting the time alloted to you.

I might live for another year, or it might only be six months. In any case, I think I can survive for a few more months with the aid of this walker and all the painkillers. But don't try telling me that nothing is ever hopeless.'

'Advances are being made all the time. Sometimes things happen amazingly quickly.'

She sat up a little more erect against the pillows.

'Do you really believe what you're saying?'

I didn't answer. I remembered her once saying that life was like your shoes. You couldn't simply expect or imagine that your shoes would fit perfectly. Shoes that pinched your feet were a fact of life.

'I want to ask you to do something,' she said, and burst out laughing. 'Can't you take those bits of paper out of your nostrils?'

'Was that all?'

'No.'

I went to the bathroom and removed the blood-soaked pieces of toilet paper. The bleeding had stopped. My nose was tender; there would be a bruise and some swelling. I could still hear the solitary dog barking mournfully somewhere outside.

I went back and sat on the side of the bed once more.

'I want you to lie down beside me. Nothing more than that.'

I did as she asked. Her perfume was strong. I could feel the contours of her body through the sheet. I lay down on her left side. That's what I had always done in the past. She reached out and switched off the bedside light. It was between four and five in the morning. The faint light from a solitary lamp post by a fountain in the courtyard seeped in through the curtains.

'I really do want to see that forest pool,' she said. 'I never had a ring from you. I don't think I ever wanted one. But I'll settle for the pool. I want to see it before I die.'

'You're not going to die.'

'Of course I'm going to die. We all reach a point where we no longer have the strength to deny what's going to happen. Death is the only constant companion a human being can have in this life. Even a lunatic usually knows when it's time to go.'

She fell silent. Her pains came and went.

'I've often wondered why you never said anything,' she said after a while. 'I can understand that you had met somebody else, or that you simply didn't want to carry on any more. But why didn't you say anything?'

'I don't know.'

'Of course you know. You always knew what you were doing, even when you claimed that you didn't. Why did you hide away? Where were you when I stood at the airport, waiting to see you off? I stood there for hours. Even when the only flight that hadn't left was a delayed charter to Tenerife, I still stood there. Afterwards, I wondered if you'd been hiding behind a column somewhere, watching me. And laughing.'

'Why should I laugh? I'd already left.'

She thought for a moment before speaking.

'You'd already left?'

'The same time, the same flight, the previous day.'

'So you'd planned it?'

'I didn't know if I was going to get on the flight. I simply went to the airport to see what would happen. A passenger didn't turn up, and I was able to rebook.'

'I don't believe you.'

'It's the truth.'

'I know it's not. You weren't like that. You never did anything without having planned it in advance. You used to say that a surgeon could never leave anything to chance. You said you were a surgeon through and through. I know you had planned it. How can you expect me to believe something that can only be a lie? You're just the same now as you were then. You lie your way through life. I caught on too late.'

Her voice was shrill. She was starting to shout. I tried to calm her down, to make her think about the people sleeping in the neighbouring rooms.

'I don't care about them. Explain to me how somebody can behave like you did towards me.'

'I've said that I don't know.'

'Have you done something similar to others? Let them get caught in your net, then left them to survive as best they can?'

'I don't understand what you're talking about.'

'Is that all you can say?'

'I'm trying to be honest.'

'You're lying. There's not a word of truth in what you say. How can you live with yourself?'

'I've nothing else to say.'

'I wonder what you're thinking.'

She suddenly tapped me on the forehead with her finger.

'What's inside there? Nothing? Only darkness?'

She lay down and turned her back on me. I hoped it was over.

'Have you really nothing to say? Not even "sorry"?'

'Sorry.'

'If I weren't so ill I'd hit you. I'd never leave you in peace again. You succeeded in almost destroying my life. All I want is for you to say something that I can understand.'

I didn't respond. Perhaps I felt a little bit relieved: lies always weigh you down, even if they seem to be weightless at first. Harriet pulled the covers up to her chin.

'Are you cold?' I asked tentatively.

She sounded perfectly calm when she replied.

'I've felt cold all my life. I've gone looking for warmth in deserts and tropical countries. But all the time I've had a little icicle hanging inside me. People always have baggage. For some it's sorrow, for others it's worry. For me, it's always been an icicle. For you it's an anthill in a living room in an old fisherman's cottage.'

'I never use that room. It's not heated during the winter and in the summer I just air it. Both my grandfather and my grandmother died in that room. As soon as I enter it, I can hear their breathing and detect their smell. One day I noticed that there were ants inside the room. When I opened the door several months later, they had started to build a nest. I left them to it.'

Harriet turned over.

'What happened? I'm not going to give up. I don't know what happened in your life. Why did you move out to the island? I gathered from the man who took me out there that you'd been living on the skerry for nearly twenty years.'

'Jansson is a rogue. He exaggerates everything. I've been living there for twelve years.'

'A doctor who retires at the age of fifty-four?'

'I don't want to talk about it. Something happened.'

'You can tell me.'

'I don't want to.'

'I shall soon be dead.'

I turned my back on her, and thought that I should never have given way. It wasn't the forest pool she wanted, it was me.

That's as far as I managed to think.

She moved to snuggle up against me. The warmth from her body enveloped me, and filled what had long seemed to be nothing but a pointless shell. That was how we had always lain when we slept together. I used to carry her into slumber on my back. Just for a brief moment, I could imagine that we had always been lying together like this. For nearly forty years. A remarkable sleep that we were only now beginning to wake up from.

'What happened to you? You can tell me now,' said Harriet.

'I made a catastrophic mistake during an operation. Afterwards, I argued that it wasn't my fault. I was found guilty. Not in court, but by the National Board of Health and Welfare. I was admonished, and couldn't cope with it. That's as much as I can bring myself to say just now. Don't ask any more questions.'

'Tell me about the forest pool instead,' she whispered.

'It's black, they say it's bottomless, and there's no shore. It's a small poor relation to all those lovely lakes with inviting waters. It's hard to imagine that it exists at all, and isn't just a drop of nature's ink that has been spilled. I've told you that I watched my father swimming there. But what I didn't say was that the experience made me realise what life was all about. People are close to each other so that they can be parted. That's all there is to it.'

'Are there any fish in that pool?'

'I don't know. But if there are, they must be completely black. Or invisible, because you can't see anything in that dark water. Black fish, black frogs, black water spiders. And down at the bottom – if there is a bottom – a solitary black eel slowly wriggling its way through the mud.'

She pressed herself up against me even harder. I thought about how she was dying, how the warmth she radiated would soon be an insidious chill. What had she said? An icicle inside her? So as far as she was concerned, death was ice, nothing more. Everybody perceived death differently, the shadow hovering behind us always takes on a different form. I wanted to turn round and hug her as tightly as I could. But something prevented me. Perhaps I was still afraid of whatever it was that had made me leave her? A feeling of being too close, something I couldn't cope with?

I didn't know. But perhaps I now wanted to know, despite everything.

* * *

I must have dozed off briefly. I was woken up by Harriet sitting on the edge of the bed. To my horror, I watched her sink down on to her knees and start crawling towards the bathroom door. She was completely naked, her breasts heavy, her body older than I had imagined. I didn't know if she was crawling to the bathroom because she was too exhausted to walk, or so as not to wake me up with the squeaking wheels of her walker. Tears welled up in my eyes, she was blurred as she closed the door. When she came back, she had managed to stand up and walk. But her legs were trembling. She snuggled up close to me again.

'I'm not asleep,' I said. 'I don't know what's happening any more.'

'You had an unexpected visitor on to your island. An old woman from your past came walking over the ice. Now you're on your way to fulfil an old promise.'

I could smell spirits. Did she have a bottle hidden among her toilet things?

'Medicines don't mix well with strong drink,' I said.

'If I'm forced to choose, I shall stick to my booze.'

'You're drinking in secret.'

'I've noticed you smelling my breath, of course. But I like drinking in secret even so.'

'What are you drinking?'

'Ordinary Swedish aquavit. You'll have to stop at one of the booze shops tomorrow. The stuff I brought with me is almost finished.'

We lay there waiting for dawn.

She occasionally dozed off. The dog outside in the night had fallen silent. I got up again and stood by the window. I had the feeling that I'd turned into my own father. That day at the forest pool I had discovered his loneliness. I now realised that it was also my own. Despite the fifty-five-year gap, we had fused together and become the same individual.

It frightened me. I didn't want it.

I didn't want to be a man who had to jump down into freezing cold water every day, in order to confirm that he was still alive.

CHAPTER 8

We left the inn shortly before nine.

Outside, there was patchy fog, a slight breeze, and it was a couple of degrees above freezing. The piano player had not returned. There was a young lady at reception. She asked if we had slept well, and had been satisfied with our stay. Harriet was standing with her walker a couple of yards away from me.

'We slept very well,' she said. 'The bed was broad and comfortable.'

I paid and asked if she had a local map. She disappeared for a few minutes, then reappeared carrying a substantial atlas.

'You can have it for nothing,' she said. 'An overnight guest from Lund left it behind a few weeks ago.'

We set off and drove straight into the fog.

We drove slowly. The fog was so thick, the road had disappeared. I thought of all the occasions on which I had rowed into patches of fog in my boat. When the mists came rolling in from the sea, I liked to rest on the oars and allow myself to be swallowed up by all the whiteness. I had always experienced it as a strange mixture of security and threat. Grandma sometimes used to sit on the bench under the apple tree and tell stories about people rowing themselves away in the fog. She maintained there was some kind of hole in the middle that people could be sucked into and never be seen again.

Now and then we would see a set of fog lights approaching, catch a fleeting glimpse of a car or lorry, and then we would be alone once more.

There was a state monopoly liquor store in one of the little towns we passed through. I bought what Harriet wanted. She insisted on paying herself. Vodka, aquavit and brandy, in half-bottles.

The fog had slowly begun to lift. I could sense that there was snow in the air.

Harriet took a swig from one of the bottles before I had time to start the engine. I said nothing, as there was nothing to say.

Then I suddenly remembered.

Aftonlöten. I remembered the name of the mountain close to the forest pool where I had watched my father swimming around like a happy walrus.

Aftonlöten.

I remember asking him what it meant. He didn't know. At least, he didn't answer.

Aftonlöten. It suggested pastures at eventide, and sounded like a word from the traditional songs shepherdesses used to sing as they brought their herds in to shelter for the night. It was an insignificant little mountain, barely a thousand feet high, between Ytterhögdal, Linsjön and Älvros.

Aftonlöten. I said nothing to Harriet as I was still not certain that I would be able to find my way to the pool.

I asked how she felt. We drove almost three miles before she answered. Taciturnity and distance are linked. It's easier to be silent when you have a long way to go.

She said she wasn't in pain. As that was an obvious untruth, I didn't bother to ask again.

We stopped for something to eat as we approached the Härjedalen border. There was one lone car parked outside. Something about the cafe and the place as a whole perplexed me, but I couldn't put my finger on why. There was a roaring fire burning in the timber-built cafe, and a smell of lingonberry juice. I remembered that smell from my childhood. I'd thought that lingonberry juice was so outdated now that it barely existed any more. But they served it here.

We sat down at one of the many empty tables and contemplated the timber-clad walls decorated with elk antlers and stuffed game birds. There was a cranium lying on a shelf. I couldn't resist investigating. It was some time before I realised that it was a bear's skull. The waitress, who had recited the menu for us, came in at that point and saw me standing there with the skull in my hand.

'It just lay down and died.' she said. 'My husband used to want me to tell everybody that he'd shot it. But now that he's no longer with us, I can tell the truth about it. It just lay down and died. It was lying on the shore at Risvattnet Lake. An old bear that simply lay down by a log pile and died.'

As she spoke, it dawned on me that I'd been here before. When I went on that trip with my father. Perhaps it was the smell of lingonberry juice that brought the distant memory to life. I'd been in this same cafe with my father. I was very young at the time; we'd had a meal and I'd drunk lingonberry juice.

Were all those stuffed birds mounted on the walls back then, staring down at hungry diners with their steely eyes? I couldn't remember. I could see in my mind's eye my father wiping his mouth with his serviette, checking the time, and urging me to hurry up and finish eating. We had a long way to go yet.

There was a map on the wall over the open fire. I checked it and found Aftonlöten, Linsjö Lake, and a mountain that I'd forgotten about.

It was called Fnussjen.

An impossible name – it must have been a joke. No more than eight hundred feet high, covered in trees, and somebody must have dreamt up a nonsense name for it. In stark contrast to Aftonlöten, which sounded attractive and even meaningful in an old-fashioned way.

We ordered beef stew. I finished before Harriet, and went to sit by the fire until she was ready.

She had some trouble in manoeuvring her walker over the threshold when we left the cafe. I tried to help her.

'I can manage, thank you.'

We walked slowly through the snow back to the car. We had never lived together; but even so, people we met seemed to regard us as an old couple blessed with no end of patience with each other.

'I haven't the strength to do anything else today,' said Harriet as we settled down in the car.

Her brow was covered in sweat as a result of the strain she had been subjected to; eyes half closed, as if she were about to fall asleep. She's dying, I thought. She's going to die here in the car. I've always wondered about when exactly I'm going to die. In my bed, in the street, in a shop, or down on my jetty, waiting for Jansson? But I'd never imagined myself dying in a car.

'I need some rest,' she said. 'I shudder to think what will happen if I don't get it.'

· 'You'll have to tell me what you can cope with.'

'That's what I'm doing. Tomorrow can be the day we go to the forest pool. Not today.'

I found a little guest house in the next town. A yellow building behind the church. We were welcomed by a friendly lady. When she saw Harriet's walker, she gave us a large room on the ground floor. I would really have preferred a room to myself, but refrained from saying anything. Harriet lay down to rest. I thumbed through a pile of old magazines on a table before dozing off. A few hours later I went out and bought a pizza at a bleak takeaway cafe where the only customer was an old man muttering away to himself, with a greyhound slumped at his feet.

We sat on the bed and ate the pizza. Harriet was very tired. When she'd finished eating, she lay down again. I asked if she wanted to talk, but she merely shook her head.

I went out as dusk was falling, and wandered around the little town. Many shops were standing empty, with contact details in the windows for anyone interested in renting the premises. These advertisements were like cries for help from a small Swedish town in deep distress. My grandparents' island was a part of this gigantic abandoned, unneeded archipelago lining the edge of Sweden, comprising not only islands along our coasts, but just as many villages and small towns in inland backwaters and in the forests. In this town there were no jetties for mooring and going ashore, no angry-sounding hydrocopters whipping up a whirlwind of snow as they approached with their cargo of post and junk mail. Nevertheless, wandering around this deserted place felt like walking around a skerry at the edge of the open sea. Blue television light spilled out of windows on to the snow; sometimes snatches of television sound could be heard, bits of different programmes leaking out from the windows. I thought of loneliness and all these people watching different programmes. Every evening people of all generations burrowed into different worlds, beamed down by the satellites.

In the old days, we used to have the same programmes to talk about. What did people talk about now?

I paused at what had once been the railway station, and tied my scarf more tightly round my neck. It was cold, and a wind was getting up. I walked along the deserted platform. A single goods wagon stood in a snow-filled siding, an abandoned bull in its stall. In the faint light from a single lamp I tried to read the old timetable still attached to the station wall in a case with a cracked glass window. I checked my watch. A southbound train would have been due at any moment. I waited, thinking that stranger things had been known to happen than a ghost train materialising out of the darkness and heading for the bridge over it frozen river.

But no train came. Nothing came. If I'd had a bit of hay with me, I'd have left it in front of the old goods wagon. I resumed my walk. The clear sky was full of stars. I searched for some kind of movement, a shooting star perhaps, or a satellite, perhaps even a whisper from one of the gods who are alleged to live up there. But nothing happened. The night sky was mute. I continued as far as the bridge over the frozen river. There was a log lying on the ice. A black line in the middle of all the white. I couldn't remember the name of the river. I thought it might be the Ljusnan, but wasn't sure.

I remained standing on the bridge for what seemed ages. I suddenly had the feeling that I was no longer alone under those high iron arches. There were other people there as well, and it dawned on me that what I could see was in fact myself. At all ages, from the little boy who had scurried around and played on my grandparents' island, to the me who, many years later, had left Harriet, and eventually the man I was now. For a brief moment I could see myself, as I had been and as the man I had become.

I searched among the figures surrounding me for one that was different, somebody I might have become: but there was no one. Not even a man who followed in the footsteps of his father and worked as a waiter in various restaurants.

I have no idea how long I stood there on the bridge. When I went back to the guest house, the apparitions had disappeared.

I lay down on the bed, rubbed up against her arm, and fell asleep.

I dreamt about climbing up the iron bridge in the middle of the night. I was perched on the very top of one of the huge arches, and knew that at any moment I was going to fall down on to the ice.

* * *

It was snowing gently when we set out the next day to find the right logging road. I couldn't remember what it looked like. There was nothing in the monotonous landscape to jog my memory. But I knew that we were close by. The pool was somewhere in the middle of the triangle formed by Aftonlöten, Ytterhögdal and Fnussjen.

Harrie appeared rather better in the morning. When I woke up, she was already washed and dressed. We had breakfast in a small dining room where we were the only guests. Harriet had also had a dream during the night. It was about us, a trip we'd made to an island in Lake Mälaren. I had no recollection of it.

But I nodded when Harriet asked me if I remembered. Of course I did. I remembered everything that had happened to us.

The snow was piled up high on both sides of the road; there were few turn-offs, and most of them hadn't been ploughed. Something from my youth came back to me without warning. Logging roads. Or perhaps I should say emotions connected with a logging road.

I'd spent a summer with one of my father's relations in Jämtland, up in the north. My grandmother was ill, so I couldn't spend the summer on her island. I made friends with a boy whose father was a district judge. We had paid a visit to the court archives, and when nobody was looking we'd opened a bundle of documents comprising records of proceedings and police investigations. We were fascinated by accounts of paternity cases, with all the amazing but compelling details of what had gone on in the back of motor cars on Saturday nights. The cars had always been parked on logging roads. It seemed to us that everybody had been conceived on the back seat of a motor car. We devoured case notes on the cross-examination of young men hauled up before the courts, who described reluctantly and laconically what had happened, or not happened, in the cars parked on the various logging roads. It was always snowing, there were never any simple and straightforward truths to rely on, there was always considerable doubt when it came to deciding if the young man was lying his way out of a corner, or if the equally young woman was right in insisting that it was him and nobody else, that back seat and no other back seat, that logging road and no other logging road. We gorged ourselves on the secret details, and I think that until reality caught up with us many years later, we dreamed about one day sharing the back seat of a car parked on snow-covered logging roads with desirable young women.

That's what life was all about. What we longed for always took place on a logging road.

Without really knowing why, I began telling Harriet about it. I'd started to turn off automatically into every side road we came to.

'I've no intention of telling you about my experiences on the back seat of motor cars,' she said. 'I didn't do it when I was going with you, and I don't do it now. There are always humiliating moments in the life of every woman. What most of us find worst is what happened when we were very young.'

'When I was a doctor, I sometimes used to talk to my colleagues about how many people didn't seem to know who their real father was. A lot of young men lied their way out of it, and others accepted a responsibility that wasn't actually theirs. Even the mothers didn't always know who the father was.'

'All I can remember about those distant and hopeless attempts at erotic adventure was that I always seemed to smell so peculiar. And the young man crawling over me smelled funny too. That's all I can remember. The excitement and confusion and the strange smells.'

Suddenly, we were confronted by an enormous monster of a combined log harvester trundling towards us. I slammed on the brakes, and skidded into a snowdrift. The driver of the monster jumped down and pushed while I reversed the car. After considerable difficulty, I managed to back out of the drift. I got out. The man was powerfully built and had chewing-tobacco stains round his mouth. In some strange way he seemed to be a reproduction of the enormous machine he'd been driving, with all its prehensile claws and cranes.

'Is yer lost?' he asked.

'I'm looking for a forest pool.'

He squinted at me.

'In t'woods?'

'Yes, a forest pool.'

'Dunnit 'ave a name?'

'No, it doesn't have a name.'

'But tha's efter it ollt' sem? Thez a helluva lotta lakes round 'ere. Tha can teck yer pick. Where d'yer reckon yours is?'

I could see that only an idiot would be out in the forest in winter looking for a forest pool without a name. So I explained the situation to him. I thought that would sound so unlikely that it had to be true.

'I promised the lady sitting in my car that she would see it. She's very ill.'

I could see that he hesitated before deciding to believe me. Truth is often stranger than fiction, I reminded myself.

'And that'll meck 'er well, willit? Seein that there lake?'

'Perhaps.'

He nodded, and thought it over.

'There's a lake at ender this muck road, mebbe that's 'er?'

'As I recall it was circular in shape, not large, and the trees came right down to the edge of the water.'

'Mm, cud be 'er then – dunno if not. Woods fuller lakes.'

He held out his hand, and introduced himself.

'Harald Svanbeck. Yer don't often see folk on this muck road this time o'year. Scarce ever. But good luck. Is it yer mam in t'car?'

'No, she's not my mother.'

'Must be some bugger's mam, eh? Gotta be.'

He clambered back up into the cabin of his monstrous contraption, started the engine, and continued on his way. I got back into the car.

'What language was he speaking, then?' Harriet asked.

'The language of the forest. In these parts, every individual has his own dialect. They understand each other. But they each speak their own language. It's the best way for them. In these regions out on the edge of civilisation, it's easy to imagine that every man and every woman is a unique member of an individual race. An individual nation, an individual stock with its own unique history. If they are totally isolated, nobody will ever miss the language that dies with them. But there's always something that survives, of course.'

We continued along the logging track. The forest was very dense, the road began to climb gently upwards. Was this something I could recall from the time I was being driven by my father in the dove-blue old Chevrolet he looked after with such tender loving care? A road sloping gently upwards? I had the distinct impression that we were on the right track. We passed a stack of newly felled logs. The forest had been raped by the enormous beast that Harald Svanbeck was in charge of. By now, all distances seemed to be endless. I glanced in the rear-view mirror and the forest appeared to be closing in behind us. I had the feeling that I was travelling backwards through time. I remembered walking through the trees the previous evening, the bridge, the forest from my past. Perhaps we were now on the way to a summer lake, with my father and myself waiting impatiently to get there?

We negotiated a series of sharp bends. The snow was piled up high on both sides of the road.

Which petered out.

And there it was, in front of me, with its covering of white. I pulled up and switched off the engine. We were there. There was nothing else to say. I had no doubts. This was the forest pool. I had returned after fifty-five years.

The white cloth was spread out to welcome us. I suddenly had the feeling that Harriet had been destined to winkle me out of my island. She was a herald angel, even if she had gone there of her own accord. Or had I summoned her? Had I been waiting all those years for her to come back?

I didn't know. But we had arrived.

CHAPTER 9

I told her that this was it, we had arrived. She gazed hard and long at all the whiteness.

'So there is water underneath all this snow, is there?'

'Black water. Everything's asleep. All the tiny creatures that live in the water are asleep. But this is the pool we've been looking for.'

We got out of the car. I lifted out the walker. It sunk down into the snow. I fetched the spade from the boot.

'Stay in the car where it's warm,' I said. 'I'll start the engine. Then I'll dig out a path for you. Where do you want to go to? As far as the water's edge?'

'I want to go to very middle of the lake.'

'It isn't a lake. It's a pool.'

I started the engine, helped Harriet back into the car, and started digging. There was a foot or more of frozen snow underneath the powdery surface layer. Digging through it all was far from easy. I could have dropped dead at any moment from the strain.

The very thought scared me stiff. I started digging more slowly, tried to listen to my heart. When I had my latest check-up, my blood pressure readings were on the high side. All my other metabolic figures were OK; but a heart attack can strike for no obvious reason. It can swoop down on you from out of the blue, as if an unknown suicide bomber had burst into one of your cardiac chambers.

It's not unusual for men of my age to dig themselves to death. They die a sudden and almost embarrassing death, clutching a spade in their stiff fingers.

It took a long time for me to dig my way out to the middle of the frozen pool. I was soaked in sweat, and my arms and back ached by the time I finally got there. The exhaust fumes formed a thick cloud behind the car. But out there, on the ice-covered pool, I couldn't even hear the engine. There was complete silence. No birds, no movement at all in the mute trees.

I wished I could have watched myself from a distance. Hidden among the surrounding trees, an observer scrutinising himself.

As I walked back to the car, it occurred to me that things might now be drawing to a close.

I would drop Harriet off wherever she wanted us to say farewell. I still knew no more than the basic fact that she lived somewhere in Stockholm. After that, I could return to my island. A fascinating thought struck me: I would send Jansson a picture postcard. I'd never have believed that I would write to him. But I needed him now. I'd buy a card with a picture depicting the endless forests, preferably one in which the trees were weighed down with snow. I would draw a cross in the middle of the trees, and write: 'That's where I am just now. I'll be back home soon. Don't forget to feed my pets.'

Harriet had already got out of the car. She was standing behind her walker. We walked side by side along the path I'd dug. I had the feeling we were part of a procession heading for an altar.

I wondered what she was thinking. She was looking round, searching for any sign of life in among the trees. But there was silence every-where, apart from the faint hum from the car's engine ticking over.

'I've always been scared of walking on ice,' she said without warning.

'But you still had the courage to go to my island?'

'Being scared doesn't mean that I haven't the courage to do things that frighten me.'

'This pool isn't frozen all the way down,' I said. 'But very nearly. The ice is over three feet thick. It could bear the weight of an elephant, if necessary.'

She burst out laughing.

'Now that would be a sight for sore eyes! An elephant standing out here on the ice, in order to calm me down! A holy elephant sent to save people who are frightened of thin ice!'

We came to the middle.

'I think I can see it in my mind's eye,' she said. 'When the ice has gone.'

'It looks its best when it's raining,' I said. 'I wonder if there's anything to beat a gentle shower of rain in the Swedish summer. Other countries have majestic buildings or vertiginous mountain peaks and deep ravines. We have our summer rain.'

'And the silence.'

We didn't speak for a while. I tried to grasp the implications of our coming here. A promise had been fulfilled, many years too late. That was all, really. Our journey was now at an end. All that remained was the epilogue, a long journey south on frozen roads.

'Have you been here since you abandoned me? Have you been here with somebody else?'

'No such thought ever occurred to me.'

'Why did you abandon me?'

The question came like a blow to the solar plexus. I could see that she was upset again. She was holding on tightly to the handle of her walker.

'The pain you caused me sent me to hell and back,' she said. 'I was forced to make such an effort to forget you, but I never succeeded in doing it. Now that I'm standing here at long last, on the lid of your forest pool, I regret having tracked you down. What good did I think it would do? I don't know any more. I'm going to die soon. Why do I spend time opening up old wounds? Why am I here?'

We probably stood there for a minute, no longer. Silent, avoiding each other's gaze. Then she turned her walker round and started retracing her steps.

There was something lying in the snow that I hadn't noticed when I was digging out the path for Harriet. It was black. I screwed up my eyes, but couldn't make out what it was. A dead animal? A stone? Harriet hadn't noticed that I'd stopped. I stepped out into the snow at the side of the path, and approached the dark object.

I ought to have understood the danger. My experience and knowledge of the ice and its unpredictability ought to have warned me. Far too late I realised that the dark patch was in fact the ice itself. I knew that for whatever reason, a small patch of ice could be very thin despite the fact that the ice all around it was very thick. I almost managed to stop and take a step backwards. But it was too late, the ice gave way and I fell through it. The water reached up to my chin. I ought to have been used to the sudden shock of entering ice-cold water, thanks to all my winter dips. But this was different. I wasn't prepared, I hadn't created the hole in the ice myself. I screamed. It wasn't until I screamed again that Harriet turned round and saw me in the water. The cold had already begun to paralyse me, I had a burning sensation in my chest, I was desperately gulping down ice-cold air into my lungs and searching frantically for firm ground under my feet. I grasped at the edges of the hole, but my fingers were already far too stiff.

I continued to scream, convinced I was face to face with death.

I knew that she was the last person capable of helping me out. She could barely stand on her own two feet.

But she astonished me as much as she astonished herself. She came towards me with her walker, as fast as she was able. She tipped the walker over, then lay down on the ice and pushed it towards the edge of the hole so that I was able to grab hold of one of the wheels. How I managed to pull myself up I shall never know. She must have pulled at me and tried to shuffle backwards through the snow. When I scrambled out, I staggered as best I could towards the car. I could hear her calling behind me, but I had no idea of what she was saying: what I did know was that if I stopped and fell over in the snow, I would never have the strength to stand up again. I couldn't have been in the water for more than two minutes, but that had almost been enough to kill me. I have no memory of how I got from the hole in the ice to the car. I said nothing, probably closed my eyes so that I couldn't see how far there was still to go to the car. When I eventually pressed my face against the boot, I had only one thought in my head: to strip off all the soaking wet clothes I had on, and roll the blanket on the back seat round my body. I have no recollection of how that was achieved. There was a strong smell of exhaust fumes around me as I wriggled out of the last piece of clothing and somehow managed to open the back door. I wrapped the blanket round me, and after that I lost consciousness.

When I woke up, she was embracing me and was as naked as I was.

Deep down in my consciousness, the cold had been transformed into a sensation of burning. When I opened my eyes, the first thing I saw was Harriet's hair and the back of her neck. My memory slowly returned.

I was alive. And Harriet had undressed and was hugging me under the blanket to keep me warm.

She noticed that I had come round.

'Are you cold? You could have died.'

'The ice simply opened up underneath me.'

'I thought it was an animal. I've never heard a scream like that before.'

'How long was I unconscious?'

'An hour.'

'So long?'

I closed my eyes. My body was scorching hot.

'I didn't want to see the lake only for you to die,' she said.

It was over now. Two old people, naked on the back seat of an old car. We had spoken about such things earlier, of young people in the backs of cars. Making love then perhaps denying it. But we two, with a combined age of 135, simply clung on to each other, one because he had survived, the other because she hadn't been left all alone in the depths of the forest.

After what might have been another hour, she moved to the front seat and got dressed.

'It was easier when I was young,' she said. 'A clumsy old woman like me finds it difficult to get dressed in a car.'

She fetched dry clothes for me from the rucksack in the boot. Before I put them on, she warmed them up by spreading them over the steering wheel, where the heat from the engine was being blown into the car. I could see through the windscreen that it had started snowing. I was worried in case the snow should start drifting, and prevent us from driving back to the main road.

I dressed as quickly as I could, fumbling as if I was drunk.

It was snowing heavily by the time we left the forest pool. But the logging road was not yet impassable.

We returned to the guest house. This time it was Harriet who went out with her walker to fetch the pizza we had for our evening meal.

We shared one of her bottles of brandy.

The last thing I saw before falling asleep was her face.

It was very close. She may have been smiling. I hope she was.

CHAPTER 10

When I woke up the next day, Harriet was sitting with the atlas open in front of her. My body felt as if it had been subjected to a severe beating. She asked how I felt. I said I was fine.

'The interest,' she said with a smile.

'Interest?'

'On your promise. After all these years.'

'What are you asking for?'

'A diversion.'

She pointed out where we were on the map. Instead of moving her finger southwards, she moved it eastwards, towards the coast, and the province of Hälsingland. It came to a halt not far from Hudiksvall.

'To there.'

'And what's in store for you there?'

'My daughter. I want you to meet her. It will take an extra day, perhaps two.'

'Why does she live there?'

'Why do you live on your island?'

Needless to say, I did as she requested. We drove towards the coast. The countryside was exactly the same all the way: isolated houses with their satellite dishes, and no sign of any people.

Late in the afternoon Harriet said she was too tired to go any further. We checked into a hotel in Delsbo. The room was small and dusty. Harriet took her medicine and painkillers, and fell asleep from sheer exhaustion. Perhaps she took a drink without my noticing. I went out, found a chemist's and bought a pharmaceutical handbook. Then I sat down in a cafe and read about her medication.

There was something unreal about sitting in a cafe with a cup of coffee and a cream bun – with several small children shouting and screaming to attract the attention of their mothers, who were absorbed in well-thumbed magazines – and discovering just how ill Harriet was.

I felt increasingly that I was paying a visit to a world I had lost contact with during my years on my grandparents' island. For twelve years I had denied the existence of anything beyond the beaches and cliffs surrounding me, a world that had no relevance for me. I had turned myself into a hermit with no knowledge of what was happening outside the cave in which I was hidden away.

But in that cafe in Delsbo, it became clear to me that I couldn't continue to live the life I was leading. I would return to my island, of course: I had nowhere else to go. But nothing would ever be the same as it was. The moment I noticed that dark shadow on the expanse of white snow and ice, a door had slammed behind me and would never be opened again.

I had bought a picture postcard in a corner shop. It depicted a fence covered in snow. I sent it to Jansson.

I asked him to feed the animals. Nothing else.

Harriet was awake when I got back. She shook her head when she saw the book I was carrying.

'I don't want to talk about my woes today.'

We went to the neighbouring grill bar for dinner.

When I saw the kitchen and breathed the smell of cooking, it occurred to me that we were living in an age of deep-frying and ready-made meals. It was not long before Harriet slid her plate away and announced that she couldn't eat another mouthful. I tried to urge her to eat a little bit more – but why? A dying person eats no more than is necessary to sustain the short life remaining.

We soon returned to our room. The walls were thin. We could hear two people talking in a neighbouring room. Their voices rose and fell. Both Harriet and I strained our ears, but we were unable to make out any words.

'Are you still an eavesdropper?' she asked.

'There are no conversations on my island for me to overhear,' I said.

'You always used to eavesdrop on my telephone conversations, despite the fact that you pretended to be uninterested and thumbed through a book or a newspaper. That's how you tried to hide your big ears. Do you remember?'

I was upset. She was right, of course. I've always been an eaves-dropper, ever since the time when I used to listen in to the angst-ridden conversations between my father and mother. I have stood behind half-open doors and listened to my colleagues, to patients, to people's intimate conversations in cafes or on trains. I discovered that most conversations contained small, almost unnoticeable lies. I used to ask myself if that's the way it's always been. Has it always been necessary for conversations between people to contain barely noticeable elements of untruth in order to get anywhere?

The conversation in the next room had come to an end. Harriet was tired. She lay down and closed her eyes.

I put on my jacket, and went out to explore the deserted little town. Wherever you looked was blue light oozing out of barred windows. The occasional moped, a car travelling far too fast, then silence again. Harriet wanted me to meet her daughter. I wondered why. Was it to show me that she had managed perfectly well without me, that she had borne the child I hadn't been privileged to give her? I felt pangs of sorrow as I trudged through the wintry evening.

I paused at a brightly lit ice rink, where a few young people were skating around with bandy sticks and a red ball. I suddenly felt very close to my own younger days. The crackling sound of skates on ice, of stick against ball, the occasional shout, skaters falling over only to scramble to their feet again immediately. That's how I remembered it, although in fact I had never laid my hands on a bandy stick: I had been shunted off to an ice-hockey rink, where the play was no doubt a lot more painful than what I was watching taking place.

Get back on your feet as soon as you fall.

That was the message to be learned from the freezing cold ice-hockey rinks of my youth. A lesson to be applied to the life that was in store for us.

Always scramble up again when you fall down. Never stay down. But that was precisely what I had done. I had stayed down after making my big mistake.

I watched them playing, and soon picked out a very little boy, the smallest of them all, albeit fat – or perhaps he was wearing more protective clothing than the rest? But he was the best. He accelerated quicker than any of the others, dribbled the ball with his stick without even needing to look at what he was doing, feinted with astonishing speed, and was always in exactly the right position to receive a pass.

A fat little lad who was a faster skater than any of the others. I tried to imagine which of the skaters out there was most like me at their age. Which one would I have been, with my much heavier ice-hockey stick? Certainly not the little boy who could skate so fast and had a much better ball sense than most. I would have been one of the also-rans – a blueberry that could be picked and replaced with any other blueberry around.

Never stay down if you don't have to.

I had done what you should never do.

I went back to the hotel. There was no night porter. The room key opened the outside door. Harriet had gone to bed. One of the brandy bottles was standing on her bedside table.

'I thought you must have run away,' she said. 'I'm going to sleep now. I've taken a dram and a sleeping pill.'

She turned on to her side, and was soon asleep. I cautiously took hold of her wrist and measured her pulse: 78 beats per minute. I sat down on a chair, switched on the television, and watched a news broadcast with the sound turned down so low that not even my eavesdropping ears were able to hear a word of what was said. The pictures seemed to be the same as usual. Bleeding, tortured, suffering specimens of humanity. And then a series of well-dressed men making endless pronouncements, displaying no sign of sympathy, only arrogant smiles. I switched off the television and lay down on the bed. I thought about the young female police officer with the blonde hair before falling asleep.

At one o'clock the next day we were approaching Hudiksvall. It had stopped snowing, and there was no ice on the roads. Harriet pointed out a road sign to Rångevallen. The surface was terrible, destroyed by monster tree-felling machines. We turned off again, this time on to a private road. The forest was very dense. I wondered what kind of a person Harriet's daughter was, living like this so remotely in the depths of the forest. The only question I had put to Harriet during our journey was whether Louise had a husband or any children. She didn't. Logs were stacked in various appropriate places by the road-side. The road reminded me of the one that had led to Sara Larsson's house.

When we eventually came to a clearing, I saw several ruined buildings and dilapidated fences. And a large caravan with a tented extension.

'We're here,' said Harriet. 'This is where my daughter lives.'

'In the caravan?'

'Can you see any other building with a roof that hasn't collapsed?'

I helped her out of the car, and fetched her walker. There was the sound of an engine coming from what might once have been a dog kennel. It could hardly be anything else but a generator. There was a satellite dish on the roof of the caravan. We stood there for several minutes without anything happening. I felt an intense desire to return to my island.

The caravan door opened. A woman emerged.

She was wearing a pink dressing gown and high-heeled shoes. It seemed to me anything but easy to estimate her age. She had pack of cards in one hand.

'This is my daughter,' said Harriet.

She pushed her walker through the snow to where the woman was trying to stand steadily on her high heels.

I stayed where I was.

'This is your father,' said Harriet to her daughter.

There was snow in the air. I thought of Jansson, and wished to goodness that he could have come to collect me in his hydrocopter.

THE FOREST

CHAPTER 1

My daughter doesn't have a well of her own.

Needless to say, there was no running water in her caravan; nor was there any sign of a pump anywhere on the site. In order to fetch water, I had to follow a path down the slope, through a copse, and eventually to another deserted farm with glassless windows and suspicious crows perched on the chimneys. In the yard was a rusty pump which produced water. As I raised and lowered the handle, the rusty iron screamed in pain.

The crows were motionless.

This was the first thing my daughter had asked me to do for her. To fetch two buckets of water. I'm just thankful that she didn't say anything else. She could have yelled at me and told me to clear off, or she could have been overcome with joy at finally meeting her father. But all she did was ask me to fetch some water. I took the buckets and followed the path through the snow. I wondered if she would normally go herself in her dressing gown and high-heeled shoes. But what I wondered most of all was what had happened all those years ago, and why nobody had told me anything about it.

It was 250 yards to the abandoned farm. When Harriet said that the woman standing by the caravan was my daughter, I knew immediately that she was telling the truth. Harriet was incapable of lying. I searched my memory for the moment when she must have been conceived. As I trudged through the snow, it struck me that the only possibility was that Harriet had discovered she was pregnant after I'd disappeared. So the moment of conception must have been a month or so before we parted.

I tried hard to remember.

The forest was silent. I felt like a gnome making his way through the snow in some ancient fairy tale. We had only ever made love on her sofa bed. So that was where my daughter must have been created.

When I left for America and Harriet had waited for me in vain at the airport, she would have known nothing about it. She only became aware of the situation later, and I had vanished by then.

I pumped up the water. Then I stood the buckets by the side of the pump and went into the abandoned house. The front door was rotten – it collapsed as I nudged it open with my foot.

I wandered round the rooms, which smelled of mould and rotten wood. It was like examining a shipwrecked liner. Bits of newspaper protruded from behind torn wallpaper. A page of *Ljusnan* from 12 March 1969: *A car crash took place on* . . . The rest of the article was missing. *In this picture, Mrs Mattsson is displaying one of her most recent tapestries created with her customary loving care* . . . The picture was torn, Mrs Mattsson's face was still visible, and one of her hands, but no tapestry. In the bedroom was what was left of a double bed. It seemed to have been chopped to pieces with an axe. Somebody had vented his fury on the bed and made certain that it could never ever be slept in again.

I tried to conjure up images of the people who had lived in the house, and one day left it, never to return. But their faces were averted. Abandoned houses are like empty showcases in a museum. I left the building and tried to come to grips with the thought that I had acquired a daughter, out of the blue, who lived in the forest to the south of Hudiksvall. A daughter who must be thirty-seven years of age, and lived in a caravan. A woman who walked through the snow in a pink dressing gown and high-heeled shoes.

One thing was clear to me.

Harriet had not prepared her for this. She knew that she had a father, of course, but not that I was him. I was not the only one to be surprised. Harriet had astounded us both.

I picked up the buckets and started to make my way back. Why was my daughter living in a caravan in the depths of the forest? Who was she? When we shook hands, I hadn't dared to look her in the eye. She was surrounded by a strong smell of perfume. Her hand was sweaty.

I put down the buckets to rest my arms.

'Louise,' I said aloud to myself. 'I have a daughter called Louise.'

The words struck me dumb, made me a little afraid, but also

84

exhilarated. Harriet had come to me over the ice in Jansson's hydro-copter, bringing with her news about life, and not just the death that would soon claim her.

I picked up the buckets again and carried them to the caravan. I knocked on the door. Louise opened it. She was still wearing the high-heeled shoes, but she had replaced the pink dressing gown with trousers and a jumper. She had a very attractive figure. She made me feel embarrassed.

The caravan was cramped. Harriet had squeezed on to a bench-cum-bed behind a little table in front of the window. She was smiling. I smiled back at her. It was warm in the caravan. Louise was busy making coffee.

Louise had a lovely voice, just like her mother's. If ice could sing, so could my daughter.

I looked round the caravan. Dried roses hanging from the ceiling, a shelf with documents and letters, an old-fashioned typewriter on a stool. A radio but no television set. I started worrying about the kind of life she led. It seemed reminiscent of my own.

And now you've turned up in my life, I thought. The most un-expected thing that has ever happened to me.

Louise produced a Thermos of coffee and some plastic mugs. I sat down on the bed next to Harriet. Louise remained standing, looking at me.

'I'm pleased to note that I haven't burst out crying,' she said. 'But I'm even more pleased to note that you haven't gone overboard and insisted how happy you are about what you've just discovered.'

'It hasn't sunk in yet. But then again, I never get so excited that I lose control of myself.'

'Maybe you think it's not true?'

I thought about all those dust-covered bundles of legal documents containing statements made by young men swearing that they were not the father.

'I'm quite sure it's true.'

'Do you feel sad because you didn't know about me sooner? Because I've come into your life so late?'

'I'm pretty immune to sadness,' I said. 'Just now I'm more surprised than anything else. Until an hour ago, I didn't have any children. I didn't think I ever would.'

'What do you do for a living?'

I looked at Harriet. So she hadn't told Louise anything at all about her father, not even that he was a doctor. That shocked me. What had she said about me? That her daughter had a father who was just a ship passing in the night?

'I'm a doctor. Or was a doctor, rather.'

Louise looked quizzically at me, coffee mug in hand. I noticed that she had a ring on every one of her fingers, and her thumbs as well.

'What sort of a doctor?'

'I was a surgeon.'

She pulled a face. I thought about my father, and his reaction when I told him at the age of fifteen what I wanted to be.

'Can you write prescriptions?'

'Not any more. I'm retired.'

'More's the pity.'

Louise put down her mug of coffee and pulled a woolly hat over her head.

'If you need a pee you go behind the caravan, then cover it up with snow afterwards. If you need to do something more substantial, you use the dry closet next to the woodshed.'

She went out, slightly unsteady on her high-heeled shoes. I turned to Harriet.

'Why didn't you tell me about her? It's disgraceful!'

'Don't you talk to me about disgraceful behaviour! I didn't know how you would react.'

'It would have been easier if you'd prepared me for it.'

'I didn't dare. Maybe you'd have thrown me out of the car and left me by the roadside. How could I know if you really wanted a child?'

Harriet was right. She couldn't have known how I would react. She had every reason to distrust me.

'Why does she live like this? What does she do for a living?'

'It's her choice. I don't know what she does.'

'But you must have some idea?'

'She writes letters.'

'Surely she can't make a living out of that?'

'It seems to be possible.'

It occurred to me that the caravan walls were thin, and that my daughter might be standing out there with her ear pressed up against the cold plastic, or whatever it was. Perhaps she had inherited my tendency to eavesdrop?

I lowered my voice to a whisper.

'Why does she look like she does? Why does she walk around in the snow wearing high heels?'

'My daughter —'

'Our daughter!'

'Our daughter has always had a mind of her own. Even when she was five, I had the feeling that she knew exactly what she wanted to do with her life, and that I would never be able to make her out.'

'What do you mean by that?'

'She's always chosen to live her life without worrying too much about what other people think. Her shoes, for example. They are very expensive. Ajello, made in Milan. Very few people dare to live the way she does.'

The door opened, and our daughter came back in.

'I need to rest,' said Harriet. 'I'm tired.'

'You've always been tired,' said Louise.

'I haven't always been dying.'

For a brief moment, they were hissing at each other, like cats. Not exactly in a nasty way, but not exactly friendly either. In any case, neither of them seemed to be surprised by the other's reaction. So Louise was aware of the fact that her mother was dying.

I stood up so that Harriet could lie down on the narrow bed. Louise put on a pair of boots.

'Let's go out for a walk,' she said. 'I need some exercise. And besides, I think we're both a bit shaken.'

There was a well-worn path heading in the opposite direction to the abandoned farm. We passed an old earth cellar and entered a dense conifer wood. She was walking quickly, and I had difficulty in keeping up with her. She suddenly turned round to face me.

'I thought I had a father who had gone to America and vanished. A father called Henry who was mad about bees, and spent his time researching into how they lived. But the years passed by, and he didn't even send me a jar of honey. I thought he was dead. But you're not dead. I've actually met you. When we get back to the caravan I'm going to take a photograph of you and Harriet. I have lots of photos of her, on her own or together with me. But I want a photo of both my parents before it's too late.'

We continued walking along the path.

It seemed to me that Harriet had told Louise the facts. Or at least as much of the facts as she could, without telling a lie. I had gone to America, and I had vanished. And in my youth I'd been interested in bees. Moreover, it was certainly true that I wasn't yet dead.

We continued walking through the snow.

She would get her photograph of her parents.

It wasn't yet too late to take the picture she needed.

CHAPTER 2

The sun had sunk down towards the horizon.

In the middle of a little field was a boxing ring, covered in snow. It looked as if somebody had thrown it out, and it had just happened to land there in the whiteness. Half hidden in the snow were a couple of ramshackle wooden benches that might well have been taken from a chapel or a cinema.

'We have boxing matches in spring and summer,' she said. 'We generally start the season in mid-May. That's when we have the weigh-in, using some old scales from a dairy.'

'We? Are you telling me that you box as well?'

'Of course. Why shouldn't I?'

'Who do you box with?'

'My friends. People from around here who have chosen to live the kind of life they think suits them best. Leif, for instance, who lives with his old mum who used to run the biggest moonshine operation for miles around. Amandus, who plays the fiddle and has very strong fists.'

'But surely you can't be a boxer and play the violin as well? How do his fingers cope?'

'You'll have to ask Amandus that. Ask the others.'

She didn't tell me who the others were. She continued along the well-trodden path leading to a barn at the other side of the boxing ring. As I observed her from behind, it struck me that her body was very much like Harriet's. But what had my daughter looked like when she was a little girl? Or when she was a teenager? I trudged along through the snow and tried to think myself back in time. Louise was born in 1967. She was a teenager when I was at the height of my career as a surgeon. I suddenly felt a surge of anger. Why had Harriet not said anything?

Louise pointed to some tracks in the snow and said they had been made by a wolverine. She opened the barn door. There was a paraffin lamp on the floor: she lit it and hung it from a hook in the ceiling. It was like entering an old-fashioned gym used by boxers or wrestlers. Dotted around on the floor were dumb-bells and weightlifting bars, a punchbag hung down from the ceiling, and on a bench was a neatly coiled skipping rope and several pairs of red and black boxing gloves.

'If it had been spring, I'd have suggested we should have a couple of rounds,' Louise said. 'I can't think of a better way of starting to get to know a father I've never met before. In more than one sense.'

'I have never, ever worn a pair of boxing gloves.'

'But you must have been in a fight or two?'

'When I was thirteen or fourteen, I suppose. But they were more like wrestling matches in the school playground.'

Louise stood by the punchbag and set it swaying gently back and forth with her shoulder. The paraffin lamp was shining just above her head. I still thought it was Harriet I was looking at.

'I'm nervous,' she said. 'Have you any more children?'

I shook my head.

'None at all?'

'No, none at all. What about you?'

'None.'

The punchbag was still swaying back and forth.

'I'm just as confused as you are,' she said. 'There have been times when I've remembered that I must have had a father, despite everything, and the thought has made me furious. I think that's why I took up boxing. So that I could knock him out on the day that he rose from the dead, and count him out into eternity, as my revenge for him abandoning me.'

The light from the lamp danced around the rough walls. I told her about how Harriet had suddenly turned up on the ice, about the forest pool, and the detour she had suddenly asked me to make.

'Didn't she say anything about me?'

'No, all she spoke about was the forest pool. Then she said that she wanted me to meet her daughter.'

'I ought to throw her out really. She's made fools of us both. But you don't throw out somebody who's ill.'

She raised her hand and stopped the punchbag swinging.

'Is it true that she's going to die soon? You're a doctor – you must know if she's telling the truth.'

'She's very ill indeed. But I don't know when she's going to die. Nobody could put a date on that.'

'I don't want her to die in my caravan,' said Louise, blowing out the paraffin lamp.

We stood there in the pitch dark. Our fingers happened to meet. She took hold of my hand. She was strong.

'I'm so glad you've turned up,' she said. 'I suppose that, deep down, I've always thought you would do one day.'

'It had never occurred to me that I might have a child.'

'You don't have a child. You have a grown-up woman approaching middle age.'

When we emerged from the barn, I could see her in front of me as a silhouette. The stars seemed to be almost within reach, glittering.

'It's never completely dark up here in the far north,' said Louise. 'When you live in a big town, you don't see the stars any more. That's why I live here. When I lived in Stockholm, I used to miss the silence, but most of all the stars. I don't understand why it doesn't seem to have occurred to anybody that in this country we have fantastic natural resources just waiting to be exploited. Why is nobody selling silence, in the same way that they sell the forests and the iron ore?'

I knew what she meant. Silence, starry skies, perhaps also solitariness – such things simply don't exist any more for most people. I was beginning to think that she was very like me, despite everything.

'I'm going to start a company,' she said. 'My boxer friends are going to be partners. We're going to start selling these glittering, silent nights. We'll all be very rich one of these days, I'm sure of it.'

'Who are these friends of yours?'

'There's a deserted village a few miles north of here. Its last inhabitant moved out one day in the 1970s. All the houses were empty, nobody even wanted them as holiday cottages. But Mr Mateotti, an old Italian shoemaker, came here while on his journey looking for silence. Now he's living in one of those houses, and he makes two pairs of shoes per year. At the beginning of May every year, a helicopter lands in the field behind his house. A man from Paris comes to pick up the shoes, pays him for his work, and passes on the orders for the shoes Giaconelli is expected to make in the coming year. There's an old rock singer living in Sparrman's village store that closed down years ago. He used to call himself the Red Bear, and he had two gold discs, making him a candidate for the Swedish King of Rock in competition with Ricky Rock and Gary Granite. His hair was bright red, and he made a scrumptious recording of "Peggy Sue". But when we celebrate midsummer and sit down to eat at our table in the boxing ring, we all want him to sing "The Great Pretender".'

I remembered that hit very well, in the original version recorded by the Platters. Harriet and I had even danced to it. I think I could remember all the words, if I put my mind to it.

But the Red Bear and his gold discs – that meant nothing to me at all.

'It sounds as if there are a lot of remarkable people living around here.'

'There are remarkable people living everywhere, but nobody notices them because they're old. We live in an age when old people are supposed to be as transparent as a sheet of glass. It's best if we don't even notice that they exist. You are becoming more and more transparent as well. My mother has been for ages.'

We stood there in silence. I could just about make out the lights from the caravan in the distance.

'Sometimes I feel an urge to lie down out here in the snow in my sleeping bag,' said Louise. 'When it's full moon, the blue light gives me the feeling of being in a desert. It's cold at night in the desert as well.'

'I've never been in a desert. Unless the shifting sands at Skagen count as a desert?'

'One of these days I really will go to bed out here. I'll take the risk of never waking up again. We don't only have rock musicians around here: we have jazz musicians as well. When I lie down out here and try to go to sleep, I'll have them standing round me, playing a slow lament.'

We set off again through the snow. An owl hooted somewhere in the distance. Stars fell out of the sky, but then seemed to be ignited again. I tried to digest what she had told me.

It turned out to be a very strange evening.

Louise prepared a meal in the caravan while Harriet and I sat squashed together on the narrow sofa bed. When I said Harriet and I would have to find somewhere to spend the night, Louise insisted that all three of us could sleep in her bed. I was going to protest, but decided not to. Louise produced a flagon of wine that seemed to be very strong and tasted of gooseberries. She then served up a stew which she claimed contained elk meat, and to go with it a variety of vegetables grown by one of her friends in a greenhouse, which he evidently used as a home as well. His name was Olof, he slept among his cucumbers, and was one of the men she boxed with in the spring.

It wasn't long before we were all drunk, especially Harriet. She kept dozing off. Louise had an amusing habit of clicking her teeth whenever she emptied a glass. I tried hard to stay sober, but failed.

Our conversation became increasingly confused and bewildering, but I managed to glean something of the kind of relationship Louise and Harriet had. They were constantly in touch, often quarrelled and hardly ever agreed about anything at all. But they were very fond of each other. I had acquired a family that oozed anger, but was held together by deep-felt love.

We talked for a long time about dogs – not the kind you take for walks on a lead, but the wild dogs that roam the African plains. My daughter said they reminded her of her friends living in the forest, a herd of African dogs wagging their tails at a herd of northern Swedish boxers. I told them that I had a dog of such mixed race that it was impossible to say exactly what its ancestry was. When Louise realised that the dog roamed around at will on my grandparents' island, she very much approved. She was also interested to hear about the old cat.

Harriet eventually fell asleep, thanks to a mixture of exhaustion, spirits and gooseberry wine. Louise gently laid a blanket over her.

'She has always been a snorer. When I was a child I used to pretend that it wasn't her snoring, but my father who came to visit every night in the form of an invisible but snoring creature. Do you snore?'

'Yes, I do.'

'Thank God for that! Here's to my father!'

'And here's to my daughter!'

She refilled our glasses carelessly and spilled wine on the table. She wiped it with the palm of her hand.

'When I heard the car driving up, I wondered what kind of an old codger Harriet had brought with her this time.'

'Does she often come visiting with different men?'

'Old codgers. Not men. She always manages to find somebody willing to drive her here, and then drive her home again. She often sits in some cafe or other in Stockholm, looking tired and miserable. Somebody always turns up to ask if he can help her, perhaps give her a lift home. Once she's in the car, with her walker stowed in the boot, she mentions that "home" is a couple of hundred miles or more north, just to the south of Hudiksvall. Surprisingly enough, hardly any of them refuse to take her. But she soon tires of the codger and ditches him for another one. My mother is very impatient. While I was growing up there would be long periods when there was always a different man in her bed on Sunday mornings. I used to love jumping up and down on them and waking them up, so that the men became aware of the unpleasant fact that I existed. But then there were times when she would go for weeks and months without so much as looking at a man.'

I went outside for a pee. The night was sparkling. I could see through the window how Louise placed a pillow under her mother's head. I almost burst into tears. I thought perhaps I ought to run away – take the car and get out of there. But I carried on observing her through the window, with a distinct feeling that she knew I was watching her. She suddenly turned her head towards the window and smiled.

I left the car where it was, and went back inside.

We sat there in the cramped caravan, drinking and conducting a tentative conversation. I don't think either of us really knew what we wanted to say. Louise produced some photo albums from a drawer. Some were faded black-and-white snaps, but most were poor-quality coloured pictures from the early 1970s, in the days when everybody had red-eye, and gaped at the photographer like vampires. There were pictures of the woman I had abandoned, and of the daughter I would have wanted more than anything in the world. A little girl, not a fully grown adult. There was something evasive in her expression. As if she didn't really want to be seen.

I leafed through the album. She didn't say much, merely answered the questions I put to her. Who had taken the picture? Where were they? The summer when my daughter was seven, she and Harriet spent some weeks with a man by the name of Richard Munter on the island of Getterön near Varberg. Munter was a powerfully built man, bald, and always had a cigarette in his mouth. I felt pangs of jealousy. This man had been together with my daughter when she was of the age I wished she still was. He had died a few years later, when his affair with Harriet was already over A bulldozer had toppled over, and he was crushed to death. All that remained of him now were poor-quality photographs with the ever-present cigarette, and the red eyes caused by the camera flash.

I closed the album: I didn't have the strength to cope with any more pictures. The level of the wine left in the flagon fell lower and lower. Harriet was asleep. I asked Louise who she wrote letters to. She shook her head.

'Not now. Tomorrow, when we've slept off the hangover. We must go to bed now. For the first time in my life I'm going to lie down between my parents.'

'There's not enough room in that bed for all three of us. I'll sleep on the floor.'

'There's room.'

She gently moved Harriet towards the wall, then folded away the table after first removing the cups and glasses. The bed was extendable, but it seemed obvious that it would be very cramped even so.

'I'm not going to get undressed in front of my father,' she said. 'Go outside. I'll bang on the wall once I've snuggled down under the covers.'

I did as I was told.

The starry sky was spinning round. I stumbled and fell down in the snow. I had acquired a daughter, and perhaps she would come to like, perhaps even to love the father she had never met before.

My whole life flashed before my eyes.

I'd managed to get this far. There might be a few crossroads yet to come. But not too many. My journey was nearly over.

Louise banged on the caravan wall. She had switched off all the lights and lit a candle standing on the tiny refrigerator. I could see two faces beside each other. Harriet was furthest away, and my daughter lay next to her. There was a narrow strip of bed left for me.

'Blow the candle out,' said Louise. 'I don't want to use it up the first night I've ever slept with my parents.'

I undressed, but kept on my vest and pants, blew the candle out and crept into bed. It was impossible to avoid touching Louise. I noticed to my horror that she was naked.

'Can't you put on a nightdress?' I asked. 'I can't possibly sleep with you next to me, naked. Surely you can understand that?'

She clambered over me and put on something that seemed to me to be a dress. Then she came back to bed.

'Time to go to sleep now,' she said. 'At long last I'm going to hear my father snoring. I shall lie awake until you've gone to sleep.'

Harriet was muttering in her sleep. Whenever she rolled over, we had to adjust as well. Louise felt warm. I only wished she had been a little girl sleeping soundly in a nightdress. Not a fully grown woman who had suddenly entered my life.

I don't know when I finally fell asleep. It was a long time before the bed seemed to stop spinning round. When I eventually woke up, I was alone.

The caravan was empty. The car was gone.

CHAPTER 3

I could see from the tracks in the snow how Louise had turned the car round and driven off. It occurred to me that all this had been planned in advance. Harriet had collected me, taken me to meet my unknown daughter, and then the pair of them had taken my car and vanished. I'd been dumped in the forest.

It was a quarter to ten. The weather had changed, and the temperature was above freezing. Water was dripping from the dirty caravan. I went back inside. I had a headache, and my mouth was parched. There was no sign of a message saying where they had gone. There was a Thermos flask of coffee on the table. I took out a cracked cup advertising a chain of health stores.

All the time the forest seemed to be creeping up on the caravan.

The coffee was strong, my hangover painful. I took my cup of coffee out into the fresh air. A cloud of damp mist hovered over the forest. A rifle shot echoed in the distance. I held my breath. It was followed by a second one, then nothing more. It seemed that all sounds were having to queue up before being allowed into the silence – and then only tentatively, one at a time.

I went back inside and started searching methodically through the caravan. Although it was small and cramped, there was a surprising amount of storage space. Louise kept everything in good order. Her favourite colour for clothes seemed to be chestnut brown, although some items were a shade of deep red. Most garments were in earth colours.

In a simple wooden chest with the year 1822 painted on the lid, I was amazed to find a large sum of money – thousand-kronor and five-hundred-kronor notes amounting to 47,500 in all. Then I began investigating drawers containing documents and letters.

The first item I found was a signed photograph of Erich Honecker. It said on the back that it dated from 1986, and had been sent by the

DDR Embassy in Stockholm. There were several more photographs in the drawer, all of them signed – Gorbachev, Ronald Reagan and Africans I had never heard of, but presumed were statesmen. There was also a photograph of an Australian prime minister whose name I couldn't make out.

I moved on to the second drawer, which was full of letters. After having read five of them, I began to understand how my daughter spent her time. She wrote letters to political leaders in all parts of the world, protesting about the way in which they were treating their own citizens and also people in other countries. In every envelope was a copy of the letter she had written in her sprawling hand, and the reply she had received. She had written to Erich Honecker in passionate English to the effect that the Berlin Wall was a disgraceful scandal. In reply she had received a photograph of Honecker on a podium waving to a blurred mass of East Germans. Louise had written to Margaret Thatcher urging her to treat the striking miners decently. I couldn't find a reply from the Iron Lady – in any case there was nothing in the envelope apart from a photograph of Thatcher clutching her handbag tightly. But where had Louise got all that money from? There was no clue here to answer that question.

That was as far as I got. I heard the sound of a car approaching, closed the drawers and went outside. Louise was driving fast. She braked abruptly in the wet snow.

Louise took the walker out of the boot.

'We didn't want to wake you up. I'm delighted to discover that my father is an expert in the art of snoring.'

She helped Harriet out of the car.

'We've been shopping,' said Harriet with a smile. 'I've bought some stockings, a skirt and a hat.'

Louise lifted some carrier bags from the back seat.

'My mother never did have any dress sense,' she said.

I carried the bags to the caravan while Louise helped Harriet to negotiate the slippery slope.

'We've eaten already,' said Louise. 'Are you hungry?'

I was in fact, but shook my head. I didn't like her borrowing my car without permission.

Harriet lay down on the bed to rest. I could see that the trip had done her good, but had exhausted her even so. She soon fell asleep. Louise produced the red hat that Harriet had bought.

'It suits her,' she said. 'It's a hat that could have been made specifically for her.'

'I've never seen her wearing a hat. When we were young, we were always bare-headed. Even when it was cold.'

Louise put the hat back in its bag, and looked round the caravan. Had I left any traces? Would she see that I'd spent the time they were away going through her belongings? She turned to look at me, then at my shoes that were standing on a newspaper next to the door. I'd had them for many years. They were very worn, and several of the lace-holes had split. She stood up, gently placed a blanket over her mother, and put on her jacket.

'Let's go out,' she said.

I was only too pleased to do so. My headache was painful.

We stood outside the caravan, breathing in the bracing air. It struck me that I had failed to write anything in my logbook for several days now. I don't like breaking my routine.

'Your car could do with a service,' said Louise. 'The brakes are out of balance.'

'It's good enough for me. Where are we going?'

'We're going to see a good friend of mine. I want to give you a present.'

I turned the car round in the slush. When we came to the main road, she told me to turn left. Several lorries laden with logs whipped up clouds of snow. After a couple of miles she told me to turn right: a sign indicated that we were heading for somewhere called Motjärvsbyn. The pine trees came to the very edge of the road, which was badly ploughed. Louise was concentrating on the road ahead. She was humming a tune: I recognised it, but couldn't remember what it was called.

We came to a fork, and Louise pointed to the left. After half a mile or so the forest receded and the road was lined with a row of cottages: but they were empty, dead, no smoke rose from their chimneys. Only the cottage at the end of the row, a two-storey wooden building with a battered, green-painted porch, showed any signs of life. A cat was sitting on the steps. A thin wisp of smoke rose up from the chimney.

'Via Salandra in Rome,' said Louise. 'That's a street I'm determined to walk along one of these days. Have you ever been to Rome?'

'I've been there several times. But I don't know the street you mention.'

Louise got out of the car. I followed her. The timber-built cottage must have been over a hundred years old; opera music could be heard from inside.

'There's a genius living in this house,' said Louise. 'Giaconelli Mateotti. He's an old man now. But he used to work for the famous shoemaking family Gatto. As a young apprentice, he was taught his trade by the one and only Angelo Gatto, who started his workshop at the beginning of the 1900s. But now Giaconelli has brought his skills to the forest. He grew tired of all the traffic, of all the important customers who were always so impatient and refused to accept the fact that patience and time were essential for the making of good shoes.'

Louise looked me in the eye, and smiled.

'I want to give you a present,' she said. 'I want Giaconelli to make you a pair of shoes. The ones you are wearing are an insult to your feet. Giaconelli has told me how our feet our constructed; the bones and muscles that enable us to walk and run, to stand on tiptoe, to dance ballet even. I know of opera singers who don't much care about directors or conductors or costumes or the high notes they have to sing – but are passionate about the shoes they wear which they believe enable them to sing properly.'

I stared at her. This was just like listening to my father. The brow-beaten waiter who had long since been banished to the grave. He had also spoken about opera singers and their shoes.

It was a strange feeling, realising that my father and my daughter had this in common.

But the shoes she was offering me? I wanted to object, but she raised her hand, walked up the steps, pushed the cat to one side and opened the front door. The opera music hit us with full force. It was coming from one of the rooms further back in the house. We passed through the rooms that Mateotti lived in, and where he kept his leather and his lasts. On one of the walls was a hand-painted motto that I assumed had been written by Mateotti himself. Somebody by the name of Chuang Chou had said: 'When the shoe fits, you don't think about the foot.'

One room was filled with wooden lasts, stacked on shelves from floor to ceiling. Each pair had a name label hanging from it. Louise pulled several lasts out and I was amazed when I read the names. Giaconelli had made shoes for American presidents, now dead; but their lasts were still here. There were conductors and actors, and people who'd achieved notoriety, for good reason or bad. It was a bewildering experience to make one's way through all these famous feet. It was as if the lasts themselves had struggled through snow and swamp so that the master I still hadn't met would be able to make his marvellous shoes.

'Two hundred individual operations,' said Louise. 'That's what's needed to make just one shoe.'

'They must be extremely expensive,' I said. 'When shoes are elevated to the level of jewels.'

She smiled.

'Giaconelli owes me a favour. He'll be pleased to reciprocate.'

Reciprocate.

When had I last heard anybody use that word in a context like that? I couldn't remember. Perhaps people who live in the depths of the forest use language in a different way? Perhaps people who live in big cities chase down words as if they were outlaws?

We continued to make our way through the old cottage. There were lasts and tools everywhere, and one room smelled strongly of the tanned hides piled up on simple trestle tables.

The opera had reached its finale. The old floorboards creaked as we walked over them.

'I hope you've washed your feet,' said Louise as we came to the final door, which was closed.

'What will happen if I haven't?'

'Giaconelli won't say anything, but he will be disappointed even if he doesn't show it.'

She knocked on the door, and opened it.

At a table with neat rows of tools sat an old man hunched over a last partly covered by leather. He wore glasses, and was completely bald apart from a few strands of hair at the back of his head. He was very thin, one of those persons who give the impression of being more or less weightless. There was nothing in the room apart from that table.

The walls were bare, there were no shelves containing lasts, nothing but naked wooden walls. The music had come from a radio set standing on one of the window ledges. Louise leaned over and kissed the old man on the top of his bald pate. He seemed to be delighted to see her, and carefully slid to one side the brown shoe he was making.

'This is my father,' said my daughter. 'He's come back after all these years.'

'A good man always comes back,' said Giaconelli. He had a thick accent.

He stood up and shook hands.

'You have a beautiful daughter,' he said. 'She's also an excellent boxer. She laughs a lot, and helps me whenever I need help. Why have you been hiding yourself away?'

He was still grasping my hand. His grip became even tighter.

'I haven't been hiding away. I didn't know that I had a daughter.'

'Deep down, a man always knows if he has a child or not. But you have turned up. Louise is happy. That's all I need to know. She's been waiting for long enough for you to come walking through the forest to visit her. Perhaps you've been on your way all these years without realising it? It's just as easy to lose your way inside yourself as it is to get lost in the woods or in a city.'

We went to Giaconelli's kitchen. Unlike his ascetic workshop, it was cluttered with all shapes and sizes of pans, dried herbs, bunches of garlic hanging from the ceiling, paraffin lamps and rows of jars with spices squeezed on to beautifully carved shelves. In the middle of the floor was a large, heavy table. Giaconelli noticed me looking at it, and stroked his hand over the smooth surface.

'Beech,' he said. 'The marvellous wood from which I make my lasts. I used to get my timber from France. It's not possible to make lasts from any other kind of wood: beech trees grow in rolling countryside, tolerate shade, and are not affected by big and unexpected variations in climate. I always used to choose personally which trees were going to be felled. I would pick them out two or three years before I needed to replenish my stocks. They were always felled during the winter and chopped into lengths of six feet, never any more, and were stored outdoors for long periods. When I moved to Sweden I found a supplier in Skåne. I'm too old now to raise the strength to drive down south to pick out individual trees myself. I find that very sad. But then, I make fewer and fewer lasts nowadays. I prowl round in my house and wonder how much longer I shall carry on making shoes. The man who chooses which trees to cut down for me presented me with this table when I celebrated my ninetieth birthday.'

The old master invited us to sit down, and produced a bottle of red wine in a raffia sleeve. His hand shook as he filled our glasses.

'A toast to the father who turned up!' he said, raising his glass.

The wine was very good. I realised I had been missing something during the years I had spent alone on my island: drinking wine with friends.

Giaconelli began telling remarkable stories about all the shoes he had made over the years, about customers who kept coming back for more, and their children who would turn up at his door after their parents had passed on. But most of his stories were about all the feet he had seen and measured before making his lasts, and how my feet would have already carried me for approaching 120,000 miles. About the significance of the ankle bone – *talus* – for the strength of a foot. He fascinated me by speaking about the apparently insignificant little cuboid bone – *os cuboideum*. He seemed to know everything there was to know about the bones and muscles of the foot. I recognised much of what he talked about from my days as a medical student – such as the incredibly ingenious anatomical constructions; how all muscles in the foot are short in order to give strength, endurance and flexibility.

Louise said she wanted Giaconelli to make a pair of shoes for me. He nodded sagely, and stared at my face for several second before turning his interest to my feet. He slid to one side an earthenware dish of almonds and other nuts, and asked me to stand on the table.

'Please take off your shoes and socks. I know some modern shoemakers measure feet with socks on, but I'm old-fashioned. I want to see the naked foot, nothing else.'

It had never occurred to me that I would ever have somebody measuring my foot in order to make me a pair of shoes. Shoes were something you tried on in a shop. I hesitated, but removed my worn-out shoes, took off my socks and clambered on to the table. Giaconelli looked at my shoes with a worried expression on his face. Louise had evidently been present before on occasions when the Italian had measured people's feet for shoes, as she withdrew into an adjacent room and returned with some sheets of paper, a clipboard and a pencil.

It was like going through a rite. Giaconelli examined my feet, stroked them with his fingers, and then asked if I was feeling well.

'I think so.'

'Are you completely healthy?'

'I have a headache.'

'Are your feet in good order?'

'Well, they don't hurt at least.'

'They're not swollen?'

'No.'

'The most important thing when making shoes is to measure the feet in calm circumstances, never at night, never in artificial light. I only want to see your feet when they are in good condition.'

I was beginning to wonder if I was the object of a practical joke. But Louise seemed completely serious, and was ready to start making notes.

It took Giaconelli over two hours to complete his examination of my feet, and to compile a list of the various measurements needed for the creation of my lasts, and thereafter of the shoes my daughter was keen to present me with. During those two hours, I learned that the world of feet is more complicated and comprehensive than one might think. Giaconelli spent ages searching for the theoretical longitudinal axis dictating whether my left or right foot pointed outwards or inwards. He checked the shape of the ball of each foot, and the instep, and investigated to see if I had any characteristic deformations: was I flat-footed, was either of my little toes unduly prominent, were my big toes higher than usual, so-called hammer toes? I gathered that there was one golden rule that Giaconelli followed meticulously: the best results were achieved using the simplest of measuring instruments. He restricted himself to two shoe heels and a shoemaker's tape measure. The tape measure was yellow and had two different calibration scales. The first scale was used to measure the foot in old French stitches, each one equal to 6.66 millimetres. The other one measured the width and circumference of the foot, using the metric system, in centimetres and millimetres.

Giaconelli also used an ancient set square, and when I stood on the sheet of indigo paper he drew a line round my feet using a simple pencil. He talked all the time, just as I recalled the older doctors doing when I started training as a surgeon – constantly describing exactly what they were doing and commenting on every incision, the blood flow, and the general condition of the patient. As he was drawing an outline of my feet, Giaconelli explained that the pencil must be held at exactly ninety degrees to the paper: if the angle was less than this, he elaborated in his heavily accented Swedish, the shoes would be at least one size too small.

He traced the outline of each foot with his pencil, always starting from the heel and following the inside of the foot to the big toe, then along the tips of the toes, and back to the heel via the outside of the foot. He instructed me to press my toes down hard on the ground. He used the word ground, even though I was standing on a sheet of paper on a table. As far as Giaconelli was concerned, people always stood on the ground, nowhere else.

'Good shoes help a person to forget about his feet,' he said. 'Nobody travels through life on a table or on a sheet of paper. Feet and the ground are linked together.'

As the left foot and the right foot are never identical, it is essential to draw outlines of both of them. When the outlines were completed, Giaconelli marked the location of the first and the fifth phalanx, and also the most prominent points of the ball of the foot and the heel. He drew very slowly, as if he were not only following the outline of my foot, but was also relating to an inner process that I knew nothing about, and could only guess at. I had noticed this characteristic in the surgeons I admired.

When I was finally allowed to get down from the table, the whole procedure was repeated once again, with me sitting in an old rattan basket chair. I assumed Giaconelli had taken it with him from Rome when he'd made up his mind to continue creating his masterpieces in the depths of the northern forests. He displayed the same degree of meticulous accuracy, but now he didn't speak: instead he hummed arias from the opera he'd been listening to when Louise and I had arrived at his house.

Eventually, when all the measuring was finished and I was allowed to put back on my socks and my old, worn-out shoes, we drank another glass of wine. Giaconelli seemed to be tired, as if the measuring had exhausted him.

'I suggest a pair of black shoes with a hint of violet,' said Giaconelli, 'and a perforated pattern on the uppers. We shall use two different leathers in order to present the design discreetly but also to add a personal touch. I have leather for the upper that was tanned two hundred years ago. That will give something special in the way of colour and subtlety.'

He poured us another glass of wine, emptying the bottle.

'The shoes will be ready a year from now,' he said. 'At the moment I am busy with a pair for a Vatican cardinal. I'm also committed to making a pair of shoes for Keskinen, the conductor, and I have promised the diva Klinkova some shoes appropriate for her concerts featuring Romantic lieder. I shall be able to start on yours eight months from now, and they'll be ready in a year.'

We emptied our glasses. He shook us both by the hand, and withdrew. As we left through the front door, we could hear once again music coming from the room he used as his workshop.

I had met a master craftsman who lived in a deserted village in the depths of the vast northern forests. Far away from urban areas, there lived people with marvellous and unexpected skills.

'A remarkable man,' I said as we walked to the car.

'An artist,' said my daughter. 'His shoes are beyond compare. They're impossible to imitate.'

'Why did he come here?'

'The city was driving him mad. The crowds, all the impatience that left him no peace and quiet in which to carry out his work. He lived in the Via Salandra. I made up my mind some time ago to go there, in order to see the place he had left behind.'

We drove through the gathering dusk. As we approached a bus stop, she asked me to pull into the side and stop.

The forest came right down to the edge of the road. I looked at her.

'Why are we stopping?'

She stretched out her hand. I took hold of it. We sat there in silence. A lorry laden with logs thundered past, whipping up a cloud of snow.

'I know you searched through my caravan while we were out. I don't mind. You'll never be able to find my secrets in drawers or on shelves.'

'I noticed that you write letters and sometimes receive answers. But probably not the answers you'd like to get?'

'I receive signed photographs from politicians I accuse of crimes. Most of them answer evasively, others not at all.'

'What do you hope to achieve?'

'To make a difference that's so small it's not even noticeable. But it's a difference, for all that.'

I had a lot of questions, but she interrupted me before I had chance to ask them.

'What do you want to know about me?'

'You lead a strange life out here in the forest. But then, maybe it's no more strange than my own. I find it hard to ask all the questions I'd like to have answers to: but I can sometimes be a good listener. A doctor has to be.'

She sat in silence for a while before she started speaking.

'You have a daughter who's been in prison. That was eleven years ago. I hadn't committed any violent crimes. Only fraud.'

She half opened the door, and immediately it became cold inside the car.

'I'm telling you the facts,' she said. 'You and Mum seem to have lied to each other. I don't want to be like you.'

'We were young,' I said. 'Neither of us knew enough about ourselves to do the right thing every time. It can sometimes be very hard to act in accordance with the truth. It's much easier to tell lies.'

'I want you to know the kind of life I've led. When I was a child, I felt like a changeling. Or, if you like, as if I'd been billeted with my mother by chance, while waiting for my real parents. She and I were at war. You ought to know that it's not easy to live with Harriet. That's something you've escaped having to go through.'

'What happened?'

She shrugged.

'The usual horror stories. One thing after another. Glue sniffing, thinner, drugs, truancy. But it didn't get me down, I pulled through. I recall that period of my life as a time playing non-stop blind man's buff. A life led with a scarf tied over my eyes. Instead of helping, all my mum did was tell me off. She tried to create an atmosphere of love between us by shouting at me. I left home just as soon as I could. I was trapped in a net of guilt: and then came all the fraud and deceit, and in the end I was locked up. Do you know how many times Harriet came to visit me while I was locked up?'

'No?'

'Once. Shortly before I was released. Just to make sure that I had no intention of moving back in with her. We didn't speak to each other for five years after that. It was a long time before we got in touch again.'

'What happened?'

'I met Janne, who came from up here in the north. One morning I woke up to find him stone-cold dead in bed beside me. Janne's funeral took place in a church not far from here. His relatives arrived. I didn't know any of them. Without warning I stood up and announced that I wanted to sing a song. I don't know where I got the courage from. Maybe I was angry to find that I was on my own again, and maybe I was annoyed by all those relatives who hadn't put in an appearance when Janne needed them. The only song I could remember was the first verse of "Sailing". I sang it twice – and looking back, I think it's the best thing I've ever done in my life. When I emerged from the church and saw those apparently endless Hälsningland forests, I had the feeling that I belonged here, in the trees and the silence. That's why I ended up here. Nothing was planned, it just happened. Everybody else around here is leaving and heading for the cities: but I turned my back on urban life. I found people here that I'd never realised existed. Nobody had told me about them.'

She stopped, and announced that it was too cold in the car to carry on talking. I had the feeling that what she had said could have been the blurb on the back of a book. A summary of a life, lived thus far. I still didn't really know anything about my daughter. But she had begun to tell me.

I switched on the engine. The headlights illuminated the darkness.

'I wanted you to know,' she said. 'One thing at a time.'

'Let it take as long as it needs,' I said. 'The best way to get to know another person is one step at a time. That applies to you just as much as it does to me. If you go too fast, you can collide, or run aground.'

'As happens at sea?'

'What you don't see is what you notice too late. That doesn't only apply to unmarked channels at sea, it applies to people as well.'

I pulled out and continued along the main road. Why hadn't I told her about the catastrophe that had blighted my life? Perhaps it was only due to exhaustion and confusion as a result of the astonishing revelations of the last couple of days. I would tell her soon enough, but not just yet. It was as if I was still trapped in that moment when I'd emerged from my hole in the ice, had the feeling that there was something behind me, looked round and saw Harriet, leaning on her wheeled walker.

I was deep in the melancholy forest of northern Sweden. But even so, most of me was still in my hole in the ice.

When I got back home, if the thaw hadn't started and the ice was still there, it would take me a long time to chop it away again and open up the hole.

CHAPTER 4

The headlight beams and shadows danced over the snow.

We got out of the car without speaking. It was a cloudless and starry sky, colder now, and the temperature was falling. Faint light seeped out from the caravan windows.

When we went inside I could hear from Harriet's breathing that all was not well. I failed to wake her up. I took her pulse: it was fast and irregular. I had my blood pressure monitor in the car. I asked Louise to fetch it. Both Harriet's diastolic and systolic readings were too high.

We carried her out to my car. Louise asked what had happened. I told her that we needed to take Harriet to an A&E department where they could examine her thoroughly. Maybe she had had a stroke, perhaps something had happened in connection with her general condition: I didn't know.

We drove through the darkness to Hudiksvall. The hospital lay in waiting, looking like an illuminated liner. We were received by two friendly nurses at the Emergency entrance; Harriet had regained consciousness, and it was not long before a doctor arrived to examine her. Although Louise looked at me somewhat oddly, I didn't mention the fact that I was a doctor myself – or, at least, had been. I merely informed them that Harriet had cancer, and that her days were numbered. She was taking medicine to ease her pain, that was all. I wrote the names of the medication on a piece of paper, and gave it to the doctor.

We waited while the doctor, who was about my age, performed the examination. He said afterwards that he would keep her in overnight for observation. He couldn't find anything specific that might have caused her reaction: it was presumably due to a deterioration in her general condition.

Harriet had fallen asleep again when we left her and emerged once more into the dark night. It was gone two by now; the sky was still cloudless. Louise suddenly stopped.

'Is she going to die now?' she asked.

'I don't think she's ready to die yet. She's a tough lady. If she has the strength to walk over the ice with her walker, I reckon she has a lot of strength left. I think she'll tell us when the time comes.'

'I always get hungry when I'm scared,' said Louise. 'Some people feel ill, but I simply have to eat.'

We got into the freezing cold car.

I had noticed an all-night hamburger restaurant on the edge of town, so we drove there. Several shaven-headed and overweight youths looking like Teddy boys from the distant fifties were sitting round one of the tables. All of them were drunk, apart from one – there was always one who stayed sober, and did the driving. A big, highly polished Chevrolet was parked outside. There was a smell of hair cream as we passed by their table.

To my astonishment, I heard them talking about Jussi Björling. Louise had also noticed their loud-voiced, drunken conversation. She pointed discreetly at one of the four men, with gold earrings, a beer belly falling out of his jeans and salad dressing smeared round his mouth.

'Bror Olofsson,' she said in a half-whisper. 'The gang call themselves the Bror Brothers. Bror has a lovely singing voice. When he was a young lad he used to sing solos in the church choir. But he stopped all that when he became a teenager and a tearaway. There are those who are convinced he could have gone far – he might even have made it to the opera stage.'

'Why are there no normal people up here?' I asked as I studied the menu. 'Why are all the people we meet so unusual? Italians who make shoes, or a retro Teddy boy who talks about Jussi Björling?'

'There's no such thing as normal people,' she said. 'That's a twisted view of the world that politicians want us to believe. That we are all a part of an endless mass of normality, with no possibility, never mind desire to claim that we are different. I've often thought that I ought to write to Swedish politicians. To the secret team.'

'What team is that?'

'That's what I call them. The ones with the power. The ones who receive my letters but never answer them – they just send pin-up photos. The secret team with all the power.'

She ordered something called the King's Platter, while I made do with a large coffee, a small bag of crisps and a hamburger. She really was hungry. She gave the impression of wanting to stuff everything on her tray into her mouth at one go.

It was not a pretty sight. Her table manners embarrassed me.

She's like an impoverished child, I thought. I remembered a trip I'd made to Sudan with a group of orthopaedists, in order to find out the best way of setting up clinics for landmine casualties requiring artificial limbs. I had watched those penniless children attacking their food in extreme desperation – a few grains of rice, a single vegetable, and perhaps a biscuit sent from some well-meaning country dedicated to assisting the Third World.

In addition to the four Teddy boys who had crept out from under a stone from another age, there were a few lorry drivers dotted around the restaurant. They were hunched over their empty trays, as if they were either asleep, or contemplating their mortality. There was also a couple of young girls, very young – they couldn't have been more than fourteen or fifteen years old. They sat there whispering to each other, occasionally erupting into laughter before reverting to whispers. I could remember that atmosphere, all those confidential certainties one could pass on and feel informed about as a teenager. We all gave promises but broke them almost immediately, promised to keep secrets but spread them as quickly as possible. Nevertheless, they were far too young to be sitting there in the middle of the night. I was shocked. Shouldn't they be in bed? Louise noticed what I was looking at. She had gobbled her slap-up meal before I had even taken the lid off my plastic beaker of coffee.

'I've never seen them before,' she said. 'They're not from these parts.'

'Are you saying you know everybody who lives in this town?'

'I just know.'

I tried to drink the coffee, but it was too bitter. It seemed to me we ought to go back to the caravan and try to get a few hours' sleep before we needed to return to the hospital. But we stayed put until dawn. The Teddy boys had gone by then. So had the two girls. It hadn't registered with me when the lorry drivers left: suddenly they were no longer there. Louise hadn't noticed when they left either.

'Some people are like migratory birds,' she said. 'Those vast distances they fly are always covered during the night. They just flew away without our noticing them.'

Louise ordered a cup of tea. The two dark-skinned men behind the counter spoke Swedish in a way that was difficult to understand, then lapsed into a language that was very melodic but filled me with melancholy. Louise occasionally asked if we ought to go back to the hospital.

'They have your mobile number if anything should happen,' I said. 'We might just as well stay here.'

What we had in prospect was boundless conversation – a chronicle embracing almost forty years. Perhaps this hamburger joint, with its neon lights and the smell of deep-frying, was the framework we required?

Louise continued telling me about her life. At one point she had dreamt about becoming a mountaineer. When I asked her why, she said it was because she was afraid of heights.

'Was that really such a good idea? Hanging from ropes on a sheer cliff face when you are scared stiff of climbing a ladder?'

'I thought I'd get more out of it than people who aren't scared of heights. I tried it once, up in Lappland. It wasn't a very steep cliff, but my arms weren't strong enough. I buried my mountaineering dreams in the heather up there in the far north. By the time I'd got as far south as Sundsvall – which wasn't all that far, let's face it – I'd stopped crying over my abandoned dream, and decided to become a juggler instead.'

'And how did that go?'

'I can still keep three balls in the air for quite a long time. Or three bottles. But I was never as good as I wanted to be.'

I waited for what was coming next. Somebody opened the squeaky outside door, and there was a blast of cold air before it closed again.

'I thought I would never find what I was looking for. Especially as I didn't know what it was. Or maybe it would be more accurate to say that I knew what I wanted, but didn't think I'd ever get it.'

'A father?'

She nodded.

'I tried to find you in the games I played. Every eleventh man I passed in the street was my father. At midsummer, every Swedish girl picks seven different wild flowers and places them under her pillow in order to dream about the man she's going to marry: I picked lots and lots of flowers in order to see you. But you never appeared. I remember once being in a church. There was an altarpiece, Jesus soaring up in a beam of light that seemed to be coming from underneath him. Two Roman soldiers were on their knees, terrified of what they had done when they nailed him to the cross. All at once, I was certain that one of those soldiers was you. His face was identical to yours. The first time I saw you, you had a helmet on your head.'

'Didn't Harriet have any photos?'

'I asked her. I searched through all her belongings. There weren't any.'

'We took lots of pictures of each other. She was always the one who kept and looked after our snaps.'

'She told me there weren't any. If she's burnt them all, you are the one she'll have to answer to.'

She went to refill her cup of tea. One of the men working in the kitchen was sitting on the floor, leaning against the wall – fast asleep. His jaw had dropped.

I wondered what he was dreaming about.

Now the story of her life featured horses and riders.

'We never had enough money to pay for me to have riding lessons. Not even when Harriet had been promoted to manageress of a shoe shop, with a better salary. Sometimes I still get angry when I remember how mean she was. I used to turn up for the riding lessons, but I was on the wrong side of the fence: I had to stand outside and watch as the other girls rode around like little female warriors. I had the feeling of being forced to act as both horse and rider. I divided myself up into two parts: part of me was the horse and the other part the rider. When I was feeling good, and found it easy to get up in the morning, I would sit on the horse and there would be no split in my life. But when I didn't feel like getting out of bed in the morning, it was as if I was the horse – as if I'd retired to a corner of the paddock and refused to respond, no matter how much they whipped me. I tried to feel that I and the horse were one and the same. I think that doing that helped me to survive all the difficulties I experienced as a child. Perhaps later as well. I sit on my horse, and my horse carries me – except when I jump off of my own accord.'

She stopped abruptly, as if she regretted saying what she had said.

* * *

Five o'clock came round. We were the only customers. The man leaning against the wall was still asleep. The other one was slowly and laboriously filling the half-empty sugar bowls.

Out of the blue, Louise suddenly exclaimed: 'Caravaggio! I've no idea why I just started thinking about him, and his furious outbursts and his life-threatening knives. Perhaps because if he'd lived in our time, he might well have painted this hamburger bar, and people like you and me.'

Caravaggio the artist? I couldn't see any paintings in my mind's eye, but I recognised the name. A vague impression of dark colours, always with dramatic motifs, edged its way into my tired brain.

'I don't know anything about art.'

'Nor do I. But I once saw a painting of a man holding a decapitated head in his hand. When I realised that the artist had depicted his own head, I felt I really had to find out more about him. I made up my mind to visit every single place where his pictures were hung. It was not enough to look at reproductions in books. Instead of making a pilgrimage to monasteries or churches, I started following in Caravaggio's tracks. As soon as I had managed to save up enough money, I set off for Madrid and other places where his paintings could be seen. I lived as cheaply as possible, sometimes even sleeping rough on park benches. But I have seen his pictures, I've got to know the people he painted and turned them into my companions. I have a long way to go yet though. You're welcome to pay for the journeys I still have to make.'

'I'm not a rich man.'

'I thought doctors were paid pretty well?'

'It's many years since I worked as a doctor. I'm a pensioner.'

'With no money in the bank?'

Didn't she believe me? I decided that it was the time of day (or night) and the stuffy atmosphere making me suspicious. The neon tubes on the ceiling were not illuminating us, they were staring down at our heads, keeping watch over us.

She continued talking about Caravaggio, and eventually I began to understand some of the passion that filled her. She was a museum, slowly developing each room with her own interpretation of the great painter's life's work. As far as she was concerned, he wasn't somebody who had lived more than four hundred years ago, but was ensconced in a deserted house in the forests surrounding her caravan.

The occasional early bird started drifting into the bar and stood at the counter, reading the menu. 'Monster Meal, Mega-Monster, Mini-Monster, Night Owl's Menu.' It occurred to me that there were important stories to be told even in scruffy restaurants like this one. Just for a moment, this unpleasant, smelly place was transformed into an art gallery.

My daughter talked about Caravaggio as if he had been a close relative, a brother, or a man she was in love with and dreamed of living with.

He was born Michelangelo Merisi da Caravaggio. His father, Fermi, had died when he was six years old. He barely remembered him; his father was just another of the shadows in his life, an unfinished portrait in one of his big inner galleries. His mother lived rather longer, until he was nineteen. But all she inspired was silence, a rancorous, soundless fury.

Louise talked about a portrait of Caravaggio made by an artist called Leoni using red and black chalk. It was like an ancient police 'Wanted' notice posted on a house wall. Red and black, charcoal and blood. He peers at us from out of the picture, attentive, evasive. Do we really exist, or are we merely figments of his imagination? He has dark hair, a beard, a powerful nose, eyes with highly arched brows – a handsome man, some would say. Others maintained that he was nothing remarkable, a criminal type, filled with violence and hatred, despite his enormous ability to depict people and movement.

As if reciting a verse of a hymn she had learned off by heart, she quoted a cardinal whose name might have been Borromeo – I'm not sure I heard it properly. He wrote that 'I became aware of an artist in Rome who behaved badly, had disgusting habits, was always dressed in ragged and filthy clothes. This painter, who was notorious for his cantankerous ways and his brutality, produced no art of significance. He used his paintbrushes to produce only taverns, drunkards, sly prophetesses and actors. Hard though it may be to understand, he took pleasure in portraying these wretched people.'

Caravaggio was a supremely gifted artist, but also a very dangerous man. He had a violent temperament, and was always looking for trouble. He fought with his fists and sometimes with knives, and once murdered a man as a result of a quarrel over a point in a tennis game. But above all else, he was dangerous because in his paintings he confessed that he was afraid. The fact that he didn't conceal his fear in the shadows made – and still makes – him dangerous.

Louise talked about Caravaggio, and she also talked about death. It is visible in all his paintings, in the hole made by a maggot in an apple on top of a basket of fruit, or in the eyes of someone who is about to be decapitated.

She said that Caravaggio never found what he was looking for. He always settled for something else. Such as the horses he painted, their frothing mouths an expression of the fury he had inside himself.

He painted everything. But he never painted the sea.

Louise said that she was so deeply moved by his work because it offered her proximity. There was always a space in his pictures where she could place herself. She could be one of the people in his canvases, and she didn't need to be afraid that they might chase her away. She had often sought consolation in his paintings, in the lovingly drawn details, where his brushstrokes had become fingertips stroking the faces he conjured up in his dark colours.

Louise transformed the foul-smelling hamburger bar into a beach on the Italian coast on 16 July 1609. The heat is oppressive. Caravaggio is walking on the sands somewhere to the north of Rome, washed ashore in the form of human jetsam. A little *felucca* (whatever that might be – Louise never explained) has sailed away. On board the ship are his paintings and paintbrushes, his oils and a kitbag with his ragged and filthy clothes and shoes. He is alone on the sands, the Roman summer is stiflingly hot, perhaps a gentle breeze cools him out there at the water's edge, but there are also mosquitoes swarming around, mosquitoes that bite him, injecting poison into his bloodstream. As he lies exhausted and curled up on the beach during the hot, humid nights, they bite him over and over again and the malaria parasites begin to multiply in his liver. The first attack of fever catches him unaware. He doesn't know he's going to die, but the paintings he hasn't yet completed but that he carries inside him will soon become petrified in his brain. 'Life is a dream impossible to pin down,' he had once said. Or perhaps it was Louise who had invented this poetic truth.

I listened in astonished admiration. Only now had I seen who she really was. I had a daughter who knew something about what it means to be a human being.

I no longer needed to doubt whether the long-dead Caravaggio was one of her closest friends. She could communicate with the dead just as well as with the living. Perhaps even better?

She carried on talking until she suddenly fell silent. The man behind the counter had woken up. He yawned as he opened a plastic bag of chips that he tipped into the deep-fryer.

We sat there for a long time without speaking. Then she stood up and went to refill her cup.

When she came back I told her how I had amputated the wrong arm of a patient. I hadn't thought about what to say, it simply tumbled out, as if it were inevitable that I should now describe the incident that I had hitherto thought was the most significant happening in my life. At first she didn't seem to understand that what I was telling her had actually happened to me. But the penny dropped in the end. That fatal mistake had happened twelve years ago. I was given a warning. That would hardly have been the end of my career if I had accepted it, but I thought it was unjust. I defended myself by insisting that I had been placed in an impossible situation. Waiting lists were growing longer and longer, but at the same time cutbacks were being enforced. All I did was work, day in and day out. And one day the safety net failed. During an operation shortly after nine o'clock in the morning, a young woman lost her healthy right arm, just above her elbow. It was not a complicated operation – not that an amputation is ever a routine matter, but there was nothing to make me aware that I had made a fatal mistake.

'How is it possible?' Louise asked when I had finished talking.

'It just is possible,' I said. 'If you live long enough, you'll realise that nothing is impossible.'

'I'm intending to live for a long time,' she said. 'Why do you sound so angry? Why do you become so unpleasant?'

I flung my arms out wide.

'That wasn't my intention. Perhaps I'm tired. It's nearly half past six in the morning. We've spent the whole night here. We need a few hours' sleep.'

'Let's go home, then,' she said, getting to her feet. 'The hospital hasn't rung.'

I remained seated.

'I can't sleep in that narrow bed.'

'Then I'll sleep on the floor.'

'It's not worth going home. We'll have to return to the hospital as soon as we get there.'

She sat down again. I could see that she was just as tired as me. The man behind the counter had fallen asleep again, his chin hanging down towards his chest.

The neon lights on the ceiling continued to stare down at us, like the scheming eyes of a dragon.

CHAPTER 5

Dawn came as a relief.

We returned to the hospital at half past eight. It had started snowing, just a few flakes. I could see my tired face in the rear-view mirror. It made me wince, gave me a feeling of death, of inexorability.

I was on a downward path, hemmed in by my own epilogue. There were a few entries and exits still to go, but not much more.

I was so absorbed in my thoughts that I missed the turning for the hospital. Louise looked at me in surprise.

'We should have turned right there.'

I said nothing, drove round the block and then took the correct turning. Standing outside the A&E entrance was one of the nurses who had received us during the night. She was smoking a cigarette and seemed to have forgotten who we were. In another age, I thought, she could have been in one of Caravaggio's paintings.

We went in. The door to Harriet's room was open. The room was empty. A nurse approached along the corridor. I asked about Harriet. She looked searchingly at us. We must have resembled a pair of woodlice that had crept out into view after a night spent under a cold stone.

'Mrs Hörnfeldt is no longer here,' she said.

'Where have you sent her?'

'We haven't sent her anywhere. She simply went away. She got dressed and vanished.'

She seemed angry, as if Harriet had let her down personally.

'But somebody must have seen her go, surely?' I said.

'The night staff kept checking regularly, but when they looked in at a quarter past seven, she had left. There's nothing we can do.'

I turned to Louise. She made a movement with her eyes that I interpreted as a signal.

'Did she leave anything behind?' Louise asked.

'No, nothing.'

'Then she must have gone home.'

'She ought to have informed us if she didn't want to stay here.'

'That's the way she is,' said Louise. 'That's my mother for you.'

We left through the A&E entrance.

'I know what she's like,' said Louise. 'I also know where she is. We have an agreement that we made when I was a little girl. The nearest cafe, that's where we'll meet. If we ever get separated.'

We walked round the hospital to the main entrance. There was a cafe area in the big foyer.

Harriet was sitting at a table with a cup of coffee. She waved when she saw us coming. She appeared almost cheerful.

'We still don't know what's wrong with you,' I said sternly. 'The doctors ought to have been given an opportunity to check the samples they've taken.'

'I've got cancer,' said Harriet, 'and I'm going to die. Time is too short for me to lie around in hospital and start panicking. I don't know what happened yesterday. I expect I drank too much. I want to go home now.'

'To my place, or to Stockholm?'

Harriet took hold of Louise's arm and pulled herself up. Her walker was standing by a newspaper stall. She grasped at the handles with her frail fingers. It was impossible to understand how she had managed to pull me out of the forest pool.

When we got back to the caravan, all three of us lay down on the narrow bed. I lay on the outside with one knee on the floor, and soon fell asleep.

In my dreams, Jansson approached me in his hydrocopter. It carved its way towards me like a sharp saw cutting through ice. I hid behind a rock until he had gone away. When I stood up I saw Harriet standing on the ice with the wheeled walker. She was naked. Next to her was a large hole in the ice.

I woke up with a start. The two women were asleep. I thought of grabbing my jacket and getting out of there. But I stayed put. Soon, I fell asleep again.

We all woke up at the same time. It was one o'clock. I went outside for a pee. It had stopped snowing and the clouds had started to part.

We drank coffee. Harriet asked me to take her blood pressure as she had a headache. It was only slightly above normal. Louise wanted me to take her blood pressure as well.

'One of my first memories of my father will be that he took my blood pressure,' she said. 'First the buckets of water, and now this.'

It was very low. I asked if she sometimes had bouts of dizziness.

'Only when I'm drunk.'

'Never on other occasions?'

'I've never fainted in my life.'

I put my blood pressure monitor away. We had finished the coffee, and it was a quarter past two. It was warm inside the caravan. Perhaps too warm? Was it the stifling air, short of oxygen, that caused them to lose their tempers? But whatever the cause, I was suddenly attacked from two sides. It started with Harriet asking me what it felt like, having a daughter, now that I'd known about it for a few days.

'What does it feel like? I don't think I can answer that one.'

'Your indifference is frightening,' she said.

'You know nothing about how I'm feeling,' I said.

'I know you.'

'We haven't met for nearly forty years! I'm not the same as I was then.'

'You're too cowardly to admit that what I say is true. You didn't have the courage then to say that you wanted us to stop seeing each other. You ran away then, and you're running away now. Can't you bring yourself to tell the truth just once? Is there no truth in you at all?'

Before I had chance to say anything, Louise chipped in that a man who had abandoned Harriet in the way I had done could hardly be expected to react to an unexpected child with anything but indifference, perhaps fear, and at most with a bit of curiosity.

'I can't go along with that,' I said. 'I've apologised for what I did, and I couldn't have known anything about a child because you never told me.'

'How could I tell you when you'd run away?'

'In the car on the way to the forest pool, you said you'd never tried to find me.'

'Are you accusing a dying person of lying?'

'I'm not accusing anybody.'

'Tell it as it is!' yelled Louise. 'Answer her question!'

'What question?'

'Why you're indifferent.'

'I'm not indifferent. I'm pleased.'

'I see no sign of pleasure in you.'

'There's not enough room in this caravan to dance on the table! If that's what you'd like me to do.'

'Don't think for one moment I'm doing this for you,' screeched Harriet. 'I'm doing it for her sake.'

We yelled and shouted. The walls of the cramped caravan came close to collapsing. Deep down, of course, I knew that what they were saying was true. I had let Harriet down, and perhaps I hadn't displayed enough ebullient happiness on meeting my daughter. Nevertheless, this was too much. I couldn't take it. I don't know how long we carried on with this pointless shouting and sparring. On several occasions I expected Louise to clench her boxer's fists and give me a telling punch. I daren't even begin to think about what level Harriet's blood pressure reached. In the end I stood up, grabbed my bag and my jacket and shoes.

'Go to hell, the pair of you!' I yelled as I stormed out of the caravan.

Louise didn't follow me out. Neither of them said a word. Everything was silent. I walked down to the car in my stockinged feet, got in and drove off. Not until I came to the main road did I stop, remove my soaking wet socks and put on my shoes over my bare feet.

I was still upset about the accusations. During the journey the exchanges came back to me in my head, over and over again. I sometimes changed what I had said, made my responses clearer, sharper. But what they had said was the same all the time.

I reached Stockholm in the middle of the night, having driven far too quickly; I slept in the car for a while until it became too cold, then continued as far as Södertälje. I hadn't the strength to drive any further. I checked into a motel, and fell asleep the moment my head touched the pillow. At about one the next day I continued my journey south, having telephoned Jansson and left a message on his answering machine: could he collect me at half past five? I wasn't sure how he felt about driving in the dark. I crossed my fingers and hoped he would check his messages and had some decent headlights on his hydrocopter.

Jansson was waiting when I arrived at the harbour. He told me he had been feeding the animals every day. I thanked him and said I was in a hurry to get home.

When we arrived, Jansson refused to accept any payment.

'I can't take a fare from my doctor.'

'I'm not your doctor. We can settle up the next time you come.'

I remained standing on the jetty until he had disappeared behind the rocks and the lights had faded away. I suddenly noticed that my cat and my dog were sitting next to me on the jetty. I bent down to stroke them. The dog seemed to be thinner than he had been. I left my rucksack on the jetty, I was too tired to see to it.

There were three of us on this island, just as there had been three of us in the caravan. But nobody would be launching an attack on me here. It was a relief to enter my own kitchen again. I fed the animals, sat down at the kitchen table and closed my eyes.

I had difficulty in sleeping that night. I got out of bed again and again. It was full moon, the sky was clear. The moonlight oozed over the rocks and the white ice. I put on my boots and fur coat and went down to the jetty. The dog didn't notice that I had gone out, and the cat opened an eye but didn't stir from the sofa. It was cold outside. My suitcase had somehow burst open, shirts and socks had fallen out. For the second time, I left it to its fate.

It was while I was standing there on the jetty that I realised I had another journey to make. For twelve years I had succeeded in convincing myself that it wasn't necessary, but the meeting with Louise and our long nocturnal conversation had changed all that. I was obliged to undertake this new journey. And I now wanted to do it.

Somewhere in Sweden there was a young woman who had lost an arm – the wrong arm amputated by me. She was twenty years old when it happened, so now she would be thirty-two. I could remember her name: Agnes Klarström. As I stood on the jetty, all the details came back to me – as if I had just reread her case notes. She came from one of the southern suburbs of Stockholm, Aspudden or Bagarmossen. It had all started as a pain in her shoulder. She was an outstanding swimmer and took part in competitions. For a long time she and her trainer assumed it was due to overexertion, but when it came to the point that she could no longer enter a pool without severe shoulder pains, she went to a doctor for a thorough examination. Then everything happened very quickly: a malignant bone tumour was confirmed, and amputation was the only possibility, despite the fact that it would be catastrophic for her swimming ambitions. Having been a swimming champion, she would be one-armed for the rest of her life.

I wasn't even down for the operation – she was the patient of one of my colleagues. But his wife was involved in a serious car crash, and his operations list was farmed out somewhat haphazardly among the other orthopaedic surgeons. Agnes Klarström was assigned to me.

The operation took longer than an hour. I can still recall all the details, how the theatre nurses washed and prepared the wrong arm. It was my responsibility to check that the correct arm would be operated on, but I relied on my staff.

That was twelve years ago now. I had ruined Agnes Klarström's life, and also my own. And what made matters even worse was that a subsequent examination of the arm with the tumour indicated that amputation had not been necessary.

It had never occurred to me that I would one day go to visit her. The only time I had ever spoken to her was immediately after the operation when she was still groggy.

It was two in the morning by now. I went back to the house and sat down at my kitchen table. I still hadn't opened the door of my ant room. Perhaps I was afraid they would come teeming out if I did so.

I rang directory enquiries, but there was nobody in Stockholm of that name. I asked the operator, who said her name was Elin, to extend the search to the whole of Sweden.

There was one Agnes Klarström who could be the one I was looking for. She lived near Flen, some fifty miles west of Stockholm: the address suggested a farm in a village called Sångledsbyn. I made a note of the address and her telephone number.

The dog was asleep. The cat was outside in the moonlight. I stood up and went to the room in which a half-finished mat was still stretched over the frame of my grandmother's loom. It had always been a significant image as far as I was concerned: this is what death always looks like when it rudely interrupts and terminates our lives. On a shelf where there had previously been reels of thread, I stored various papers I had been keeping for many years. A thin file containing documents, from my rather poor school-leaving report that my father was so proud of that he learned it off by heart, to the accursed copy of the notes of the amputation. The file was sparse because I have always had no difficulty in discarding papers that most people regard as important to keep. On top was the will that a ridiculously expensive lawyer had drawn up for me. Now I was forced to change it, because I had acquired a daughter. But that was not the reason I had come to the room with the loom that still smelled of my grandmother. I took out the operation notes from 9 March 1991. I spread the sheet of paper out on the table in front of me and read it from first to last.

Every word was like a sharp stone paving the path to my ruin. From the very first words: *Diagnosis: chondrosarcoma of the proximal humerus sin*, to the last one of all, *Bandaging.*

Bandaging. That was all. The operation was over, the patient was wheeled away to the recovery room. Minus an arm, but still with that confounded tumour in the bone of the other upper arm.

I read: *Pre-op assessment. Twenty-year-old right-handed woman, previously basically healthy, examined in Stockholm due to swollen left upper arm. MRI scan shows low-grade chondrosarcoma left upper arm. Subsequent scan confirms diagnoisis, patient agrees to amputation of proximal humerus which allows adequate margin. Operation: intubation narcosis, sunbed position, arm exposed. Usual antibiotic prophylaxis. Incision from coracoid process along lower edge of deltoid to the anterior fold of the axilla. Ligation of a cephalic vein and detachment of pectoralis. Identification of vascular structure, ligation of veins and securing of arteries with double ligatures. Extrusion of nerves from wound, and division. Then separation of deltoid muscle from humerus, and of latissimus dorsi and teres major. Separation of long and short head of biceps, also of coracobrachialis slightly below amputation level. Humerus sawn off at surgical neck and filed. Stump covered by triceps, which are separated, and by coracobrachialis. Pectoralis sewn to lateral edge of humerus using osteosutures. Drain inserted and skin flaps stitched together with no tension. Bandaging.*

I supposed Agnes Klarström must have read this text many times, and had it explained to her. She must have noticed that among all the Latin terms, an everyday word suddenly cropped up: she had been operated on in a 'sunbed position'. As if she had been lying on a beach or a veranda, with her arm exposed, and the operating theatre lights the last thing she saw before she lost consciousness. I had submitted her to an outrageous injustice while she was resting on a sunbed.

Could it possibly be a different Agnes Klarström? She had been young then – maybe she had married and acquired a new surname? Her entry in the telephone directory had evidently not indicated if she was Miss, or Mrs, or had any other title.

It was a scary but also a crucial night. I could no longer run away. I must speak to her, explain what was impossible to explain. And tell her that in so many ways I had also amputated myself.

I lay awake on top of the bed for a very long time before falling asleep. When I opened my eyes again, it was morning. Jansson would not be delivering any post today. I would be able to cut my way into my hole in the ice without interruption.

I had to use a crowbar in order to break through the thick ice. My dog sat on the jetty, watching my exertions. The cat had vanished into the boathouse looking for mice. I finally managed to create a big enough hole and stepped down into the burning cold. I thought about Harriet and Louise, and wondered if I would have enough courage today to ring Agnes Klarström and ask her if she was the woman I was looking for.

I didn't ring that day. Instead, in a fit of frenzied activity, I gave the house a spring clean, as there was a thick layer of dust everywhere. I managed to start my ancient washing machine and washed my bedlinen, which was so filthy that it could easily have been a homeless tramp who'd been sleeping in my bed. Then I went for a walk round the island, surveyed the icy wastes with my binoculars, and accepted that I must make up my mind what to do next.

An old woman standing on the ice, a daughter I didn't know I had in a caravan. At the age of sixty-six I was having to accept that everything I'd thought was definite and done with was starting to change.

After lunch I sat down at the kitchen table and wrote two letters. One was to Harriet and Louise, and the other to Agnes Klarström. Jansson would be surprised when I handed over two letters. To be on the safe side, I secured them with Sellotape. I wouldn't put it past him to try to read all my correspondence.

What did I write? I told Harriet and Louise that my fury had passed. I understood them, but I wasn't able to see them at the moment. I had returned to my island to look after my abandoned animals. But I took it for granted that we should meet again soon. Our conversations and our social intercourse must continue, obviously.

It took a long time to write those few lines. By the time I thought I had written something that might suffice, the kitchen floor was covered in scrunched-up paper. What I had put wasn't actually true. My fury had not passed, my animals could have survived for a while longer – Jansson could have managed. Nor was I entirely sure that I wanted to meet them again in the near future. I needed time to think things over. Not least to decide what to say to Agnes Klarström, if I could find her.

The letter to Agnes Klarström did not take long to write. I realised that I had been carrying it around in my head for many years. I just wanted to meet her, that was all. I sent her my address and signed it: she would no doubt never be able to forget that name. I hoped I was writing to the right person.

When Jansson arrived the following day, it had turned windy. I noted in my logbook that the temperature had fallen during the night, and the squally wind was veering between west and south-west.

Jansson was on time. I gave him three hundred kronor for collecting me, and insisted that he accepted the payment.

'I'd like you to post these two letters for me,' I said, handing them to him.

I had taped all four corners on each of them. He made no attempt to disguise his astonishment that I was holding two letters in my hand.

'I write when I have to. Otherwise not.'

'That picture postcard you sent me was very pretty.'

'A fence covered in snow? What's pretty about that?'

I was getting impatient.

'How is the toothache?' I asked, in an attempt to cover up my irritation.

'It comes and goes. It's worst up here on the right.'

Jansson opened his mouth wide.

'I can't see anything wrong,' I said. 'Talk to a dentist.'

. Jansson tried to close his mouth. There was a creaking sound. His jaw locked, and he stood there with his mouth half open. I could see that it was painful. He tried to speak, but it was impossible to understand what he said. I pressed gently with my thumbs on either side of his face, feeling for his jawbone, and massaged until he could close his mouth again.

'That hurt.'

'Try to avoid yawning or opening your mouth too wide for a few days.'

'Is this an indication of some serious illness?'

'Not at all. You don't need to worry.'

Jansson drove off with my letters. The wind bit into my face as I walked back to the house.

That afternoon I opened the door to the ant room. Still more of the tablecloth seemed to have been swallowed up by the constantly growing anthill. But generally speaking, the room and the bed where Harriet had slept were still as they were when we'd left them.

Days passed and nothing happened. I walked over the ice until I came to the open sea. I measured the thickness of the ice in three different places. I didn't need to consult my earlier logbooks in order to establish that the ice had never been as thick as this before, for as long as I'd lived on the island.

I peeped under the tarpaulin and tried to judge if I'd ever be able to put to sea again in my boat. Had it been beached for too long? Would I have the strength and energy to carry out the necessary repairs and spruce it up again? I replaced the tarpaulin without having answered my question.

One evening the telephone rang. A rare thing. More often than not it would be some telephone company or other urging me to change my supplier, or to install broadband. When they discovered where I lived and that I was an old-age pensioner, they usually lost interest. Besides, I haven't the slightest idea what broadband is.

A female voice I didn't recognise said: 'Agnes Klarström here. I've received your letter.'

I held my breath. Didn't say a word.

'Hello? Hello?'

I said nothing. After further attempts to lure me out of my cave, she hung up.

So I'd found her. The letter had reached the address it was sent to. She lived near Flen.

There was an old map of Sweden in one of the kitchen drawers. I think it used to belong to my grandfather. He sometimes used to go on about how he would like to visit Falkenberg before he died. I've no idea why he wanted to go there; but he had never been to Stockholm, nor had he ever ventured outside the borders of Sweden. He took his dream of visiting Falkenberg with him to his grave.

I spread the map out over the table and located Flen. The scale wasn't big enough for me to pin down Sångledsbyn. It would take me two hours at most to drive there. I had made up my mind: I was going to pay her a visit.

Two days later I walked across the ice to my car. I hadn't left a note on my door this time or told Jansson. The dog and the cat had been supplied with sufficient food. The sky was blue, it was dead calm, plus two degrees. I drove north, turned off inland and reached Flen shortly after two in the afternoon. I found a book shop, bought a large-scale map and tracked down Sångledsbyn. It was only a couple of miles away from Harpsund, which is the location of the summer residence of Swedish prime ministers. Once upon a time, a man had lived there who made a fortune out of cork. He had left his home to the state. There was an oak tree in the grounds around which many a visiting foreign statesman, their retinue and their hosts had gathered – not many of the younger generation would ever have heard of them.

I knew all that about Harpsund because my father had once worked there as a waiter when the then prime minister, Tage Erlander, had been entertaining foreign guests. He never tired of talking about the men – they were all men, no women – sitting around the table conducting important discussions about world politics. This had been during the Cold War; he had made a special effort to move without making a noise, and could recall details of the menu, and the wines. Unfortunately there had also been an incident that came close to causing a scandal. He used to describe it as if he had been party to something top secret, and was chary about revealing any details to me and my mother. One of the guests had become extremely drunk. He had delivered an incomprehensible 'thank you' speech at the wrong time, which had caused a bit of a problem for the waiters: but they had saved the day and delayed the serving of the dessert, which had been about to begin. Shortly afterwards the drunken man had been found dead to the world on the lawn at the front of the house.

'Fagerholm got himself drunk in most unfortunate circumstances,' my father used to say in serious tones.

My mother and I never discovered who this Fagerholm was. It was only much later on, when my father had died, that I realised he must have been one of the Finnish trade union leaders of the day.

However, living close to Harpsund now was a woman whose arm I had cut off.

Sångledsbyn consisted of a few farms spread along the shore of an oval-shaped lake. The fields and meadows were covered in snow. I had taken my binoculars with me and climbed to the top of a hillock in order to get a better overview. People occasionally crossed over the farmyards, between outhouses and barns, or house and garage. None of those I saw could have been Agnes Klarström.

I gave a start. A dog was sniffing at my feet. A man in a long over-coat and wellington boots was standing on the road below. He shouted for the dog, and raised a hand in greeting. I hid my binoculars in a pocket and went down to the road. We spoke briefly about the view, and the long, dry winter.

'Is there somebody in this village by the name of Agnes Klarström?' I asked.

The man pointed at the house furthest away.

'She lives there with her bloody kids,' he replied. 'I didn't used to have a dog until that lot came here. Now everybody has a dog.'

He shook his head in annoyance, and continued on his way. I didn't like what I'd heard. I didn't want to get involved with something that would bring even more disorder into my life. I decided to go home and went back to the car. But something made me stay on even so. I walked through the village until I came to a cart track where the

131

snowplough had been busy. If I went along it, I could approach the rear of the last house through a clump of trees.

It was late afternoon, and dusk would soon close in. I made my way along the track and stopped when I came to a spot where I could see the house through the trees. I shook the snow off some branches and created a good view. The house was obviously well looked after. A car was parked outside, with the cable from an engine heater trailing through the snow to an electric socket in the wall.

Suddenly a young girl appeared. She was looking straight at me and my binoculars. She produced something that had been hidden behind her back. It appeared to be a sword. She started running straight at me with the sword raised above her head.

I dropped my binoculars and fled. I stumbled over a tree root or a large stone and fell down. Before I could get to my feet, the girl with the sword had caught up with me.

She was glaring at me with hatred in her eyes.

'Perverts like you,' she said, 'they're everywhere. Peeping Toms skulking in the bushes with their binoculars.'

A woman came running after her. She stopped by the girl and snatched away the sword with her left and only hand – and I realised it must be Agnes Klarström. Perhaps, hidden away at the back of my subconscious mind, there was an image of the young girl from twelve years ago who had lain in the sunbed position in front of my well-scrubbed hands in their rubber gloves.

She was wearing a blue jacket, zipped up to her neck. The empty right sleeve was fastened to her shoulder with a safety pin. The girl by her side was eyeing me with contempt.

I wished Jansson could have come to rescue me. For the second time recently the ice under my feet had given way, and I was drifting without being able to clamber ashore.

CHAPTER 6

I stood up, brushed off the snow and explained who I was. The girl started kicking out at me, but Agnes snapped at her and she slunk away.

'I don't need a guard dog,' said Agnes. 'Sima sees absolutely everything that's going on, everybody who approaches the house. She has the eyes of a hawk.'

'I thought she was going to kill me.'

Agnes eyed me up and down, but didn't respond.

We went into the house and sat down in her office. Somewhere in the background rock music was blaring out at top volume. Agnes seemed not to hear. When she took off her jacket, she did it just as quickly as if she'd had two arms and two hands.

I sat down on a visitor chair. Her desk was empty. Apart from a pen: nothing else.

'How do you think I reacted when I received your letter?' Agnes asked.

'I don't know. I suppose you must have been surprised. Perhaps furious?'

'I was relieved. At last, I thought! But then I wondered: Why just now? Why not yesterday, or ten years ago?'

She leaned back in her chair. She had long, brown hair, a simple hairslide, bright blue eyes. She gave the impression of being strong, decisive.

She had placed the samurai sword on a shelf next to the window. She noticed me looking at it.

'I was once given it by a man who was in love with me. When we fell out of love, for some strange reason he took the scabbard with him, but left this incredibly sharp sword with me. Maybe he hoped I would use it to split open my stomach in desperation after he'd left me?'

She spoke quickly, as if time was short. I told her about Harriet and Louise, and how I now felt duty-bound to track her down, and find out if she was still alive.

'Did you hope I wouldn't be? That I'd died?'

'There was a time when I did. But not any more.'

The telephone rang. She answered, listened to what was said, than replied briefly but firmly. There were no empty places in her home for errant girls. She already had three teenagers to look after.

I entered a world I knew nothing about. Agnes Klarström ran a foster home where she lived with three teenage girls who, in my day, would have been classified as tearaways. The girl Sima came from one of Gothenburg's sink estates. It wasn't possible to say for certain how old she was. She had come to Sweden as a lone refugee, hidden in a long-distance lorry via the southern port of Trelleborg. During her journey from Iran, she had been advised to dump all her identification papers the moment she set foot on Swedish soil, change her name and lose all traces of her orginal identity to avoid deportation should she be caught. All she had was a slip of paper with the three Swedish words it was assumed she needed to know.

Refugee, persecuted, alone.

When the lorry eventually stopped outside Sturup airport, the driver pointed to the terminal building and said she should go there and look for a police station. She was eleven or twelve at the time; now she was about seventeen, and the life she had led in Sweden meant that she only felt safe with the samurai sword in her hands.

One of the other girls in the household had run away two days ago. There was no fence round the property, no locked doors. Nevertheless, anybody who left was regarded as a runaway. If it happened too often, Agnes would eventually lose patience. When found, the girl in question would be faced with a new home where the gates would be substantial and the keyrings large.

The runaway, an African from Chad, called Miranda, had probably gone to stay with one of her friends who, for some reason, was called Teabag. Miranda was sixteen and had come to Sweden with her family as a refugee, as part of a UN quota.

Her father was a simple man, a carpenter by trade and very religious, who had soon buckled in the face of the endless cold weather and the feeling that nothing had turned out as he had hoped. He had locked himself into the smallest of the three rooms in which the large family lived, a room with no furniture, only a small pile of African sand that had been in their battered suitcases when they arrived in their new homeland. His wife used to place a tray with food and drink outside the door three times a day. During the night, when everybody else was asleep, he would go to the bathroom, and perhaps also go out for lonely walks around town. At least, they assumed he did, because they would sometimes find wet footprints on the floor when they woke up the next morning.

Miranda eventually found this too much to bear, and one evening she had simply left, perhaps hoping to go back to where she came from. The new homeland had turned out to be a dead end. Before long she was being picked up by the police for petty theft and shoplifting and ended up being shunted around from one penal institution to another.

And now she had run away. Agnes Klarström was furious, but was determined not to rest until the police had made a determined effort to find her and bring her back.

There was a photograph of Miranda pinned up on the wall. The girl's hair was plaited and arranged artistically, clinging to her skull.

'If you look carefully, you notice that she has plaited in the word "fuck" next to her left temple,' said Agnes.

I could see that she was right.

There was also a third girl in the foster home that was Agnes Klarström's mission and source of income. She was the youngest of the three, only fourteen, and a skinny creature reminiscent of a timid caged animal. Agnes knew next to nothing about her. She was a bit like the child in the old folk tale who suddenly finds herself standing in a town square, having forgotten her name and where she came from.

Late one evening two years previously, an official at the railway station in Skövde had been about to close down for the night when he found her sitting on a bench. He told her to leave, but she didn't seem to understand. All she could do was hold up a piece of paper on which it said 'Train to Karlsborg', and he began to wonder which of the pair of them was going mad, as there hadn't been a train from Skövde to Karlsborg for the last fifteen years.

A few days later she started appearing on newspaper placards as 'The Railway Child in Skövde'. Nobody seemed to recognise her, although there were pictures of her wherever you looked. She didn't have a name, psychologists examined her, interpreters who spoke every language under the sun tried to get her to say something, but nobody had any idea where she came from. The only clue to her past was the mysterious slip of paper with the words 'Train to Karlsborg'. They turned the little town of Karlsborg on the shores of Lake Vättern inside out, but nobody recognised her and nobody could understand why she had been waiting for a train that stopped running fifteen years ago. An evening newspaper had conducted a poll of its readers and given her the name Aida. She was given Swedish citizenship and a personal identity number after doctors agreed that she must be about twelve years old, thirteen at most. Because of her thick, black hair and olive-coloured skin, it was assumed that she came from somewhere in the Middle East.

Aida didn't speak a word for two years. Only when every other possibility had been exhausted and Agnes Klarström took her in was any progress made. One morning Aida came to the breakfast table and sat down. Agnes had been talking to her ever since she'd arrived, trying to stir up some reaction in Aida, and now she asked in a friendly tone what she would like.

'Porridge,' she said in almost perfect Swedish.

After that, she started talking. The psychologists who came flocking round assumed that she had picked up the language by listening to everything said by all those trying to make her speak. A significant fact supporting this theory was that Aida knew and understood a large number of psychological and medical terms that would otherwise hardly be normal vocabulary for a girl of her age.

She talked, but she had nothing at all to say about who she was, or what she was supposed to do in Karlsborg. Whenever anybody asked her what her name was, she replied as one might have expected:

'I'm called Aida.'

She appeared on all the newspaper placards again. There were voices muttering in dark corners, suggesting that she had fooled everybody and that her silence had been a smokescreen to overcome all resistance and guarantee her full citizenship in Sweden. But Agnes thought there was a different explanation. The very first time they had met,

Aida had stared at her amputated arm. It was as if the sight of it rang a bell with her, as if she had been swimming in deep water for years, but had now finally reached the shallows where she could stand up. Perhaps Agnes's stump signified something Aida recognised and made her feel secure. Perhaps she had seen people having limbs chopped off. Those doing the chopping were her enemies, and those on the receiving end were the only people she could trust.

Aida's silence was due to her having seen things that no human being, least of all a young child, should ever be exposed to, and consequently she never said anything about her past life. It was as if she was slowly liberating herself from the remains of horrific experiences, and might now be in a position slowly to start on a journey towards a life worth living.

And so Agnes Klarström now ran her little foster home caring for these three girls, with financial support from various local councils. Lots of people were begging her to open her doors to more girls skulking around in the outer reaches of society. But she refused: in order to provide the help and feeling of security necessary to make a real impact, she needed to keep her activities on a small scale. The girls in her care often ran away, but they nearly always came back again. They stayed with her for a long time, and when they finally left her for good, they always had a new life in store for them. She never took in more than three girls at a time.

'I could have a thousand girls if I wanted,' she said. 'A thousand abandoned, wild girls who hate being alone and the feeling of not being welcome wherever they go. My girls realise that without money all you receive is contempt. So they disfigure themselves, they stab people they've never met before – but deep down they are screaming in pain from a wound they don't understand.'

'How come you got involved in all this?'

She pointed at the arm I had amputated.

'I used to be a swimmer, as you might recall. There must have been something about that in my records. I wasn't just a hopeful, I really could have become a champion. Won medals. I can say, without bitterness, that my strong point was not my legs, but the strength I had in my arms.'

*   *   *

A young man with a ponytail marched into the room.

'I've told you before that you must knock first,' she shouted. 'Out you go! Try again!'

The young man gave a start, went out, knocked and came in.

'Half right. You must wait until I tell you to come in. What do you want?'

'Aida's upset. She's threatening everybody. Mainly me. She says she's going to strangle Sima.'

'What's happened?'

'I don't know. Maybe she's just miserable.'

'She'll have to learn to cope with that. Leave her alone.'

'She wants to speak to you.'

'Tell her I'm coming.'

'She wants you to come now.'

'I'll be there in a minute.'

The young man left the room.

'He's not up to it,' she said with a smile. 'I think he needs somebody snapping at his heels all the time. But he doesn't mind my criticising him. After all, I can always blame everything on my arm. He's come to me thanks to some unemployment benefit scheme or other. His dream is to be in one of those television reality programmes where the participants get to screw each other in front of the cameras. If he can't manage that, then he hopes to become a presenter. But simply helping my girls seems to be beyond him. I don't think Mats Karlsson is going to make much of a career for himself in the media.'

'You sound cynical.'

'Not at all. I love my girls, I even love Mats Karlsson. But I'm not doing him a favour by encouraging his flawed dreams, or letting him think that he's making a positive contribution here. I'm giving him an opportunity to see himself for what he is, and perhaps carve out a meaningful life. Maybe I'm wrong in underestimating him. One day he might have his long hair cut off, and try to make something of his life.'

She stood up, escorted me out into a lounge and said she would be back shortly. The rock music coming from somewhere upstairs was still excessively loud.

Melted snow was dripping from the roof outside the windows, song-birds were flitting around like hastily formed shadows.

I gave a start. Sima had entered the room behind my back, without a sound. This time she wasn't holding a sword. She sat down on a sofa and tucked her legs underneath herself. But she was on guard the whole time.

'Why were you watching me through your binoculars?'

'You weren't the one I was looking at.'

'But I saw you. Paedophile!'

'What do you mean by that?'

'I know your type! I know what you're like.'

'I came here to meet Agnes.'

'Why?'

'That's something between us.'

'You fancy her, do you?'

I was shocked, and blushed.

'I think it's time to conclude this conversation.'

'What conversation? Answer my question!'

'There's nothing to answer.'

Sima looked away, and seemed to have tired of trying to talk to me. I felt offended. The accusation that I was a paedophile was beyond anything I could ever have imagined. I looked furtively at her. She was intent on chewing her fingernails. Her hair seemed to be a mixture of red and black, and was tousled, as if she had combed it while in a temper. Behind that hard exterior, I thought I could discern a very small girl in clothes much too big and black for her.

Agnes came into the room. Sima immediately withdrew. The lion-tamer had arrived, and the beast had slunk away, I thought. She sat down on the same chair that Sima had occupied, and tucked her legs underneath her, as if she were imitating her foster-daughter.

'Aida is a little girl, and words have suddenly started pouring out of her,' she said.

'What's happened?'

'Nothing at all. She's just been reminded of who she is. A big, hopeless nothing, as she puts it. A loser among lots of other losers. If somebody started a Loser Party in Sweden, there'd be no shortage of members to contribute lots of experience. I'm nearly thirty-three years old. What about you?'

'Twice that.'

'Sixty-six. That's old. Thirty-three isn't much at all. But it's enough to realise that there has never been so much tension in this land of ours as there is today. But nobody seems to have noticed. At least, none of the people you might think ought to have their fingers on the pulse. There's an invisible network of walls in Sweden, and it's getting worse by the day – dividing people up, increasing the distance between them. Superfically, the opposite might seem to be the case. Get on a tube train in Stockholm and go to the suburbs. It's not very far in terms of miles, but nevertheless, the distance is enormous. It's rubbish to talk about entering another world. It's the same world. But every station on the way out from the city centre is another wall. When you eventually get to the outskirts, it's up to you if you choose to see the truth of the matter or not.'

'And what is the truth?'

'That what you think is the periphery is in fact the centre, and it's slowly recreating Sweden. The country is slowly rotating, and outer and inner, near and far, centre and outskirts are changing. My girls exist in a no-man's-land in which they can see neither backwards nor forwards. Nobody wants them, they are superfluous, rejected. It's no wonder that every morning when they wake up, the only thing they can be sure about is their own worthlessness, staring them in the face. So they don't want to wake up! They don't want to get out of bed! They've had bitterness drilled into them since they were five, six years old.'

'Is it really as bad as that?'

'It's worse.'

'I live on an island. There aren't any suburbs there, just little skerries and rocks. And there certainly aren't any screwed-up girls who come running at you wielding a samurai sword.'

'We treat our children so badly that, in the end, they have no means of expression except through violence. That used to apply to boys only. Now we have incredibly tough girl gangs who don't think twice about inflicting harm on others. We really have reached rock bottom when girls are so desperate that they think their only choice is to behave like the very worst of the gangsters among their boyfriends.'

'Sima called me a paedophile.'

'She calls me a whore when the mood takes her. But the worst thing is what she calls herself.'

'What does she say?'

'That she's dead. Her heart can't cope. She writes strange poems, and then leaves them on my desk or in my pockets without saying a word. It could well be that ten years from now, she'll be dead. Either by her own hand or somebody else's. Or she'll have an accident, full of drugs or other shit. That's a highly probable end to the wretched saga of her life. But I can't give up on her. I know she has an inner strength. If only she can overcome that feeling of uselessness that pursues her everywhere. I have no alternative but to succeed with her. She's riddled with decay and disillusionment: I have to revitalise her.'

She stood up.

'I must get on to the police and nag them to put more effort into looking for Miranda. Why don't you take a walk to the barn, and then we can continue our conversation later?'

I left the room. Sima was peering out from behind the curtains, following my every move. Several kittens were clambering over the bales of hay in the barn. Horses and cows were in boxes and pens. I recognised vaguely the smell from my very earliest childhood when my grandparents used to keep animals on the island. I stroked the horses' muzzles, and caressed the cows. Agnes Klarström seemed to have her life under control. What would I have done if a surgeon had done the same to me? Would I have become a bitter wino and rapidly drunk myself to death on a park bench? Or would I have won through? I don't know.

Mats Karlsson came into the barn and started feeding the animals with hay. He worked slowly, as if he were being forced to do something he hated doing.

'Agnes asked me to tell you to go back to the house,' he said suddenly. 'I forgot to say.'

I went back inside. Sima was no longer at the window. There was a light breeze, and it had started snowing again. I felt cold and tired. Agnes was standing in the hall, waiting for me.

'Sima's run away,' she said.

'But I saw her only a few minutes ago.'

'That was then. She's disappeared now. In your car.'

I felt for the car key in my pocket. I knew I had locked the car. As you grow older, you find you have more and more keys in your pocket. Even if you live alone on a remote island in the archipelago.

'I can see that you don't believe me,' she said. 'But I saw the car leaving. And Sima's jacket is nowhere to be seen. She has a special getaway jacket she always wears when she does a runner. Maybe she believes it has the power to make her invulnerable, invisible. She's taken that sword with her as well. The stupid girl!'

'But I have the car keys in my pocket.'

'Sima used to have a boyfriend – his name was Filippo – a nice guy from Italy, who taught her all there is to know about opening locked cars and starting engines. He would always steal cars from outside swimming pools or buildings containing illegal casinos. He knew that the car owners would be preoccupied for quite a long time. Only hopeless amateurs stole cars from ordinary car parks.'

'How do you know all this?'

'Sima told me. She trusts me.'

'But nevertheless she steals my car and vanishes.'

'You could interpret that as a sign of trust. She expects us to understand what she's done.'

'But I want my car back!'

'Sima usually burns out engines. You took a risk in coming here. But you couldn't know that, of course.'

'I met a man with a dog. He used expressions like "bloody kids".'

'So do I. What sort of a dog was it?'

'I don't know. It was brown and shaggy.'

'Then the man you met was Alexander Bruun. A former swindler who worked in a bank and cheated customers out of their money. He was arrested for fraud, but wasn't even sent to prison. Now he's living the life of Riley on all the money he embezzled and the police never found. He hates me, and he hates my girls.'

She rang the police from her office and explained what had happened. I grew increasingly worried as I listened to what sounded like a cosy chat with a police constable who didn't seem to think there was anything urgent about catching the runaway who was evidently intent on smashing up my already ailing car.

She hung up.

'What are they going to do?' I asked.

'Nothing.

'But they have to do something, surely?'

'They haven't the resources available to start looking for Sima and your car. It will eventually run out of petrol. And so Sima will abandon it and take a train or a bus. Or steal another car. She once came back on a milk float. She always comes back eventually. Most people who run away don't have any specific destination in mind. Have you never run away?'

It seemed to me that the only honest answer to that was that I'd been running away for the last twelve years. But I didn't say that. I didn't say anything at all.

We had dinner at six o'clock. Agnes, Aida, Mats Karlsson and me. Aida had laid places for the two girls who had run away.

We ate a tasteless fish au gratin. I ate far too quickly, as I was worried about my car. Aida seemed to be inspired by the fact that Sima had run away, and spoke non-stop. Karlsson listened attentively and kept encouraging her, while Agnes ate in silence.

When we'd finished eating, Aida and Mats cleared away and took care of the washing-up. Agnes and I went out to the barn.

I apologised to her. I explained as clearly as I could what had gone wrong that fateful day. I spoke slowly and at length, so as not to omit any details. But the fact was that I could have explained what had happened in just a few words. Something had taken place that should never have been possible. Just as an airline pilot has ultimate responsibility and has to ensure that a thorough test of his aeroplane has been done before he takes off, I had a responsibility to ensure that it was the correct arm that had been washed and exposed for amputation: and I had failed in that responsibility.

We each sat on our bale of hay. She looked hard at me all the time as I talked. When I finished, she stood up and fed the horses with carrots from a sack. Then she came to sit beside me on the bale of hay,

'My God, but how I've cursed you!' she said. 'You will never be able to understand just how much it means to somebody who loves swimming to be forced to give it up. I used to imagine how I would track you down, and cut off your arm with a very blunt knife. I would wrap you up in barbed wire and dump you in the sea. There's a limit to how long you can keep hatred going. It can give you a sort of illusory strength, but the fact is that it's nothing more than an all-consuming parasite. The girls are all that matter now.'

She squeezed my hand,

'Anyway, that's enough of that,' she said. 'If we go on we'll only get sentimental. I don't want that. A person with only one arm can easily get emotional.'

We went back into the house. Very loud music was coming from Aida's room. Screeching guitars, thumping bass drums. The walls were vibrating. The mobile phone Agnes had in her pocket rang. She answered, listened, said a few words.

'That was Sima,' she said. 'She sends you her greetings.'

'Sends me her greetings? Where is she?'

'She didn't say. She just wanted Aida to phone her.'

'I didn't hear you saying anything about her coming back here with my car.'

'I was listening. She did all the talking.'

Agnes got to her feet and went upstairs. I could hear her shouting to make herself heard through the music. I had found Agnes Klarström, and she hadn't shouted at me. She hadn't drowned me in a torrent of accusations. She hadn't even raised her voice when she described how she wanted to kill me in her dreams.

I had a lot to think about. Within a few short weeks three women had unexpectedly entered my life. Harriet, Louise and now Agnes. And perhaps I should add Sima, Miranda and Aida.

Agnes returned. We drank coffee. There was no sign of Mats Karlsson. The rock music continued thudding away.

The doorbell rang. When Agnes answered it, there were two policemen with a girl I assumed must be Miranda. The officers were holding her arms as if she were dangerous.

She had one of the most beautiful faces I had ever seen. A Mary Magdalene gripped by Roman soldiers.

Miranda said nothing, but I gathered from the conversation between Agnes and the police officers that she had been caught by a farmer in the act of trying to steal a calf. Agnes protested indignantly – why on earth would Miranda want to steal a cow? The conversation became more and more heated, the policemen seemed tired, nobody was listening to what the others said, and Miranda just stood there.

The police left, without it having become clear whether or not the alleged attempt to steal a calf had succeeded. Agnes asked Miranda a few questions in a stern voice. The girl with the beautiful face answered in such a low voice that I couldn't catch what she said.

She went upstairs, and the loud music stopped. Agnes sat down on the sofa and examined her fingernails.

'Miranda is a girl I would have loved to have as my own daughter. Of all the girls who have been here, who've come and gone, I think she is the one who will do best in life. As long as she discovers that horizon she has inside her.'

She showed me to a room behind the kitchen, where I could sleep. She left me to it as she had a lot to do in the office. I lay down on the bed and pictured my car in my mind's eye. Smoke was coming from the engine. Next to Sima in the passenger seat was the newly sharpened sword. What would my grandparents have said if they'd still been alive and I'd tried to tell them about all this? They would never have believed me, never have understood. What would my browbeaten and kicked-around waiter of a father have said? My weeping mother? I switched off the light and lay there in the darkness, surrounded by whispering voices telling me that the twelve years I had spent on my island had robbed me of contact with the world I lived in.

I must have fallen asleep. I was woken up by the feel of something cold against my neck. The bedside lamp was switched on. I opened my eyes and saw Sima standing over me, with the sword pressed against my neck. I don't know how long I held my breath until she removed the sword.

'I liked your car,' she said. 'It's old and it doesn't go very fast, but I liked it.'

I sat up. She placed the sword on the window ledge.

'The car's standing outside,' she said. 'It's not damaged.'

'I don't like people taking my car without permission.'

She sat down on the floor, her back against the radiator.

'Tell me about your island,' she said.

'Why should I? How do you know I live on an island?'

'I know lots of things.'

'It's a long way out to sea, and just now it's surrounded by ice. In the autumn, storms can be so bad that they throw boats up on to land if you don't moor them properly.'

'Do you really live there all alone?'

'I have a cat and a dog.'

'Don't you feel scared of all that empty space?'

'Rocks and juniper bushes don't often run at you with a sword. It's people who do that.'

She sat there for a moment without saying anything, then got to her feet and picked up the sword.

'I might come and visit you one of these days,' she said.

'I very much doubt that.'

She smiled.

'So do I. But I'm often wrong.'

I tried to go back to sleep. I gave up at about five o'clock. I got dressed and wrote a note to Agnes, saying that I'd gone home. I slid it under the locked door of her office.

The house was asleep when I drove off.

There was a smell of burning from the engine, and when I stopped for petrol at an all-night filling station, I also topped up the oil. I arrived at the harbour shortly before dawn.

I walked out on to the pier. A fresh wind was getting up. Despite the vast stretch of ice, the wind brought with it the salty smell of the open sea. A few lamps illuminated the harbour, where a few abandoned fishing boats were gnawing at the car tyres.

I waited for it to get light before starting off for home over the ice. I had no idea how I was going to adjust my life in order to cope with everything that had happened.

Standing alone out there on the pier, in the bitterly cold wind, I started to cry. Every single door inside me was swinging back and forth in the wind, which seemed to be getting stronger all the time.

THE SEA

CHAPTER 1

It was the beginning of April before the thaw came. This was the longest the sea had been frozen during all the years I had lived here. I could still walk over the channels to the mainland at the end of March.

Jansson came by in his hydrocopter every third day, and reported on the condition of the ice. He thought he could recall a winter in the 1960s when the ice had remained for as long as this in the outer archipelago.

The white-painted landscape was dazzling when I climbed up the hill behind the house and gazed towards the horizon. Sometimes I hung Grandfather's ice prods round my neck, collected an old ski pole and went for wintry walks around the skerries and rocks where the old herring-fishing grounds used to be: my grandfather and his father before him used to land catches that nobody nowadays could even dream of. I walked around the skerries where nothing grows and remembered how I used to row out to them as a child. You could find all kinds of remark-able flotsam and jetsam hidden in the crevices. I once discovered a doll's head, and on another occasion a watertight box containing several 78 rpm gramophone records. My grandfather asked somebody who knew about such things, and heard that they were German songs from the war that had ended when I was a little boy. I didn't know where the records were now. On another rocky islet I had found a large waterproof logbook that some raving or desperate sea captain had thrown into the sea. It had been from a cargo ship taking timber from the sawmills of northern Sweden to Ireland, where it was used for housebuilding. The vessel had weighed 3,000 tons and was called *Flanagan*. Nobody could say how or why the logbook had ended up in the water. Grandfather had spoken to a retired schoolteacher who used to spend his summers on Lönö, in what used to be the cottage of a former pilot, Grundström. He had translated the text, but there was nothing unusual noted in the logbook on the day it had been thrown into the sea. I can still remember the date: 9 May 1947. The last entry had been a note about 'greasing the anchor gear as soon as possible'. Then nothing more. The logbook was incomplete, but had been thrown into the sea. It had been on its way from Kubikenborg with a cargo of timber for Belfast. The weather was fine, the sea almost dead calm, and a note made that morning said there was a south-easterly breeze blowing at one metre per second.

As the long winter progressed, I often thought about that logbook. It seemed to me that my life after the catastrophic error was a bit like throwing my unfinished logbook into the sea and then sailing on without leaving any trace behind. The insignificant notebook I was now keeping, recording such things as vanished waxwings and the ill health of my pets, wasn't even of any interest to me. I made notes because it was a daily reminder of the fact that I was living a life of no substance. I wrote about waxwings to confirm the existence of a life in a vacuum.

I suddenly started to think about my parents. I would often wake up during the night with my head full of remarkable memories, long since forgotten, that had returned in my dreams. I could picture my father on his knees, lining up his tin soldiers and moving them in a reconstruction of Waterloo, or Narva. My mother was generally sitting in her armchair, watching him with an expression of great tenderness – his games always took place in absolute silence: she just sat there.

The march of the tin soldiers ensured that there would be moments of genuine peace in our home, albeit only occasionally. In my dreams I relived my fear of the arguments that sometimes flared up. My mother would be crying, and my father making a feeble attempt to show his anger by cursing the restaurant owner who employed him. I was slowly dreaming my way back to my roots. I had the feeling that I was walking along with a pickaxe in my hand, searching the ground for something that had gone missing.

Even so, it was a winter characterised by things that had been reclaimed. Harriet had presented me with a daughter, and Agnes didn't hate me.

It was also a winter of letters. I wrote, and I received answers. For the first time in the twelve years I had lived on the island, there was now a point in Jansson's visits. He still regarded me as his doctor, and demanded consultations for his imagined pains. But now he brought me mail, and sometimes I would hand him a reply.

I wrote my first letter the very day I got back home. I had walked over the ice in the grey light of dawn. My animals gave the impression of being starved, despite the fact that I had left more than enough food to feed them properly. When I was satisfied that they had eaten as much as they wanted, I sat down at the kitchen table and wrote a letter to Agnes.

'I apologise for leaving so abruptly. I suppose I was overwhelmed by meeting the person who had suffered so much because of me. There was a lot I would have liked to talk to you about, and you might well have had a lot of questions for me. I am now back again on my island. The sea all around me is still frozen hard. I hope that my sudden departure will not result in our losing contact with each other.'

I didn't change a single word. The following day I asked Jansson to post it for me. He didn't seem to have noticed that I'd been away. He was curious about the letter, of course, but said nothing. He didn't even have any pains that day.

In the evening I started writing a letter to Harriet and Louise, despite the fact that I'd not had a reply to my previous one. It became far too long, and it had become clear that I couldn't write a letter addressed to both of them: I didn't have much idea how close they were. I tore the letter up, and started again. The cat was lying on the sofa, fast asleep, the dog was lying next to the stove, breathing heavily. I tried to see if it had pains in its joints. It probably wouldn't live beyond the coming autumn. The same applied to the cat.

I wrote to Harriet and asked how she was. It was a silly question, as I knew that she was ill, of course. But I asked, even so. The impossible question was the obvious one to ask. Then I wrote about the journey we had made together.

'We went to that forest pool. I very nearly drowned. You pulled me out of the water. It's only now, when I'm back at home, that I realise fully how close I was to drowning.'

I shuddered at the thought of drowning. But that didn't prevent me from opening up the hole in the ice for my bath every morning. However, after a few days I realised that I didn't need my bath as badly as I used to do. Having met Harriet and Louise, it didn't seem as essential for me to expose myself to the cold. My morning baths became less frequent.

That same evening I also wrote a letter to Louise. I read about Caravaggio in an old encyclopedia from 1909, the so-called Owl edition. I started my letter with a quotation from the encyclopedia: 'His striking, albeit sombre colours and his bold reproductions of nature aroused widespread and justified attention.' I tore the sheet of paper up. I couldn't pretend that what I had written was my own opinion. Nor did I want to admit that I had stolen the quotation from a reference book almost a hundred years old, even though I had updated the language.

I started again. It turned out to be a very short letter.

'I slammed the door of your caravan as I left. I shouldn't have done that. I couldn't handle my confusion. I apologise for that. I hope we shall not continue with our lives pretending the other doesn't exist.'

It was not a good letter. I discovered two days later just how badly it had been received. The telephone rang in the middle of the night. I groped around half asleep, stumbling over my frightened animals, before I was able to lift the receiver. It was Louise. She was furious. She was shouting so loudly, she almost burst my eardrums.

'I'm so angry with you. How could you write such a letter? You slam the door shut the moment things turn unpleasant.'

I could hear that she was slurring her words. It was three in the morning. I tried to calm her down. That only made her more furious. So I said nothing. I let her carry on ranting.

This is my daughter, I kept telling myself. She's saying what she needs to say. And I knew my letter was not a good one.

I don't know how long she carried on screaming down the line. But suddenly, in mid-sentence, there was a click and the call was over. The silence echoed. I stood up and opened the door to the living room. The anthill was growing bigger. Or so I fancied, at least. But do anthills really grow during the winter when the insects are hibernating? I knew as little about that as I did about the best way to respond to Louise. I understood why she was angry. But did she understand me? Was there anything to understand, in fact? Can you regard a grown woman, whose existence you knew nothing about, as your daughter? And who was I to her?

I got no more sleep that night. I was gripped by a fear that I was unable to cope with. I sat at the kitchen table, clutching at the blue waxed tablecloth that had covered it ever since Grandmother's day. I was over-whelmed by emptiness and powerlessness. Louise had dug her claws deep into my innermost being.

* * *

I went out as dawn broke. It seemed to me it would have been better if Harriet had never appeared out there on the ice. I could have lived my life without a daughter, just as Louise could have got by without a father.

Down by the jetty I wrapped myself up in my grandfather's old fur coat and sat down on the bench. Both the dog and the cat had wandered off on their separate ways, as their tracks in the snow showed. They seldom went anywhere together. I wondered if they sometimes lied to each other about their intentions.

I stood up and bellowed straight out into the mist. The noise died away into the grey light. My routine had been disturbed. Harriet had appeared from nowhere, and turned my life upside down. Louise had shouted a truth into my ear, and I had no defence against it. Perhaps Agnes would also attack me with unexpected fury in due course?

I flopped back down on to the bench. I was reminded of Grandma's words, her fear. If you went out walking in the mist, you might disappear and never be heard of again.

I had lived alone on this island for twelve years. Now it felt as if it had been invaded by three women.

I ought really to invite them all to visit me when summer comes. One beautiful summer's evening they could take it in turns to attack me. Eventually, when there was barely anything left of me, Louise could don her boxing gloves and knock me out for the final count.

They would be able to count up to a thousand, and still I wouldn't get up.

A few hours later, I opened up my hole in the ice and stepped into the freezing cold water. This morning I forced myself to stay there for an unusually long spell.

Jansson turned up on time but he had nothing for me, nor I for him. Just as he was about to leave, I remembered that it was ages since he had complained of having toothache.

'How are your teeth?'

Jansson looked surprised.

'What teeth?'

I asked no more. The hydrocopter vanished into the mist.

On my way back from the jetty, I paused by the boat and raised the tarpaulin once again. The hull was going rotten. If I left it untended for another year, it would be beyond repair.

That same day I wrote another letter to Louise. I apologised for everything I could remember and also for everything I'd forgotten, and for the annoyance I would cause her in the future. I concluded the letter with a few lines about the boat:

'I have an old wooden boat that used to be my grandfather's. It's on trestles under a tarpaulin. It's a disgrace that I treat the boat so badly. I just haven't looked after it properly. I often think that ever since I came to live on this island, I've also been lying on trestles under a tarpaulin. I'll never be able to sort out the boat until I've sorted out myself.'

A couple of days later I gave the letter to Jansson, and the following week he brought a reply. After a few days of thaw, it had turned cold again. Winter refused to loosen its grip. I sat down at the kitchen table to read the letter. I had shut the cat and the dog out – sometimes I simply couldn't bear to see them.

Louise wrote: 'I sometimes feel that I've lived my life with dry and chapped lips. Those are words that came to me one morning when life felt worse than usual. I don't need to tell you about the life I've led because you already have an indication of what it's been like. Filling in the details would change nothing. Now I'm trying to find a way of living with the knowledge that you exist, the troll who emerged from the forest that turned out to be my father. Even though I know Harriet ought to have explained, I can't help feeling upset with you as well. When you stormed off, it felt as if you'd punched me in the face. At first it was a relief you'd gone. But the feeling of emptiness became too much. And so I hope we might be able to find a way of becoming friends at least, one of these days.'

She signed the letter with an ornate L.

What a mess, I thought. Louise has every reason in the world to direct her anger at the pair of us.

The winter wore on, with letters travelling back and forth between the caravan and the island. And occasionally I would receive a letter from Harriet, who was back in Stockholm by now. It was not explained how she got there. She said she felt very tired, but the thought of the forest pool and the fact that Louise and I had met at last kept her going. I asked questions about her condition, but never received an answer.

Her letters were characterised by quiet, almost reverential resignation, in stark contrast to what Louise wrote, where between the lines there was always a hint of imminent anger.

Every morning when I woke up, I resolved to start making a serious attempt to put my life in order. I could no longer allow the days to slide past without anything constructive being done.

But I got nowhere. I made no decisions. I occasionally lifted the tarpaulin over the boat and had the feeling that I was in fact looking at myself. The flaking paint was mine, as were the cracks and the damp. Perhaps also the smell of wood slowly rotting away.

The days were getting longer. Migratory birds started returning. The flocks usually passed by during the night. Through my binoculars I could see seabirds on the outermost edge of the ice.

My dog died on 19 April. I let him out as usual when I came downstairs to the kitchen in the early morning. I could see that he had difficulty in getting out of his basket, but I thought he would live through the summer. After my usual dip through my hole in the ice, I went down to the boathouse to look for some tools I needed to repair a leaking pipe in the bathroom. I thought it was odd that the dog hadn't appeared, but didn't go in search of him. It wasn't until around dinner time that I realised he hadn't been seen all day. Even the cat seemed concerned. She was sitting on the steps outside the front door, looking pensive. I went out and called for him, but he didn't appear. I realised something must have happened. I put on a jacket and started searching. After almost an hour I found him on the far side of the island, by the unusual rock formations that rose up out of the ice like gigantic pillars. He was lying in a little depression, sheltered from the wind. I don't know how long I stood looking at him. His eyes were open, glistening like crystals – just like the seagull I had found earlier in the winter, frozen to death by the jetty.

He could hide from the wind, but there was nowhere to hide from death.

I carried his body back to the house. It was heavier than I had expected. The dead are always heavy. I fetched a pickaxe and slowly hacked a big enough hole under the apple tree. The cat sat on the steps, watching the whole procedure. The dog's body was stiff as I pressed him down into the hole, then filled it in.

I leaned the pickaxe and the spade against the house wall. The morning fog had returned, but now my eyes had misted over too. I was grieving for my pet.

I noted the death in my logbook, and calculated that the dog had been nine years and three months old. I had bought him as a puppy from one of the old trawlermen who used to breed dogs of doubtful descent.

For some time I considered acquiring another dog; but the future was too uncertain. Before long my cat would also be gone. Then there would be nothing to tie me down to the island if I no longer wanted to stay here.

I wrote to Louise and Harriet about the death of the dog. Both times I burst into tears.

Louise understood how I must miss him, while Harriet wondered how I could possibly feel sad about an old cripple of a dog who was finally at peace.

Weeks passed, and still I didn't start work on the boat. It was as if I were waiting for something to happen. Perhaps I ought to write a letter to myself, and explain what my plans for the future were?

The days became longer. The snow in the rock crevices started to melt. But the sea was still frozen.

In the end, the ice began to lose its grip. I woke up one morning to find navigable channels running all the way to the open sea. Jansson arrived in his motorboat: he had put the hydrocopter in store. He had decided to buy a hovercraft in time for next winter. I'm not sure that I understood what a hovercraft was, despite the fact that he gave me a detailed description without my asking for it. He begged me to examine his left shoulder. Could I feel that there was a lump there? Might it be a tumour?

There was nothing. Jansson was still as fit as a fiddle.

That same day I removed the tarpaulin from the boat, and started to scrape the shell. I managed to clear the stern of old paint.

My intention was to continue the following day. But something happened to prevent that. As I was on my way down to take my morning bath, I discovered that a little motorboat was beached by the jetty.

I stopped dead and held my breath.

The door to the boathouse was open.

Somebody had come to pay me a visit.

CHAPTER 2

There was a glint of light inside the boathouse. Sima emerged from the darkness, sword in hand.

'I thought you were never going to wake up.'

'How did you get here? What's that boat you've beached down by the jetty?'

'I took it.'

'Took?'

'From the harbour. It was locked. But the chain that can stop me hasn't been invented yet.'

'You mean you stole the boat?'

My cat had come to the jetty, and was observing Sima from a distance.

'Where's your dog?'

'He's dead.'

'What do you mean, dead?'

'Dead. There's only one kind of dead. When you're dead, you're not alive. Unalive. Dead. My dog is dead.'

'I had a dog once. It's dead as well.'

'Dogs die. My cat won't live much longer either. She's also old.'

'Are you going to shoot it? Do you have a rifle?'

'I wouldn't dream of telling you. I want to know what you're doing here, and why you stole a boat.'

'I wanted to see you.'

'Why?'

'Because I didn't like you.'

'You wanted to see me because you don't like me?'

'I want to know why I don't like you.'

'You're mad. How come you know how to handle a boat?'

'I spent some time at a reform school on the shore of Lake Vättern. They had a boat.'

'How did you know where I lived?'

'I asked an old bloke sweeping up leaves outside the church. It wasn't hard. I just asked about a doctor who'd hidden himself away on an island. I told him I was your daughter.'

I gave up. She had an answer to every question. Hugo Persson was employed to keep the churchyard in good order, and I knew he was a gossip. He had presumably told the girl how to get here – it wasn't difficult: straight out towards Mittbåden where the lighthouse was, then through the Järnsundet channel with the high cliffs on either side, and so to my island, where there were two broom beacons close to the rocks at the mouth of the inlet to my boathouse.

I could see that she was tired. Her eyes were dull, her face pale, her hair carelessly pinned up with cheap hairslides. She was dressed entirely in black, and her trainers had a red stripe.

'Come with me to the house,' I said. 'You must be hungry. I'll get you some food. Then I'll call the coastguards and tell them that you're here, and that you've stolen a boat. They can come and fetch you.'

She said nothing, nor did she threaten me with her sword. When we'd settled down in the kitchen, I asked her what she wanted.

'Porridge.'

'I didn't think people ate porridge any more.'

'I've no idea what people do. But I want porridge. I can make it myself.'

I had some oats, and a tin of apple sauce that wasn't too far past its use-by date. She made the porridge very thick, pushed the tin of apple sauce out of the way and filled up her bowl with milk. She ate slowly. The sword was lying on the table. I asked if she wanted coffee or tea. She shook her head. She wanted only porridge. I tried to work out why she'd come to the island to visit me. What did she want? The last time we'd met, she had come running at me with the sword brandished over her head. Now she was sitting at my kitchen table, eating porridge. It didn't make sense. She rinsed out her bowl and stood it on the draining board.

'I'm tired. I need to get some sleep.'

'There's a bed in that room over there. You can sleep there. But I should warn you that there's an anthill in the room. And as it's spring now, they've started to become active.'

She believed me. She'd been doubtful about whether my dog was dead, but she believed what I said about the anthill. She pointed at the sofa in the kitchen.

'I can sleep there.'

I gave her a pillow and a blanket. She didn't take any clothes off, nor did she remove her shoes; she just pulled the blanket over her head and fell asleep. I waited until I was sure, then went to get dressed.

Accompanied by the cat, I went back to the inlet. The boat was a Ryd with a Mercury outboard motor, 25 h.p. The bottom of the boat had scraped hard against the stones on the seabed. There was no doubt that she had beached the boat intentionally. I tried to see if the plastic had split, but I couldn't find any holes.

It was a post day: Jansson would notice the boat. I had only a few hours in which to decide what to do. It wasn't a foregone conclusion that I would in fact call the coastguards. If possible, I would prefer to persuade her to go back to Agnes without the authorities being involved. I also had my own interests to think about. It was hardly appropriate for an old doctor to be visited by runaway girls who stole boats.

With the aid of a boathook and a plank used as a lever, I managed to get the boat back into the water. I used the boathook to propel it as far as the jetty and tied it to the stern of my little rowing boat. There was an electric starter, but it needed a key and, needless to say, that hadn't been in the ignition when Sima stole the boat. She had used the drawstring, and I did the same. The engine started at the fourth attempt. The propeller and pinion were undamaged. I reversed away from the jetty, and aimed the boat at two rocky skerries known as the Sighs. Between them was a small natural harbour hidden from view. I could leave the stolen boat there for the time being.

It is not clear why the two skerries are known as the Sighs. Jansson maintains that a long time ago, there was a wildfowler in these parts by the name of Måsse who used to sigh every time he shot an eider.

I don't know if it's true. The skerries are not named on any of my charts. But I like the idea of barren rocks rising out of the sea being called the Sighs. You sometimes get the feeling that trees are whispering, flowers murmuring, berry bushes humming unknown melodies, and that the wild roses in the crevices behind Grandma's apple tree are playing beautiful tunes on invisible instruments. So why shouldn't skerries sigh?

*   *   *

It took me almost an hour to row back to the jetty. No chance of a morning bath today. I walked back up to the house. Sima was asleep under the blanket. She hadn't moved at all since lying down. As I watched her, I heard the throbbing sound of Jansson's boat. I walked back down to the jetty and waited for him. There was a gentle north-easterly breeze, the temperature was around plus five, and spring still seemed a long way off. I noticed a pike near the end of the jetty, but then it darted away.

Jansson had problems with his scalp today. He was afraid that he was starting to go bald. I suggested he should consult a hairdresser. Instead, he unfolded a page he'd ripped out from some weekly magazine or other and asked me to read it. It was a whole-page advertisement for a miraculous potion that promised immediate results; I noticed that one of the ingredients was lavender. I thought of my mother, and told Jansson that he shouldn't believe everything he read in expensive advertisements.

'I want you to give me some advice.'

'I already have done. Consult a hairdresser. He will no doubt know a lot more about hair loss than I do.'

'Didn't you learn anything about baldness when you trained as a doctor?'

'Not a lot, I have to admit.'

He took off his cap and bowed his head as if he were suddenly expressing subservience. As far as I could tell his hair was thick and healthy, not least on the crown of his head.

·'Can't you see that it's getting thinner?'

'That's only natural as you grow older.'

'According to that advert, you're wrong.'

'In that case I suggest you order the stuff and massage it into your scalp.'

Jansson crumpled up the page.

'I sometimes wonder if you really are a doctor.'

'Whatever, I can tell the difference between people with genuine aches and pains, and hypochondriac postmen.'

He was about to respond when I noticed that his gaze deviated from my face and focused on something behind my back. I turned round. Sima was standing there. She had the cat in her arms, and the samurai sword was hanging from her belt. She said nothing, only smiled. Jansson stared. Within days the whole of the archipelago would know that I was being visited by a young lady with dark eyes, tousled hair and a samurai sword.

'I think I'll go ahead and order that lotion,' Jansson said in a friendly voice. 'I'd better not disturb you any longer. I haven't got any post for you today.'

I watched as he backed away from the jetty. When I turned round, Sima was on her way to the house. She had put the cat down halfway up the hill.

She was sitting at the kitchen table, smoking, when I entered.

'Where's the boat?' she asked.

'I've moved it to where it can't be seen.'

'Who was that you were talking to down by the jetty?'

'His name's Jansson, and he delivers mail out here in the archipelago. It wasn't good for him to have seen you here.'

'Why not?'

'He gossips. He blabs.'

'That doesn't bother me.'

'You don't live here. But I do.'

She stubbed out her cigarette in one of Grandma's old coffee saucers. I didn't like that.

'I dreamt that you were pouring an anthill over me. I tried to defend myself with the sword, but the blade broke. Then I woke up. Why do you have an anthill in that room?'

'There was no reason for you to go in there.'

'I think it's pretty cool. Half the tablecloth has been swallowed up by it. In a few years the whole table will have been covered.'

I suddenly noticed something I had overlooked before. Sima was agitated. Her movements were nervous, and when I looked at her out of the corner of my eye, I could see that she was rubbing her fingers together.

It struck me that many years ago I had seen that same strange, nervous finger-rubbing in a patient whose leg I'd been forced to amputate, because of complications to do with his diabetes. He had an acute fear of germs, and was unstable mentally, suffering deep depressions.

The cat jumped up on to the table. Until a few years ago I always used to shoo it down again, but I no longer did. The cat has beaten me. I moved the sword so that she wouldn't injure her paws. When I touched the hilt of the sword, Sima gave a start. The cat rolled up into a ball on the waxed cloth and started purring. Sima and I watched her in silence.

'Come clean,' I said. 'Tell me why you're here and where you think you're going to. Then we can work out the best way of proceeding without unnecessary problems.'

'Where's the boat?'

'I've moored it in a little cove between two small islands known as the Sighs.'

'Why would anybody call an island a sigh?'

'There's a reef out here called the Copper Bottom. And some shallows just off Bogholmen are called the Fart. Islands have names just like people do. Sometimes nobody knows where they come from.'

'So you've hidden the boat?'

'Yes.'

'Thank you.'

'I don't know if that's anything to thank me for. But if you don't come clean soon I shall pick up the phone and ring the coastguard. They'll be here within half an hour and take you away.'

'If you touch that phone I shall cut your hand off.'

I took a deep breath and said: 'You don't want to touch that sword because I've had hold of it. You're afraid of germs. You're terrified your body is going to be invaded by contagious diseases.'

'I don't know what you're talking about.'

I was right. A sort of invisible shudder passed right through her body. Her hard exterior had been penetrated. So she counter-attacked. She grabbed my ancient cat by the scruff of its neck and threw her in the direction of the firewood box. Then she started screaming at me in her native language. I stared at her, and tried to tell myself that she wasn't my daughter, wasn't my responsibility.

She suddenly stopped yelling.

'Aren't you going to pick the sword up? Aren't you going to take hold of the hilt? Cut me to pieces?'

'Why are you so horrible?'

'Nobody treats my cat the way you've just done.'

'I can't stand cat fur. I'm allergic.'

'That doesn't give you the right to kill my cat.'

I stood up to let the cat out. She was sitting next to the outside door, eyeing me suspiciously. I went out with her, thinking that Sima might need to be alone for a while. The sun had broken through the cloud cover, it was dead calm, and the warmest spring day so far. The cat disappeared round the corner of the house. I glanced surreptitiously in through the window. Sima was standing at the sink, washing her hands. Then she dried them carefully, rubbed the hilt of the sword with the towel and put the sword back on the table.

As far as I was concerned, she was a totally incomprehensible person. I couldn't imagine what was going on inside her head. I hadn't the slightest idea.

I went back inside. She was sitting at the table, waiting. I didn't mention the sword. She looked at me and said:

'Chara. That's what I'd like to be called.'

'Why?'

'Because it's beautiful. Because it's a telescope. It's on Mount Wilson, near Los Angeles. I shall go there before I die. You can see stars through the telescope. And things you could never imagine. That telescope is more powerful than any other.'

She started whispering now, as if in raptures, or as if she wanted to confide in me a highly valuable secret.

'It's so powerful that you can stand here on earth and make out an individual person on the moon. I would like to be that person.'

I sensed what she was trying to say. A harassed little girl running away from everything, especially from herself, thought that although she was invisible here on earth, she might become visible through that powerful telescope.

I had the feeling I was beginning to grasp a small fragment of who she was. I tried to keep the conversation going by talking about the starry skies we had here in the islands on clear, moonless autumn nights. But she drew back into her shell, not wanting to talk; she seemed to regret having said what she had.

We sat in silence for a while. Then I asked her once again why she had come here.

'Oil,' she said. 'I intend going to Russia and becoming rich. There's oil in Russia. Then I shall come back here and be a pyromaniac.'

'What do you intend burning down?'

'All the houses I've been forced to live in against my will.'

'Are you intending to burn down my house?'

'That's the only one I shall leave alone. That and Agnes's. But I shall burn down all the rest.'

This girl was mad. Not only did she run around brandishing a lethal sword, she also had the most confused ideas about her own future.

She seemed to read my mind.

'Don't you believe me?'

'To be honest, no.'

'Then you can go to hell.'

'Nobody speaks like that in my house. I can have the coastguards here faster than you think.'

I slammed my fist down on Grandma's old coffee saucer that Sima had used as an ashtray. Shards of china shot across the kitchen. She sat there motionless, as if my outburst had nothing to do with her.

'I don't want you to get angry,' she said calmly. 'I only want to spend one night here. Then I shall go away.'

'Why did you come here at all?'

Her reply surprised me.

'But you invited me here.'

'I've no recollection of that.'

'You said you didn't think I would ever come. I wanted to prove to you that you were wrong. Besides, I'm on my way to Russia.'

'I don't believe a word you say. Can't you tell me the truth?'

'I don't think you want to hear that.'

'Why wouldn't I?'

'Why do you think I have the sword with me? I want to be able to defend myself. There was a time when I couldn't. When I was eleven.'

I realised that this was probably true. Her vulnerability cut right through her anger.

'I believe you. But why have you come here? You can't really mean that you are on your way to Russia?'

'I know I shall be successful there.'

'What will you do? Dig for oil with your bare hands? They won't even let you into the country. Why can't you stay with Agnes?'

'I have to move on. I left a note saying I was heading north.'

'But this is south!'

'I don't want her to find me. She's like a dog sometimes. She can sniff down anybody who runs away. I only want to stay here for a short time. Then I shall be off.'

'You must realise that this isn't possible.'

'I'll let you if you allow me to stay.'

'Let me what?'

'What do you think?'

It suddenly dawned on me what she was offering.

'Who do you think I am? I shall forget you ever said that. I didn't hear anything.'

I was so upset that I stormed out. I thought about the rumours that Jansson was no doubt busy spreading all over the islands. I would be Fredrik, the man who was secretly taking advantage of young girls imported from some Arabian country or other.

I sat down on the jetty. What Sima had said didn't only embarrass me, it also saddened me. I was beginning to understand the scale of the burdens she was dragging around with her.

After a while she came down to the jetty.

'Sit here,' I said. 'You can stay here a few days.'

I could feel her anxiety. Her legs were shaking. I couldn't just throw her out. Besides, I needed time to think. A fourth woman had now invaded my life, and she needed my help, though I had no idea how to give it.

We ate the last hare steak from the freezer. Sima poked around at the food rather than eating it. She didn't say much. Her worries seemed to be increasing all the time. She didn't want to sleep in the room with the anthill. I made a bed up for her in the kitchen. It was barely nine o'clock when she said she wanted to turn in.

The cat would have to spend the night out. I went upstairs and lay down on my bed to read. It was all quiet down in the kitchen, but I could see light coming from the kitchen window. She still hadn't switched the light off. As I drew my curtains, I could see my cat sitting in the light from the kitchen.

She would soon be leaving me as well. It was as if she had already turned into an ethereal being.

I was reading one of my grandfather's books from 1911 about rare birds, especially waders. I must have dozed off without putting the light out. When I opened my eyes, it still wasn't eleven o'clock. I had been asleep for half an hour at most. I got up and opened the curtains slightly. The kitchen light was out, and the cat had vanished. I was just going to lie down again when I heard something. There were sounds coming from the kitchen. I opened my door and listened intently. Sima was crying. I hesitated. Should I go downstairs? Did she want to be left in peace? After a while the sobbing seemed to fade away. I closed the door as quietly as I could, and went back to bed. I knew exactly where to put my feet in order to avoid making the floorboards creak.

The book about waders had fallen on to the floor. I didn't pick it up, but lay in the dark and wondered what I should do. The only right and proper thing to do was to phone the coastguards. But why should I always do the right and proper thing? I decided to phone Agnes. She could decide. Despite everything, Agnes was the person closest to Sima in this life, if I had understood the facts correctly.

I woke up as usual shortly after six. The thermometer outside the bedroom window showed plus four degrees. It was foggy.

I got dressed and went downstairs. I was still treading carefully as I assumed Sima would still be asleep. I thought I would take the coffee pot with me to the boathouse where I have an electric hotplate. It's been there since my grandfather's day. He used it to boil mixtures of tar and resin to make his boat watertight.

The kitchen door was ajar. I opened it slowly as I knew it creaked. Sima was lying on top of the bed in her underclothes. The lamp in the corner by the sofa was switched on and acted like a spotlight to reveal that her body and the sheet were covered in blood.

I couldn't believe what I saw. I knew it was true, but it felt as if it couldn't possibly have happened even so. I tried to shake some life into her, at the same time looking for the deepest cuts. She hadn't used a sword, but one of my grandfather's old fish knives. For some reason that made me even more desperate, as if she had dragged him, the friendly old fisherman, into her wretched misery. I yelled at her to wake up, but her body was inert, her eyes closed. The worst wounds were around her abdomen, her stomach and her wrists. Strangely enough, there were also wounds in the back of her head. How she had managed to stab herself there was beyond me. The most serious one of all was in her right arm – I had noticed the previous day that she was left-handed – she must have lost a lot of blood. I made a pressure bandage from some kitchen towels. Then I took her pulse. It was faint. All the time I was trying to shake her into life. I didn't know if she had taken any pills as well, or perhaps used some drug or other – there was a smell in the kitchen I didn't recognise. I sniffed quickly at an ashtray, another of Grandma's old coffee saucers that she had taken from a cupboard. She had presumably been smoking hash or pot. I cursed the fact that all my medical instruments were down at the boat-house. I ran out, stumbling over the cat sitting just outside the door, fetched a blood pressure cuff and returned to the kitchen. Her blood pressure was very low. She was in a serious condition.

I phoned the coastguard. Hans Lundman answered. I used to play with him in the summers when I was a child. His father, who was a pilot, and my grandfather were good friends.

Hans is a sensible man. He knows people wouldn't ring the coast-guard in the early hours of the morning unless it was urgent.

'What's happened?'

'I have a girl in my cottage who needs to be taken to hospital immediately.'

'It's foggy,' said Lundman, 'but we'll be there within half an hour.'

It was thirty-two minutes before I heard the powerful engines of the coastguard boat. They were the longest minutes of my life. Longer than when I was mugged in Rome and thought I was going to die. I was powerless. Sima was on her way out of this world. I had no way of assessing how much blood she'd lost. There was nothing I could do for her apart from the pressure bandage. When it became clear that my shouting at her to wake up didn't help, I pressed my mouth close to her ear and whispered that she had to stay alive, she couldn't just die, it wasn't right, not here in my kitchen, not now when spring had arrived, not on a day like the one that had just begun. Could she hear me? I don't know. But I continued whispering in her ear. I told her fragments of fairy tales I remembered from my own childhood,

I told her about the lovely smells that filled the island when the hawthorn and lilac had come into blossom. I said what we would be having for dinner, and described the remarkable birds that waded along the water's edge before darting forward to snap up their prey. I was talking to save her life, and my own – I was terrified that she might die.

I heard Hans Lundman and his assistant approaching and shouted to them to hurry. They quickly transferred her into a stretcher from the bed, and we were off without delay. I ran down to the boat in my stockinged feet, carrying my cut-down wellington boots in my hand. I didn't stop to close the door behind me.

We sailed into the fog. Lundman was at the wheel, and he asked me how things stood.

'I don't know. Her blood pressure is falling.'

We were off at full throttle, straight into the whiteness. His assistant, whom I didn't know, was looking in anguish at Sima, strapped in the stretcher. I wondered if he was about to faint.

An ambulance was waiting on the quayside. Everything was enveloped in the white fog.

'Let's hope she makes it,' said Lundman as we left.

He looked worried. Presumably he knew from experience when a person was close to death.

It took us forty-three minutes to get to the hospital. The ambulance woman sitting beside the stretcher was called Sonja, and in her forties. She set up a drip and worked calmly and methodically, occasionally communicating with the hospital about Sima's condition.

'Has she taken anything? Tablets?'

'I don't know. She might have been smoking pot.'

'Is it your daughter?'

'No. She simply turned up out of the blue.'

'Have you contacted her relatives?'

'I don't know who they are. She lives in a foster home. I've only met her once before. I don't know why she came to me.'

'Ring the care home.'

She reached for a mobile phone hanging from the wall of the ambulance. I rang directory enquiries and was put through to Agnes's house. When the answering machine responded, I explained the situation precisely, said which hospital we were heading for, and left a telephone number that Sonja had given me.

'Ring again,' she said. 'People wake up if you keep on trying.'

'She might be out in the shed.'

'Doesn't she have a mobile?'

I didn't have the strength to phone any more.

'No,' I said. 'She doesn't have a mobile. She's unusual.'

It wasn't until Sima had been taken into A&E and I was sitting on a bench in a corridor that I got through to Agnes. I could hear her anxious breathing.

'How is she?'

'She's in a very bad way.'

'Tell me exactly how things are.'

'There's a risk that she might die. It depends how much blood she's lost, how deep the trauma is. Do you know if she took sleeping pills?'

'I don't think so.'

I passed the nurse the phone.

'It's the girl's guardian. Talk to her. I've explained that it's serious.'

I walked along the corridor. An elderly man naked from the waist down was lying on a trolley, whimpering. The nurses were trying to calm a hysterical mother with a screaming infant in her arms. I continued until I reached the A&E entrance. An ambulance was standing there, empty and unlit. I thought of what Sima had said, about the telescope that could home in on an individual person standing on the moon. Try to stay alive, I whispered to myself. Chara, little Chara, perhaps one day you will become that person who went unnoticed here on earth, but got her own back standing on the moon and waving down to the rest of us.

That was a prayer, or perhaps an invocation. Sima, lying in intensive care and trying to stay alive, needed all the help she could get. I don't believe in God. But you can create your own gods whenever you need them.

I stood there appealing to a place near Los Angeles called Mount Wilson. If Sima survived, I would pay for her to go there. I would find out who this Wilson was, the man who had given his name to the mountain.

There's nothing to prevent a god having a name. Why shouldn't the Creator have the name Wilson?

If she died, it would be my fault. If I'd gone downstairs when I heard her crying, she might not have injured herself. I'm a doctor, I ought to have understood. But above all else, I am a human being who ought to have recognised some of the enormous loneliness that a little girl can feel.

Without warning, I found myself longing for my father. I hadn't done so since he died. His death had caused me great pain. Even though we had never spoken intimately to each other, we had shared an unspoken understanding. He had lived long enough to experience my success in training to become a doctor – and never concealed his surprise and pride over it. During his final days, when he was confined to bed with his excruciatingly painful cancer that had spread from a little black spot on the heel of his foot to become metastases all over him that he compared to moss on a stone, he often spoke about the white coat that I would be privileged to wear. I thought his concept of power being embodied in that white coat was embarrassing. It was only afterwards that I realised he envisaged me as the one who would gain revenge on his behalf. He had also worn a white jacket, but people had trampled all over him. I would be the means through which he got his own back. Nobody belittled a doctor in a white coat.

I missed him now. And that magical trip to the black forest pool. I wanted to turn the clock back, I wanted to undo most of my life. My mother also flitted before my eyes. Lavender and tears, a life I had never understood. Had she carried around an invisible sword? Perhaps she was standing on the far bank of the river of life, waving to Sima?

In my mind, I also tried to talk to Harriet and Louise. But they remained silent, as if they thought I ought to be able to sort this out myself.

I went back inside and found a small waiting room that was empty. After a while, I was informed that Sima's condition was still critical. She was going to be moved to an intensive care ward. I shared the lift with her. Both men in charge of her trolley were black. One of them smiled at me. I smiled back, and had an urge to tell him about that remarkable telescope on Mount Wilson. Sima was lying with her eyes closed; she had a drip and was being fed oxygen through a nose catheter. I bent over her and whispered into her ear: 'Chara, when you are well again you will visit Mount Wilson and see that there is somebody standing on the moon who looks remarkably like you.'

A doctor came and said nothing was certain, but that they would probably need to operate and that Sima was not reacting to anything they attempted. He asked me several questions, but I had to tell him that I simply didn't know if she was suffering from any illnesses, or if she had tried to commit suicide before. The woman who would be able to answer questions like that was on her way here.

Agnes arrived shortly after ten. It occurred to me to wonder how she could drive a car with only one arm. Did she have a specially adapted vehicle? But it wasn't important. I took her behind the curtain to where Sima was lying. Agnes sobbed quietly, but I didn't want Sima to hear anything like that and took Agnes out again.

'There's no change,' I said. 'But the very fact that you've come makes everything better. Try talking to her. She needs to know that you're here.'

'Will she be able to hear what I say?'

'We don't know. But we can hope.'

Agnes spoke to the doctor. No illnesses, no medication, no previous suicide attempts as far as she was aware. The doctor, who was about my age, said that the situation was unchanged but slightly more stable since Sima had been admitted. There was no reason for the moment to be unduly worried.

Agnes was relieved. There was a coffee machine in the corridor. Between us we managed to scrape together the necessary small change for two cups of awful coffee. I was surprised by the adroitness with which she used one hand where I needed two

I told Agnes what had happened. She shook her head slowly.

'She might well have been on the way to Russia. Sima always tries to climb mountains. She's never satisfied with walking along normal paths like the rest of us.'

'But why should she want to come and visit me?'

'You live on an island. Russia is on the other side of the sea.'

'But when she gets to the island I live on, she tries to take her own life. I don't get it.'

'You can never tell by looking at a person just how badly damaged he or she is inside.'

'She told me a few things.'

'So perhaps you have some idea.'

At about three o'clock, a nurse came to say that Sima's condition had stabilised. If we wanted to go home, we could. She would phone us if there was any change. As we had nowhere to go to we stayed there for the rest of the day and all night. Agnes curled up on a narrow sofa and dozed. I spent most of the time on a chair leafing through well-thumbed magazines in which people I'd never heard of, pictured in dazzlingly bright colours, trumpeted to the world how important they were. We occasionally went to get something to eat, but we were never away for long.

Shortly after five in the morning, a nurse came to the waiting room to inform us that there had been a sudden change. Serious internal bleeding had occurred, and surgeons were about to operate in an attempt to stabilise her condition.

We had taken things too much for granted. Sima was suddenly drifting away from us again.

At twenty past six the doctor came to see us. He seemed to be very tired, sat down on a chair and stared at his hands. They hadn't been able to stop the bleeding. Sima was dead. She had never come round. If we needed support, the hospital offered a counselling service.

We went in together to see her. All the tubes had been removed, and the machines switched off. The yellow pallor that makes the newly dead look like a waxwork had already taken a grip of her face. I don't know how many dead people I have seen in my life. I have watched people die, I have performed post-mortem examinations, I have held human brains in my hands. Nevertheless, it was me who burst into tears; Agnes was in so much pain that she was incapable of reaction. She grasped my arm; I could feel that she was strong – and I wished that she would never let go.

I wanted to stay there, but Agnes asked me to go back home. She would stay with Sima, I had done all that I could, she was grateful, but she wanted to be on her own. She accompanied me to my taxi. It was a beautiful morning, still chilly. Yellow coltsfoot were in bloom on the verge leading up to A&E.

A coltsfoot moment, I thought. Just now, this morning, when Sima was lying dead inside there. Just for a brief moment she had sparkled like a ruby. Now it was as if she had never existed.

The only thing about death that scares me is its utter indifference.

'The sword,' I said. 'And she had a case as well. What do you want me to do with that?'

'I'll be in touch,' said Agnes. 'I can't say when. But I know where to find you.'

I watched her go back into the hospital. A one-armed sorrowful angel, who had just lost one of her wicked but remarkable children.

I got into the taxi and said where I wanted to go to. The driver eyed me suspiciously. I realised that I made a dodgy impression, to say the least. Dishevelled clothes, cut-down wellington boots, unshaven and hollow-eyed.

'We usually ask for payment in advance for long journeys like this,' the driver said. 'We've had some bad experiences.'

I felt in my pockets and realised that I didn't even have my wallet with me. I turned to the driver.

'My daughter has just died. I want to go home. You'll be paid. Please drive slowly and carefully.'

I started to weep. He said nothing more until we pulled up at the quayside. It was ten o'clock. There was a slight breeze that hardly disturbed the water in the harbour. I asked the taxi driver to stop outside the red wooden building that housed the coastguard. Hans Lundman had seen the taxi approaching and had come out of the door. He could see from my face that the outcome had not been good.

'She died,' I said. 'Internal bleeding. It was unexpected. We thought she was going to make it. I need to borrow a thousand kronor from you to pay for the taxi.'

'I'll put it on my credit card,' said Lundman, and headed for the taxi.

He'd finished his shift several hours previously. I realised that he had stayed on in the hope of being there when I got back to the quayside. Hans Lundman lived on one of the islands in the southern archipelago.

'I'll take you home,' he said.

'I don't have any money at home,' I said. 'I'll have to ask Jansson to take some out of the bank for me.'

'Who cares about money at a time like this?' he said.

I always feel at ease when I'm at sea. Hans Lundman's boat was an old converted fishing vessel that progressed at a stately pace. His work occasionally forced him to hurry, but he never rushed otherwise.

We berthed at the jetty. It was sunny, and warm. Spring had sprung. But I felt devoid of any such feelings.

'There's a boat out there at the Sighs,' I said. 'Moored there. It's stolen.'

He understood.

'We'll discover it tomorrow,' he said. 'It just so happens that I'll be passing there on patrol tomorrow. Nobody knows who stole it.'

We shook hands.

'She shouldn't have died,' I said.

'No,' said Lundman. 'She really shouldn't.'

I remained on the jetty and watched him reverse out of the inlet. He raised his hand in greeting, then was gone.

I sat down on the bench. It was much later when I returned to my house, where the front door was standing wide open.

CHAPTER 3

The oaks were unusually late this year.

I recorded in my logbook that the big oak tree between the boat-house and what used to be my grandparents' henhouse didn't start turning green until 25 May. The cluster of oaks around the inlet on the north side of the island – the inlet that for some incomprehensible reason had always been known as the Quarrel – started to come into leaf a few days earlier.

They say that the oaks on these islands were planted by the state at the beginning of the nineteenth century, so that there would be ample timber to make the warships being built in nearby Karlskrona. I remember lightning striking one of the trees when I was a child, and my grandfather sawing down what remained of the trunk. It had been planted in 1802. Grandfather told me that was in the days of Napoleon. I had no idea who Napoleon was at the time, but I realised that it was a very long time ago. Those annual rings had dogged me throughout my life. Beethoven was alive when that oak was still a sapling. The tree was in its prime when my father was born.

As so often out here in the archipelago, summer came gradually, but you could never be certain that it was here to stay. My feeling of loneliness usually decreased as it grew warmer. But that was not the case this year. I just sat there with my anthill, a sharp sword and Sima's half-empty suitcase.

I often spoke to Agnes on the telephone during this period. She told me that the funeral had taken place in Mogata church. Apart from Agnes and the two girls who lived with her – the ones I had met: Miranda and Aida – the only other person to attend was a very old man who claimed to be a distant relative of Sima's. He had arrived by taxi, and seemed so frail that Agnes was afraid he would drop dead at any moment. She had not managed to establish just how he was related to Sima. Perhaps he had mistaken her for somebody else? When she showed him a photograph of Sima, he hadn't been at all sure that he recognised her.

But so what? Agnes had said. The church ought to have been full of people bidding farewell to this young person who had never had an opportunity to discover herself, or explore the world.

The coffin had been adorned with a spray of red roses. A woman from the parish, accompanied by a restless young boy in the organ loft, sang a couple of hymns; Agnes said a few words, and she had asked the vicar not to go on unnecessarily about a conciliatory and omniscient God.

When I heard that the grave would only bear a number, I offered to pay for a headstone. Jansson later delivered a letter from Agnes with a sketch of the stone, how she thought it ought to look. Above Sima's name and dates, she had drawn a rose.

I rang her the same evening and asked if it shouldn't be a samurai sword instead. She understood my way of thinking, and said she had considered it herself.

'But it would cause an uproar,' she said.

'What shall I do with her belongings? The sword and the suitcase?'

'What's in the suitcase?'

'Underclothes. A pair of trousers and a jumper. A scruffy map of the Baltic and the Gulf of Finland.'

'I'll come and collect it. I'd like to see your house. And above all, I want to see the room where it happened.'

'I've already said that I ought to have gone down to her. I shall always regret not having done so.'

'I'm not accusing you of anything. I just want to see the place where she began to die.'

Initially she planned to visit me during the last week of May, but something cropped up. She cancelled her visit twice more. The first time Miranda had run away, and the second occasion she was ill. I had put the sword and the case with Sima's clothes in the room with the anthill. One night I woke up out of a dream in which the ants had engulfed the case and the sword in their hill. I raced downstairs and wrenched open the door. But the ants were still continuing to climb and conquer the dining table and the white tablecloth.

I moved Sima's belongings to the boathouse.

Jansson later told me that the coastguards had found a stolen motor-boat moored in the Sighs. Hans Lundman was as good as his word.

'One of these days they'll be all over us,' said Jansson menacingly.

'Who will?'

'These gangsters. They're everywhere. What can you do to defend yourself? Jump into your boat and sail out to sea?'

'What would they want to come here for? What is there around here worth stealing?'

'The very thought makes me worry about my blood pressure.'

I fetched the monitor from the boathouse. Jansson lay down on the bench. I let him rest for five minutes then strapped up his arm.

'It's excellent. 140 over 80.'

'I think you're wrong.'

'In that case I think you should find yourself another doctor.'

I returned to the boathouse and stayed there in the darkness until I heard him backing away from the jetty.

I spent the days before the oak trees started to turn green sorting out my boat at last. When I eventually managed to remove the heavy tarpaulin, which took considerable effort, I found a dead squirrel beneath the keelson. I was surprised, as I had never seen a squirrel out here on the island, and never heard it claimed that there were any.

The boat was in much worse condition than I had feared. After two days assessing what needed to be done I was ready to give up even before I'd started. Nevertheless, the following day I began scraping off all the old, flaky paint on the hull. I phoned Hans Lundman and asked him for advice. He promised to call on me one of these days. It was slow going. I wasn't used to this kind of exertion, my only regular activities being a morning bath and writing up my logbook.

The same day that I started scraping off the paint, I dug out the logbook I'd kept during my very first year out here on the island. I looked up today's date. To my astonishment I read: 'Yesterday I drank myself silly.' That was all. I now remembered it happening, but very vaguely and certainly not why. The previous day I had recorded that I'd repaired a downpipe. The following day I had laid out my nets and caught seven flounders and three perch.

I put the logbook away. It was evening now. The apple tree was in blossom. I could picture Grandma sitting on the bench beside it, a shimmering figure that melted into the background, the tree trunk, the rocks, the thorn thicket.

The following day Jansson delivered letters from both Harriet and Louise. I had eventually brought myself to tell them about the girl who had come to my island, and her death. I read Harriet's first; as always, it was very short. She wrote that she was too tired to write a proper letter. I read it, and frowned. It was difficult to read her handwriting, much more so than before. The words seemed to be writhing in pain on the page. And to make matters worse, the content was bewildering. She wrote that she was better, but felt worse. She made no mention of Sima's death.

I put the letter to one side. The cat jumped up on to the table. I sometimes envy animals that don't have the worry of disturbing mail. Was Harriet befuddled by painkillers when she wrote the letter? I was worried, picked up the telephone and rang her. If she was drifting into the very last phase of her life, I wanted to know about it. I let it ring for ages, but there was no answer. I tried her mobile number. Nothing. I left a message and asked her to return the call.

Then I opened the letter from Louise. It was about the remarkable cave system in Lascaux in the west of France, where in 1940 some boys stumbled upon cave paintings 17,000 years old. Some of the animals depicted on the rock walls were four metres high. Now, she wrote, 'These ancient works of art are under threat of being ruined because some madmen have installed air conditioning in the passages because the American tourists cannot handle the temperature! But freezing temperatures are essential if these cave paintings are to survive. The rock walls have been attacked by a strain of mould that is difficult to deal with. If nothing is done, if the whole world fails to unite in defence of this, the most ancient art museum we possess will disappear.'

She intended to act. I assumed that she would write to every politician in Europe, and I felt proud. I had a daughter who was prepared to man the barricades.

The letter had been written in short bursts on several occasions. Both the handwriting and pen used varied. In between serious and agitated paragraphs, she had interposed notes about mundane happenings. She had sprained her foot while fetching water. Giaconelli had been ill. They had suspected pneumonia, but now he was on the mend. She sympathised with the sorrow I felt at the death of Sima.

'I'll be coming to visit you shortly,' she concluded. 'I want to see this island where you've been hiding yourself away all these years. I sometimes used to dream that I had a father who was just as frighteningly handsome as Caravaggio. That is not something anybody could accuse you of being. But still, you can no longer hide from me. I want to get to know you, I want my inheritance, I want you to explain to me all the things that I still don't understand.'

Not a word about Harriet. Didn't she care about her mother, who was busy dying?

I tried Harriet's numbers again, but still no answer. I called Louise's mobile, but no answer there either. I climbed the hill behind the house. It was a beautiful early-summer day. Not really warm yet, but the islands had begun to turn green. In the distance I could see one of the year's first sailing boats on its way to somewhere unknown from a home harbour that was also unknown. I suddenly felt an urge to drag myself away from this island. I had spent so much of my life wandering back and forth between the jetty and the house.

I just wanted to get away. When Harriet appeared out there on the ice with her walker, she shattered the curse that I'd allowed to imprison me here, as if in a cage. I realised that the twelve years I had lived on the island had been wasted, like a liquid that had drained out of a cracked container. There was no going back, no starting again.

I walked round the island. There was a pungent smell of sea and soil. Lively oystercatchers were scurrying about at the water's edge, pecking away with their red beaks. I felt as if I were walking round a prison yard a few days before I was due to emerge through the front gates and become a free man again. But would I do that? Where could I go to? What kind of a life would be in store for me?

I sat down under one of the oaks in the Quarrel. It dawned on me that I was in a hurry. There was no time to waste.

That evening I rowed out to Starrudden. The sea bottom was smooth there. I laid out a flounder net, but didn't have much hope of catching anything – maybe the odd flounder or a perch that would be appreciated by the cat. The net would be clogged up by the sticky algae that now proliferates in the Baltic.

Perhaps this sea stretching out before me on these beautiful evenings is in fact slowly deteriorating into a marsh?

Later that evening I did something I shall never be able to understand. I fetched a spade, and opened up my dog's grave. I dug up the whole cadaver. Maggots had already eaten away the mucous membranes around its mouth, eyes and ears, and opened up its stomach. There was a white clump of them clustered around its anus. I put down the spade, and fetched the cat that was fast asleep on the kitchen sofa. I carried her to the grave and set her down next to the dead dog. She jumped high into the air, as if she'd been bitten by an adder, and ran away as far as the corner of the house, where she paused, wondering whether to continue her flight. I gathered a handful of the fat maggots and wondered whether I ought to eat them – or would the nausea be too much for me? Then I threw them back on to the dog's body, and filled in the grave as fast as I could.

It made no sense. Was I preparing the way for opening up a similar grave inside myself? In order to summon up enough courage to face in cold blood all the things I'd been burdened with for so long?

I spent ages scrubbing my hands under the kitchen taps. I felt sick at what I'd done.

At about eleven I phoned Harriet and Louise again. Still no answer.

Early the next morning I took in the net. There were two thin flounders and a dead perch. As I had feared, the net was clogged up with mud and algae. It took me over an hour to get it somewhere near clean and hang it up on the boathouse wall. I was glad that my grandfather hadn't lived to see the sea he loved being choked to death. Then I went back to scraping the boat. I was working half naked and tried to make peace with my cat, who was wary after the previous night's meeting with the dead dog. She wasn't interested in the flounders, but took the perch to a hollow in the rocks and chewed away.

At ten o'clock I went in and phoned again. Still no answer. There wouldn't be any postal delivery today either. There was nothing I could do.

I boiled a couple of eggs for lunch and leafed through an old brochure advertising paints suitable for a wooden boat. The brochure was eight years old.

After the meal I lay down on the kitchen sofa for a rest. I was worn out and soon fell asleep.

It was almost one o'clock when I was woken up with a start. Through the open kitchen window I could hear the sound of an old compression-ignition engine. It sounded like Jansson's boat, but he wasn't due today. I got up, stuck my feet into my cut-down wellington boots and went outside. The noise was getting louder. I had no doubt now that it was Jansson's boat. It makes an uneven noise because the exhaust pipe sometimes dips down under the surface of the water. I went down to the jetty to wait. The prow eventually appeared from behind the rocks furthest away. I was surprised to note that he was only travelling at half-throttle, and the boat was moving very slowly.

Then I understood why. Jansson was towing another craft, an old cow ferry tied to the stern of his boat. When I was a child I had watched ferries like this one taking cows to islands with summer pasture. I hadn't seen a single ferry like this during all the twelve years I'd lived on the island.

On the deck of the cow ferry was Louise's caravan. She was standing in the open door, exactly as I remembered seeing her the first time I met her. Then I noticed another person standing by the rail. It was Harriet, with her walker.

If it had been possible, I'd have jumped into the water and swum away. But there was no escape. Jansson slowed down and untied the tow rope, giving the ferry a push to ensure that it glided in towards the shallowest part of the inlet. I stood there as if paralysed, watching it beach itself. Jansson moored his boat at the jetty.

'I never thought I'd have a use for this old ferry again. The last time I had it out was to take a couple of horses to Rökskär. But that must have been twenty-five years ago, if not more,' he said.

'You could have phoned,' I said. 'You could have warned me.'

Jansson looked surprised.

'I thought you knew they were coming. Louise said you were expecting them. We'll be able to tow the caravan up with your tractor. It's a good job it's high tide, otherwise we'd have had to pull it through the water.'

This explained why nobody had answered my telephone calls. Louise helped Harriet ashore with her walker. I noticed that Harriet was even thinner and much weaker now than when I'd left them so abruptly in the caravan.

I clambered down on to the shore. Louise was holding Harriet by the arm.

'It's pretty here,' said Louise. 'I prefer the forest. But it's pretty.'

'I suppose I ought to say "welcome",' I said.

Harriet raised her head. Her face was covered in sweat.

'I'll fall if I let go,' she said. 'I'd like to lie down on the bed among the ants again.'

We helped her up to the house. I asked Jansson to see if he could start my old tractor. Harriet lay down on the bed. She was breathing heavily and seemed to be in pain. Louise gave her a pill and fetched a glass of water. Harriet swallowed the pill with great difficulty. Then she looked at me.

'I haven't got much longer to live,' she said. 'Hold my hand.'

I took her warm hand.

'I want to lie here and listen to the sea and have you two close to me. That's all. The old lady promises not to give you any unnecessary trouble. I shan't even scream when the pain becomes too much to bear. When that happens, I shall take my tablets or Louise will give me an injection.'

She closed her eyes. We stood watching her. She soon fell asleep. Louise walked round the table, contemplating the expanding anthill.

'How many ants are there?' she whispered.

'A million, perhaps more.'

'How long have you had it?'

'This is the eleventh year.'

We left the room.

'You could have rung,' I said.

She stood in front of me and took a firm hold of my shoulders.

'If I had you'd have said no. I didn't want that to happen. Now we are here. You owe it to my mum and me, especially to her. If she wants to lie listening to the sea instead of to hooting motor cars when she dies, that's what she's going to do. And so you can be grateful that I won't need to harass you for the rest of your life complaining about what you did.'

She turned on her heel and went outside. Jansson had managed to start the tractor. Just as I had suspected all these years, he was pretty good at starting difficult engines.

We tied a few ropes to the caravan and managed to unload it from the cow ferry. Jansson was in charge of the tractor.

'Where do you want it to stand?' he shouted.

'Here,' said Louise, pointing to a patch of grass beyond the narrow strip of sand on the other side of the boathouse. 'I want a beach of my own,' she went on. 'I've always dreamed of that.'

Jansson displayed great skill with the tractor as he manoeuvred the caravan into position. We placed old fish boxes and driftwood where necessary until it was level and steady.

'It'll be OK now,' said Jansson, sounding satisfied. 'This is the only island out here with a caravan.'

'Thank you. You're invited to coffee,' said Louise.

Jansson looked at me. I said nothing.

It was the first time he'd been inside the house as long as I'd lived there. He looked inquisitively around the kitchen.

'It looks just as I remember it,' he said. 'You haven't changed much. Unless I'm much mistaken this is the same tablecloth as the old couple used to have.'

Louise brewed some coffee and asked if I had any buns. I didn't. So she went to her caravan to fetch something.

'She's a very elegant woman,' said Jansson. 'How did you manage to find her?'

'I didn't find her. She's the one who found me.'

'Did you advertise for a woman? I've considered doing that.'

Jansson isn't exactly quick-witted. You couldn't accuse him of indulging in too much activity behind the eyes. But it was beyond belief that he could imagine that Louise was a lady I had somehow picked up, complete with caravan and a dying old woman.

'She's my daughter,' I said. 'I told you I had a daughter. I distinctly remember doing so. We were sitting on the bench by the jetty. You had earache. It was last autumn. I told you I had a grown-up daughter. Have you forgotten?'

Jansson had no idea what I was talking about. But he didn't dare to argue. He didn't dare to risk losing his personal physician.

Louise came back with an assortment of buns and biscuits. Jansson and my daughter seemed to hit it off from the start. I would have to explain to Louise that she could hold sway over her caravan, but when it came to my island, nobody but me was allowed to lay down the law. And one of the laws that applied was that Jansson must on no account be invited to drink coffee in my kitchen.

Jansson towed away his cow ferry and disappeared round the headland. I didn't ask Louise how much she'd paid him. We went for a walk round the island as Harriet was still asleep. I showed her where my dog was buried. Then we clambered southwards over the rocks and followed the shore.

Just for a short time, it was like having acquired a little child. Louise asked about everything – plants, seaweed, the neighbouring islands barely visible through the mist, the fish in the depths of the sea that she couldn't see at all. I suppose I could answer about half her questions. But that didn't matter to her – the important thing was that I listened to what she said.

There were a few boulders on Norrudden, a headland on the north side of the island, that centuries ago the ice had shaped into throne-like constructions. We sat down.

'Whose idea was it?' I asked.

'I think we both hit on it at about the same time. It was time to visit you, and for the family to get together before it was too late.'

'What do your friends in the forest up north have to say about this?'

'They know that I'll come back one of these days.'

'Why did you have to lug the caravan with you?'

'It's my shell. I never leave it behind.'

She told me about Harriet. Harriet had been driven to Stockholm by one of Louise's boxer friends called Sture who made a living by drilling wells.

Then Harriet suddenly took a turn for the worse. Louise travelled down to Stockholm to look after her mother, as she had refused to go into a hospice. Louise had insisted on being authorised to administer the painkilling drugs Harriet needed. All that was possible now was palliative care. Every effort to prevent the cancer from spreading had been abandoned. The final countdown had begun. Louise was in constant touch with the home-nursing authorities in Stockholm.

We sat on our thrones, gazing out over the sea.

'I can't see her lasting more than another month at most,' said Louise. 'I'm already giving her enormous doses of painkillers. She's going to die here. You'd better prepare yourself for that. You're a doctor – or, at least, were one. You're more familiar with death than I am. But I've realised that death is always a lonely business. Nevertheless, we can be here and help her.'

'Is she in a lot of pain?'

'She sometimes screams.'

We continued our walk along the shore. When we came to the headland reaching out towards the open sea, we paused again. My grandfather had placed a bench there: he'd made it himself from an old threshing machine and some rough oak planks. When he and Grandma had quarrelled, as they sometimes did, he used to go and sit there until she came to fetch him and tell him that dinner was ready. Their anger had always subsided by then. I had carved my name on the bench when I was seven years old. My grandfather was no doubt less than pleased, but he never said anything.

Eider and scoter and a few mergansers were bobbing up and down on the waves.

'There's a deep underwater ravine just offshore here, where the birds are,' I said. 'The average depth is fifteen to twenty metres, but there is this sudden abyss fifty-six metres deep. When I was a lad I used to lower a grappling iron from the rowing boat, and always imagined that it was bottomless. We've had visits by geologists trying to work out why it exists. As far as I can understand, nobody has been able to give a satisfactory answer. I rather like that. I have no faith in a world in which all riddles are solved.'

'I believe in a world where people fight back,' said Louise.

'I assume you're thinking about your French caves?'

'Yes, and much more besides.'

'Are you writing protest letters?'

'The latest ones were to Tony Blair and President Chirac.'

'Have they replied?'

'Of course not. But I'm working on other courses of action.'

'What?'

She shook her head. She didn't want to go into that.

We continued our walk and came to a stop at the boathouse. The sun was shining on the lee wall.

'You fulfilled one of the promises you made to Harriet,' said Louise. 'She has another request now.'

'I'm not going back to that forest pool.'

'No, she wants something to take place here. A midsummer party.'

'Meaning what?'

Louise was annoyed.

'What can you mean by a midsummer party apart from what the words say? A party that takes place at midsummer?'

'I'm not accustomed to throwing parties here on my island. No matter whether it's summer or winter.'

'Then it's about time you did. Harriet wants to sit out on a sunny summer evening with some other guests, to eat some good food, drink some good wine, and then go back to bed and die soon after.'

'That's something we can arrange, of course. You, me and her. We can set up a long table on the grass in front of the currant bushes.'

'Harriet wants guests. She wants to meet people.'

'Who, for instance?'

'You're the one who lives here. Invite some of your friends. There don't need to be all that many.'

Louise set off for the house, without waiting for a reply. I could invite Jansson, Hans Lundman and his wife Romana, who works as an assistant at the meat counter in the big indoor food market in our nearest town.

Harriet would be able to partake of her last supper out here on my island. That was the least I could do for her.

CHAPTER 4

It rained more or less non-stop until midsummer. We established simple routines based on Harriet's deteriorating condition. To start with, Louise slept in her caravan; but when Harriet screamed out two nights in succession, she moved into my kitchen. I offered to help by giving Harriet her medication but Louise wanted to keep that responsibility. She used a mattress on the kitchen floor, and stored it in the vestibule every morning. She told me the cat would sleep at her feet.

Harriet slept most of the time, lost in a trance induced by the drugs. She had no appetite, but with boundless patience, Louise forced down her a sufficient amount of nutrition. I was touched by the extraordinary tenderness she displayed towards her mother. It was a side of her I'd not seen before. I kept my distance, and would never have dreamt of intervening.

In the evenings, we would sit in Louise's caravan or in my kitchen, talking. She had taken over the cooking. I would phone in her shopping lists and Jansson would deliver the goods. The week before midsummer, it was clear that Harriet didn't have long to go. Every time she woke up, she asked about the weather, I realised that she was thinking about her party. The next time Jansson came, when it had been raining constantly with winds blowing in from the Arctic, I invited him to a party the following Friday.

'Is it your birthday?'

'Every Christmas, you complain that I haven't put up any lights. Every midsummer you moan because I decline to drink a toast with you on the jetty. Now I'm inviting you to a party. Is it that hard to understand? Seven o'clock, weather permitting.'

'I can feel in my bones that warm weather is on its way.'

Jansson claims that he can divine water using a dowsing rod and that he can feel the weather in his bones.

I didn't comment on his bones. Later that same day I phoned Hans Lundman and invited him and his wife.

'I'm working then, but I should be able to swap shifts with Edvin. Is it your birthday?'

'It's always my birthday,' I said. 'Seven o'clock, weather permitting.'

Louise and I made preparations. I dug out some of my grandparents' summer furniture that had been stored away for years. I painted it and repaired a rotten table leg.

The day before Midsummer Eve, it was pouring with rain. A gale was blowing from the north-west, and the temperature sank to twelve degrees. Louise and I struggled up the hill and saw boats riding out the storm in a sheltered bay on the other side of Korsholmen, the island nearest to mine.

'Will the weather be like this tomorrow as well?' Louise asked.

'According to Jansson's bones, it will be fine and sunny,' I said.

The next day, the wind dropped. The rain ceased, the clouds dispersed and the temperature rose. Harriet had had two bad nights when the painkillers didn't seem to work. Then things appeared to improve. We prepared for the party. Louise knew exactly what Harriet wanted.

'Simple extravagance,' she said. 'It's a hopeless task, of course, trying to mix simplicity and extravagance, but sometimes you have to attempt the impossible.'

It was a strange midsummer party that I don't think any of those present will ever forget, even if our memories of it differ somewhat. Hans Lundman rang in the morning and asked if they could bring with them their granddaughter, who was paying them a visit and couldn't be left on her own. Her name was Andrea, and she was sixteen years old. I knew that she had a mental handicap, and that she found it difficult to understand some things, or to learn. But she also had boundless confidence in people she'd never met before. She would shake anybody at all by the hand, and as a child was more than happy to sit on the knee of total strangers.

Of course she was welcome. We set the table for seven people rather than six. Harriet, who by now was practically bedbound, was sitting in her chair in the garden by five in the afternoon. She was wearing a light-coloured summery dress chosen by Louise, who had also combed her grey hair into a pretty bun. Louise had made her up as well. Harriet's haggard face had regained some of the poise it had possessed earlier in her life. I sat down beside her with a glass of wine in my hand. She took it from me and half emptied it.

'Serve me some more,' she said. 'To make sure I don't fall asleep, I've reduced my intake of all the stuff that keeps my pains at bay. But I do still have pain, and it's going to get worse. However, what I want now is white wine instead of white tablets. Wine!'

I went to the kitchen, where a row of bottles were uncorked and ready to serve. Louise was busy with something about to go into the oven.

'Harriet wants some wine,' I said.

'Give her some, then! This party is for her. It's the last time she'll be able to drink herself tipsy. If she gets drunk, we can all be happy.'

I took the bottle out into the garden. The table was laid very attractively. Louise had decorated it with flowers and leafy twigs. She'd covered the cold dishes already on the table with some of Grandma's worn-out towels.

We toasted each other. Harriet took hold of my hand.

'Are you angry because I want to die in your house?'

'Why ever should I be?'

'You didn't want to live with me. Perhaps you don't want me to die in your house either.'

'It wouldn't surprise me if you were to outlive the lot of us.'

'I'll be dead before long. I can feel death tugging at me. The earth is pulling me down. Sometimes, when I wake up during the night, just before the agony gets so bad that I need to scream, I have time to ask myself if I'm scared of what lies in store. I am. But I'm scared without being scared. It's more of a vague worry, being on the way to open a door without being at all sure what's behind it. Then the pains strike home, and that's what I'm scared of. Nothing else.'

Louise came and sat down next to me, glass in hand.

'The family,' she said. 'I don't know now if I want to use the surname Welin or Hörnfeldt. Maybe I'll be Louise Hörnfeldt-Welin. Occupation: letter writer.'

She had a camera with her, and took a picture of Harriet and me sitting there, with glasses in our hands. Then she took a picture with herself in it as well.

'I have an old-fashioned camera,' she said. 'I have to send the films away to be developed. But now I've got that snap I've always dreamt about.'

We drank a toast to the summer evening. I thought about the fact that Harriet was forced to wear a pad under her flimsy summery dress, and that the beautiful Louise really was my daughter.

Louise went to her caravan to change her clothes. The cat suddenly jumped up on to the table. I shooed her down. She looked offended, and slunk away. We sat there in silence, listening to the muted murmuring of the sea.

'You and I,' said Harriet. 'You and I. And then, suddenly, it's all over.'

By seven o'clock it was dead calm and plus seventeen degrees.

Jansson and the Lundmans arrived together. The boats formed a friendly little convoy of two, both with flags fluttering from the stern. Louise stood waiting for them on the jetty, looking radiant. Her dress was almost provocatively short, but she had pretty legs and I recognised the red shoes she had on – she'd been wearing them when she stepped out of the caravan and I saw her for the first time. Jansson had squeezed himself into an old suit that was on the tight side, Romana was glittering in red and black and Hans was dressed all in white and sported a yachtsman's cap. Andrea was wearing a blue dress with a yellow hairband. We moored the boats, spent a few minutes on the little jetty chatting about the summer that had arrived at last, then proceeded up to the house. Jansson's eyes looked slightly glazed and he stumbled a couple of times, but nobody minded – least of all Harriet who heaved herself up off her chair without assistance and shook hands with everybody.

We had decided to tell the truth: Harriet was Louise's mother, I was her father, and once upon a time Harriet and I were almost married. Now Harriet was ill, but not so bad that we couldn't all sit out under the oak trees this evening and have dinner.

On reflection, it seemed to me that, at the beginning, our party was reminiscent of a little orchestra, with all the individual members tuning their instruments. We talked and talked, and gradually achieved the right sound. At the same time we ate, drank toasts, carried dishes back and forth, and sent our laughter echoing across the skerries. Harriet seemed in perfectly good health while this was all happening. She spoke to Hans about emergency flares, about the price of groceries to Romana, and she asked Jansson to tell us about the strangest delivery he'd made during all his years as a postman. It was her party, she was the one who dominated, conducted and blended all the sounds to form a melodious chord. Andrea said nothing. Soon after the start she had clung tightly to Louise, who allowed herself to be held. We all got drunk, of course, Jansson first – but he never lost control. He helped Louise to carry plates and didn't drop a single one. As dusk fell, he was the one who lit the candles and the citronella spirals Louise had bought to keep the mosquitoes away. Andrea was giving the adults searching looks. Harriet, who was sitting opposite her, occasionally stretched out her hand and touched Andrea's fingertips. I felt very sad as I sat there, watching those fingers touching. One of them would soon die, the other would never really understand what it meant to live. Harriet noticed me watching them and raised her glass. We touched glasses and drank.

Then I gave a speech. It wasn't prepared at all, not consciously anyway. I talked about simplicity and extravagance. About perfection, which may not exist, but whose existence can be sensed when in the company of good friends on a lovely summer's evening. The Swedish summer was unpredictable, and never very long. But it could be stunningly beautiful, as it was this very evening.

'You are my friends,' I said. 'You are my friends and my family, and I have been an inhospitable prince on this little island of mine, and never welcomed any of you here. I thank you for your patience, I shudder to think what you may have thought in the past. I hope this will not be the only time we meet like this.'

We drank. A gentle evening breeze blew through the crowns of the oak trees, and made the candle flames flutter.

Jansson tapped his glass and stood up. He was swaying slightly, but was able to stand upright. He said nothing. But then he started singing. In a staggeringly sonorous baritone voice he sang 'Ave Maria' in a way that sent shivers down my spine. I think everybody around the table had a similar reaction. Hans and Romana looked just as astonished as I must have done. Nobody seemed to know that Jansson had such a powerful voice. I had tears in my eyes. Jansson stood there, with all his imagined aches and pains, in a suit that was too small for him, singing in a way that gave the impression that a god had come down to join us and celebrate this summer evening. Only he could explain why he had kept this voice of his a secret.

Even the birds fell silent and listened. Andrea was open-mouthed. These were powerful, magic moments. When he had finished and sat down, nobody said a word. In the end, Hans broke the silence and said the only thing it was possible to say.

'Well, I'll be damned!'

Jansson was bombarded with questions. Where did he learn to sing like that? Why had he never sung before? But he didn't answer. Nor did he want to sing any more.

'I've delivered my thank-you speech,' he said. 'I sang. I only wish this evening would go on for ever.'

We carried on drinking and eating. Harriet had put down her conductor's baton, and now conversations criss-crossed haphazardly. We were all drunk. Louise and Andrea sneaked down to the boathouse and the caravan. Hans got it into his head that he and Romana should dance. They hopped and bounced round the back of the house dancing what Jansson maintained was a polka, and reappeared round the other side doing what looked more like a hambo.

Harriet was enjoying herself. I think there were moments during the evening when she felt no pain, and forgot that she would soon die. I served more wine to everybody except Andrea. Jansson staggered off to have a pee behind the bushes, Hans and Romana began an arm-wrestling match, and I switched on my radio: music, something dreamy for the piano by Schumann, I thought. I sat down beside Harriet.

'Things turned out for the best,' she said.

'What do you mean?'

'We would never have been able to live together. Before long I'd have tired of all your eavesdropping and searching through my private papers. It was as if I had you under my skin. You made me itch. But as I was in love with you, I ignored that. I thought it would pass. And it did. But only when you'd gone away.'

She raised her glass and looked me in the eye.

'You've never been a good person,' she said. 'You've always shrugged off your responsibilities. You'll never become a good person. But maybe a bit better than you are now. Don't lose Louise. Look after her and she'll look after you.'

'You should have told me,' I said. 'I had a daughter for all those years without knowing.'

'Of course I should have told you. I could have found you if I'd really tried. But I was so angry. It was my way of getting revenge. Keeping your child for myself. I'm being punished for that now.'

'How?'

'I feel regret.'

Jansson staggered up to us and sat down on the other side of Harriet, oblivious to the fact that we were deep in conversation.

'I think you're an extraordinary woman, no hesitation in coming aboard my hydrocopter and then venturing out on to the ice.'

'It was an experience,' said Harriet. 'But I wouldn't want to repeat that journey out to the island.'

I got up and walked up the hill. The sounds from the other side of the house reached me in the form of clinking crockery and sporadic shouts. I thought I could see Grandma sitting down there on the bench by the apple tree, and Grandfather on his way up the path from the boathouse.

It was an evening when the living and the dead could have a shared party. It was an evening for those who still had a long time to live, and for those like Harriet who were standing close to the invisible border-line, waiting for the ferry that would transport them over the river, for the final crossing.

I went down to the jetty. The caravan door was open. I walked over to it and peered in surreptitiously through the window. Andrea was trying on Louise's clothes. She was tottering on high-heeled light blue shoes, and was wearing a strange dress covered in glistening sequins.

I sat down on the bench, and suddenly remembered that evening at the winter solstice. When I'd been in the kitchen thinking that nothing in my life would ever change. That was six months ago, and everything had changed. Now the summer solstice had begun to project us back towards darkness. I was listening to voices on my island that is normally so quiet. Romana's shrill laughter, and then Harriet's voice, as she raised herself above death and all that pain and shouted for more wine.

More wine! It sounded like a hunting call. Harriet had mobilised the last of her strength in order to fight the final battle. I went back to the house and uncorked the bottles we had left. When I came out, Jansson was embracing Romana in a swaying, semi-conscious dance. Hans had moved over to Harriet. He was holding her hand, or perhaps it was the other way round, and she was listening as he laboriously and unsuccessfully tried to explain to her how lighthouses in shipping channels made it safer for vessels to sail along them even at very high speeds. Louise and Andrea emerged from the shadows. Nobody apart from Harriet noticed pretty Andrea in Louise's imaginative creations. She was still wearing the light blue shoes. Louise saw me looking at Andrea's feet.

'Giaconelli made them for me,' she whispered in my ear. 'Now I'm giving them to that girl who has so much love inside her but nobody will ever have the courage to accept it. An angel will wear light blue shoes created by a master.'

The long night passed slowly in a sort of dream, and I no longer recall clearly what happened or what was said. But on one occasion when I went for a pee, Jansson was sitting on the front steps, sobbing in Romana's arms. Hans was dancing a waltz with Andrea, Harriet and Louise were whispering confidentially to each other, and the sun was climbing unobtrusively out of the sea.

The band that made its way along the path to the jetty at four in the morning was anything but steady on its feet. Harriet was supported by her walker and assisted by Hans. We stood on the jetty and said our goodbyes, untied the mooring ropes and watched the boats leave.

Just before Andrea was about to clamber down into the boat with the light blue shoes in her hand, she came up to me and hugged me with her thin, mosquito-bitten arms.

Long after the boats had vanished round the headland I could still feel that embrace, like a warm film round my body.

'I'll go back to the house with Harriet,' said Louise. 'She needs a really good wash. It'll be easier if we're on our own. If you're tired you can have a lie-down in the caravan.'

'I'll start collecting the plates and things.'

'We can do that tomorrow.'

I watched her helping Harriet back to the house. Harriet was exhausted now. She could barely hold herself upright, despite leaning on the walker and her daughter.

My family, I thought. The family I didn't get until it was too late.

I fell asleep on the bench, and didn't wake up until Louise tapped me on the shoulder.

'She's asleep now. We ought to get some sleep as well.'

The sun was already high over the horizon. I had a headache, and my mouth was dry.

'Do you think she enjoyed it?' I asked.

'I hope so.'

'Did she say anything?'

'She was almost unconscious when I put her to bed.'

We walked up to the house. The cat, who had disappeared for most of the night, was lying on the kitchen sofa. Louise took hold of my hand.

'I wonder who you are,' she said. 'One day I'll understand, perhaps, But it was a good party. And I like your friends.'

She unrolled the mattress on the kitchen floor. I went up to my room and lay on the bed, taking off nothing but my shoes.

In my dreams I heard the cries and shrieks of seagulls and terns. They came closer and closer, then suddenly dived down towards my face.

When I woke up I realised that the noises were coming from downstairs. It was Harriet, screaming in pain again.

The party was over.

CHAPTER 5

A week later the cat vanished. Louise and I searched every nook and cranny among the rocks, but found nothing. As usual I thought about my dog. He would have found the cat immediately. But he was dead, and I realised that the cat was probably dead now as well. I lived on an island of dead animals, with a dying person who was struggling through her final painful days together with an ever growing anthill that was slowly threatening to take over the entire room.

The cat was never seen again. The heat of high summer formed an oppressive blanket over my island. I used my outboard motor to get the boat to the mainland, and bought an electric fan for Harriet's room. The windows were left open all night. Mosquitoes danced on the old mosquito windows my grandfather had made long ago. There was even a date, written in carpenter's pencil, on one of the frames: 1936. I began to think that despite the poor start, this July heatwave would turn the summer into the hottest I'd experienced here.

Louise went swimming every evening. Things had gone so far now that we were always within earshot of Harriet's room. One of us needed to be on hand at all times. Her agonising pains were coming increasingly often. Every third day Louise phoned the home health service for advice. The second week in July, they wanted to send a doctor to examine her. I was on the porch changing a light bulb when Louise talked to them. To my surprise, I heard her say that a visit wouldn't be necessary as her father was a doctor.

I made regular trips to the mainland in order to collect new supplies of Harriet's medication from the chemist's. One day Louise asked me to buy some picture postcards It didn't matter what of. I bought the entire stock of cards from one shop, and postage stamps to go with them. When Harriet was asleep, Louise would sit down and write to all her friends in the forest. Occasionally she would also work away at a letter I gathered was going to be very long. She didn't say who it was to. She never left her papers on the kitchen table, but always took them with her to the caravan.

I warned her that Jansson would certainly read every single card she gave him for posting.

'Why would he want to do that?'

'He's curious.'

'I think he'll respect my postcards.'

We said no more about the matter. Every time Jansson moored his boat by the jetty, she would hand him a bundle of newly written cards. He would put them in his sack without even looking at them.

Nor did he complain about his aches and pains any more. This summer, with Harriet lying in my house, dying, Jansson seemed to have suddenly been cured of all his imagined ailments.

As Louise was looking after Harriet, I was responsible for the cooking. Of course, Harriet was really the key person in the house, but Louise ran the household as if it were a ship and she was the captain. I had nothing against that.

The hot days were a torment for Harriet. I bought another fan, but it didn't help much. I rang Hans Lundman several times to ask what the coastguard's meteorologist had to say about the weather forecast.

'It's a strange heatwave,' he said. 'Ridges of high pressure usually move on, pass over, albeit sometimes very slowly. But this is different. It's just hanging there. Those who know about these things say it's a similar to the heatwave that covered Sweden in the incredibly hot summer of 1955.'

I remembered that summer. I was eighteen and spent most of my time sailing in my grandfather's dinghy. It was a restless summer for me, and my teenage pulse had been racing. I often lay naked on the hot rocks, dreaming of women. The prettiest of my women teachers kept wandering through my dreamworld, and one after another had become my lovers.

That was almost fifty years ago.

'There must be some kind of prediction as to when it will start getting cooler?'

'Just at the moment there is no movement at all. Fires are starting all over the place. There are fires in the most unexpected places.'

We had to struggle through it. Dark clouds would sometimes gather over the mainland, and we could hear the sound of distant thunder. We sometimes found ourselves without electricity, but my grandfather had devoted a lot of time to creating a clever system of lightning conductors which protected both the main house and the boathouse.

When the electric storms finally came to the island, one evening after one of the hottest days of all, Louise told me how scared she was. Most of our alcohol had been drunk at the midsummer party. There was only a half-bottle of brandy left. She poured herself a glass.

'I'm not making it up, you know,' she said. 'I really am scared.'

She sat under the kitchen table and would groan as another thunder-clap shook the house. When the storm had passed over, she crept out with her glass empty and her face white.

'I don't know why,' she said, 'but nothing scares me as much as the lightning flashes and then the thunderclaps they fling at me.'

'Did Caravaggio paint thunderstorms?' I wondered.

'I'm sure he was just as scared as I am. He often painted things he was scared of. But not thunderstorms, as far as I know.'

The rain that followed the thunderstorms freshened up the soil and also the people who lived here. When the storm had passed over, I went to check on Harriet. She was lying with her head high in an attempt to ease the pains coming from her spine. I sat on the chair by the side of her bed and took hold of her thin, cold hand.

'Is it still raining?'

'It's stopped now. Lots of angry little becks are running down from the rocks into the sea.'

'Is there a rainbow?'

'Not this evening.'

She lay quietly for a while.

'I haven't seen the cat,' she said.

'She's vanished. We've looked for her, but haven't found her.'

'Then she'd dead. Cats hide themselves away when they sense that their time is up. Some tribesmen do the same thing. The rest of us just hang on for as long as we can while others sit around and wait for us to die at long last.'

'I'm not waiting for that.'

'Of course you are. You have no choice. And waiting makes people impatient.'

She was speaking in short bursts, as if she were climbing up an endless staircase and had to keep stopping to get her breath back. She reached tentatively for her glass of water. I handed it to her, and supported her head while she drank.

'I'm grateful to you for taking me in,' she said. 'I could have frozen to death out there on the ice. You could have pretended not to see me.'

'The fact that I abandoned you once doesn't necessarily mean that I'd do the same again.'

She shook her head, almost imperceptibly.

'You have told so many lies, but you haven't even learned how to do it properly. Most of what you say has to be true. Otherwise the lies don't work. You know as well as I do that you could have abandoned me again. Have you left anybody else besides me?'

I thought it over. I wanted to answer truthfully.

'One,' I said. 'Just one other person.'

'What was her name?'

'Not a woman. I'm referring to myself.'

She shook her head slowly.

'There's no point in going on and on about what has passed. Our lives turned out as they did, it's all behind us. I shall soon be dead. You'll carry on living for a while longer, but then you'll be gone too. And all traces will fade away.'

She reached out her hand and took hold of my wrist. I could feel her rapid pulse.

'I want to tell you something you've probably gathered already. I've never loved another man in my life as much as I've loved you. The reason why I tracked you down was to find my way back to that love. And to give you the daughter I robbed you of. But most of all, I wanted to die close to the man I've always loved. I must also say that I've never hated anybody as much as I've hated you. But hatred hurts, and I've more than enough pain to be going on with. Love gives a feeling of freshness, of peace, possibly even a feeling of security which makes facing up to death not quite so frightening as it would otherwise be. Don't respond to anything I've just said. Just believe me. And ask Louise to come. I think I've wet myself.'

I fetched Louise, who was sitting on the steps outside the front door.

'It's beautiful here,' she said. 'Almost like the depths of the forest.'

'I'm scared stiff of big forests,' I said. 'I've always been frightened of getting lost if I strayed too far away from the path.'

'What you're scared of is yourself. Nothing else. The same applies to me. And Harriet. And the lovely little Andrea. Caravaggio as well. We are scared of ourselves, and what we see of ourselves in others.'

She went to change Harriet's pad. I sat down on the bench under the apple tree, next to the dog's grave. In the far distance I could hear the dull thudding from the engines of a large ship. Had the navy already started their regular autumn manoeuvres?

Harriet had said that she'd never loved anybody as much as she'd loved me. I felt touched. I hadn't expected that. I was beginning to appreciate just what I had done.

I abandoned her because I was afraid of being abandoned myself. My fear of tying myself down, and of feelings that were so strong that I couldn't control them, resulted in my always drawing back. I didn't know why that should be. But I knew that I wasn't the only one. I lived in a world where many other men were just as afraid as I was.

I had tried to see myself in my father. But his fear had been different. He had never hesitated to show the love he felt for my mother and for me, despite the fact that my mother wasn't easy to live with.

I have to come to grips with this, I told myself. Before I die, I must know why I've lived. I have some time left – I must make the most of it.

I felt very tired. The door to Harriet's room was ajar. I went upstairs. When I'd gone to bed, I left the light on. The wall behind the bed had always been decorated with sea charts my grandfather had found washed up on the shore. They were water-damaged but you could make out they depicted Scapa Flow in the Orkney Isles, where the British fleet was based during the First World War. I had often followed the narrow channels surrounding Pentland Firth, and imagined the British ships sitting there, terrified of the periscopes of German U-boats.

I fell asleep with the light still on. At two o'clock I was woken up by Harriet's screams. I stuck my fingers in my ears and waited for the painkillers to kick in.

We were living in my house in a silence that could be shattered at any moment by a roar of intense pain. I found myself thinking more and more frequently that I hoped Harriet would die soon. For all our sakes.

The heatwave lasted until 24 July. I noted in my logbook that there was a north-easterly wind and the temperature had started to fall. Troughs of low pressure queuing up over the North Sea brought changeable weather. In the early hours of 27 July, a northerly gale raged over the archipelago. A few tiles next to the chimney were ripped off the roof and smashed on the ground below; I managed to climb up on to the roof and replace them with spares that had been stored in a shed since the barn was demolished in the late 1960s.

Harriet's condition grew worse. Now that the weather had started to deteriorate she was awake for only short periods of every day. Louise and I shared the chores, but Louise washed her mother and changed her pads for which I was grateful.

Autumn was creeping up on us. The nights were getting longer, the sun was losing its strength. Louise and I prepared ourselves for the fact that Harriet could die at any moment. When she was conscious, we would both sit by her bed. Louise wanted her to see the pair of us together. Harriet didn't say much. She might ask about the time, and if it would soon be time to eat. She was becoming more and more confused. Sometimes she thought she was in the caravan in the forest, at other times she was convinced she was in her flat in Stockholm. She was not aware of being on the island, in a room with an anthill. Nor did she seem to be aware that she was dying. When she did wake up, it seemed to be the most natural thing in the world. She would drink a little water, perhaps swallow a few spoonfuls of soup, then drop off to sleep again. The skin on her face was now stretched so tightly round her cranium that I was afraid it might split and expose her skull. Death is ugly, I thought. There was now almost nothing left of the beautiful Harriet. She was a wax-coloured skeleton under a blanket, nothing more.

One evening at the beginning of August, we sat down on the bench under the apple tree. We were wearing warm jackets, and Louise had one of my old woolly hats on her head.

'What are we going to do when she dies?' I wondered. 'You must have thought about it. Do you know if she has any specific wishes?'

'She wants to be cremated. She sent me a brochure from an undertaker's some months ago. I may still have it, or I might have thrown it away. She had marked the cheapest coffin and an urn on special offer.'

'Does she have any sepulchral rights?'

Louise frowned. 'What does that mean?'

'Is there a family grave? Where are her parents buried? There's usually a link to a particular town or village. In the old days, they used to talk about sepulchral rights.'

'Her relatives are spread all over the country. I've never heard her mention visiting her parents' grave. She's never expressed any specific wish regarding her own grave. Although she did say quite firmly that she didn't want a headstone. I think she would prefer to have her ashes cast into the wind. You can actually do that nowadays.'

'You need permission,' I said. 'Jansson has told me about old fishermen who wanted their ashes scattered over the ancient herring grounds.'

We sat without speaking, thinking about what to do. I had bought a plot in a cemetery: there was probably no reason why Harriet shouldn't lie by my side.

Louise put her hand on my arm.

'We don't really need to ask permission, in fact,' she said. 'Harriet could be one of those people in this country who don't exist.'

'Everybody has a personal identity number,' I said. 'We're not allowed to disappear when it suits us.'

'There are always ways of getting round things,' Louise said. 'She will die here, in your house. We'll burn her just like they cremate dead people in India. Then we'll scatter her ashes over the water. I'll terminate the contract on her flat in Stockholm and empty it. I won't supply a forwarding address. She'll no longer collect her pension. I'll tell the home health-care people that she's died. That's all they want to know. Somebody might start to wonder, I expect, but I shall say that I haven't had any contact with my mother for several months. And she left here after a short visit.'

'Did she?'

'Who do you think is going to ask Jansson or Hans Lundman about where she's gone to?'

'But that's just it. Where has she gone to? Who took her to the mainland?'

'You did. A week ago. Nobody knows she's still here.'

It began to dawn on me that Louise was serious. We would take care of the funeral ourselves. Nothing more was said. I got very little sleep that night. But I eventually began to think it might just be possible.

Two days later, when Louise and I were having dinner, she suddenly put down her spoon.

'The fire,' she said. 'Now I know how we can light it without giving anybody cause to wonder what's happening.'

I listened to her suggestion. It seemed repulsive at first, but then I began to see that it was a beautiful idea.

The moon vanished. Darkness enveloped the archipelago. The last sailing boats of summer headed back to their home ports. The navy conducted manoeuvres in the southern archipelago. We occasionally heard the rumble of distant gunfire. Harriet was now sleeping more or less round the clock. We took it in turns to stay with her. While I was a medical student, I had sometimes earned some extra pocket money by doing night duty. I could still remember the first time I watched a person die. It happened without any movement, in complete silence. The big leap was so tiny. In a split second the living person joined the dead.

I recall thinking: This person who is now dead is someone who has in reality never existed. Death wipes out everything that has lived. Death leaves no trace, apart from the things I've always found so difficult to cope with. Love, emotions. I ran away from Harriet because she came too close to me. And now she will soon be gone.

Louise was often upset during those last days. I experienced an increasing fear that I myself was approaching the end. I was afraid of the humiliations in store for me, and hoped I would be granted a gentle death, one which spared me from having to lie in bed for a long time before I reached the final shore.

Harriet died at dawn, shortly after six o'clock, on 22 August. She had endured a restless night – the painkillers didn't seem to help. I was making coffee when Louise came into the kitchen. She stood beside me and waited until I had counted up to seventeen.

'Mum's dead.'

We went to the room where Harriet lay. I felt for a pulse, and used my stethoscope to search for any sign of heart activity. She really was in fact dead. We sat down on her bed. Louise was crying quietly, almost silently. All I felt was a worryingly selfish feeling of relief that it wasn't me lying there dead.

We sat there without speaking for about ten minutes, I listened again for any heart activity – nothing. Then I draped one of Grandma's embroidered towels over Harriet's face.

We drank coffee, which was still hot. At seven o'clock I telephoned the coastguard. Hans Lundman answered.

'Many thanks for your hospitality,' he said. 'I should have rung earlier.'

'Thank you for coming.'

'How's your daughter?'

'She's fine.'

'And Harriet?'

'She's left.'

'Andrea is staggering around on those beautiful light blue shoes. Pass that message on to Louise.'

'I'll do that. I'm ringing to say that I'm intending to have a big bonfire today, to get rid of lots of rubbish. Just in case anybody contacts you to report a fire on the island.'

'The drought's over for this year.'

'But somebody might think that my house is on fire.'

'Thank you for letting us know.'

I went outside down to the boathouse and collected the tarpaulin I'd prepared as a shroud. There wasn't a breath of wind. It was overcast. I had soaked it in tar. I spread it out on the ground. Louise had dressed Harriet in the pretty dress she'd worn at the midsummer party. She'd combed her hair and made up her face. She was still crying, just as quietly as before. We stood for a while, embracing each other.

'I shall miss her,' said Louise. 'I've been so angry with her for so many years. But now I realise that she has opened up a gap inside me. It will remain open, and blow sorrow over me for the rest of my life.'

I checked Harriet's heartbeat one last time. Her skin had already started to assume the yellow colour that follows death.

We waited another hour. Then we carried her outside and rolled her up in the tarpaulin. I had already prepared the bonfire that would transform her body to ashes, and placed at the ready a drum of petrol.

We lifted her up into my old boat, and balanced it on top of the pyre. I soaked the body and the worn-out hull with petrol.

'We'd better make ourselves scarce,' I said. 'The petrol will flare up. If you stand too near, you could catch fire.'

We stepped back. I looked at Louise. She wasn't crying any more. She gave me the nod. I lit a ball of cotton waste soaked in tar, and threw it on to the boat.

The fire flared up with a roar. There was a crackling and sizzling from the tar-soaked tarpaulin. Louise took hold of my hand. So my old boat had come in useful after all. It was the vehicle in which I sent Harriet into another world, in which neither she nor I believed, but which we no doubt hoped for, deep down.

While the fire was burning away, I went to fetch an old metal saw from the boathouse. I started to cut Harriet's walker. It soon became obvious that the saw wasn't up to the job. I put the walker in the dinghy, together with a couple of herring-net sinkers and chains. I rowed out towards Norrudden, and heaved the walker with its chains and sinkers overboard. Nobody ever fished or anchored there. So nothing would ever hook it and reel it back to the surface.

The smoke from the fire was billowing up into the sky. I rowed back to the island, and remembered that before long Jansson would arrive. Louise was squatting down, watching the boat burn.

'I wish I could play an instrument,' she said. 'Shall I tell you what kind of music Mum liked to listen to?'

'Wasn't her favourite music traditional jazz? We used to go to jazz concerts in the Old Town in Stockholm when we were going out together.'

'You're wrong. Her favourite was "Sail Along Silvery Moon". A sentimental song from the fifties. She always wanted to hear it. I wish I could have played it for her now. As a sort of recessional hymn.'

'I've no idea how it goes.'

She hummed the tune hesitantly. Maybe I'd heard it before, but not played by a jazz band.

'I'll have a word with Jansson,' I said. 'Harriet left the island yesterday.

I took her to the mainland. Some relative or other came to collect her. He was taking her to hospital in Stockholm.'

'Tell him she sent him her greetings,' said Louise. 'If you do that, he won't wonder why she left.'

Jansson was on time, as usual. He had with him a surveyor who had official business to carry out on Bredholmen. We nodded in acknow-ledgement. Jansson stepped on to the jetty and stared up at the bonfire.

'I phoned Lundman,' he said. 'I thought your house was on fire.'

'I'm burning my old boat,' I said. 'I couldn't make it seaworthy again. No point in having it lying around for another winter.'

'You did the right thing,' said Jansson. 'Old boats refuse to die unless you cut them up or burn them.'

'Harriet has left,' I said. 'I took her to the mainland yesterday. She sent her greetings.'

'That was kind of her,' said Jansson. 'Pass on greetings from me. I liked her very much. A fine old lady. I hope she was feeling a bit better?'

'She had to go to the hospital. I don't think she was any better. But she sent her greetings anyway.'

Jansson was pleased to hear Harriet had thought of him. He continued on his way with the surveyor. A few drops of rain started to fall, but it soon cleared up. I went back to the fire. The stern of the boat had collapsed. It was no longer possible to distinguish between charred wood and the tarpaulin with its contents. There was no smell of burnt flesh from the fire. Louise had sat down on a stone. I suddenly thought of Sima, and wondered if my island somehow attracted death to it. Sima had cut herself here, Harriet had come here to die. My dog was dead and my cat had vanished.

I felt despondent. Was there anything about me that I could be proud of? I wasn't an evil person. I wasn't violent, I didn't commit crimes. But I had let people down. My mother had been in a care home alone for nineteen years after my father died, and I only ever visited her once. So much time had passed before I got round to seeing her that she no longer knew who I was. She thought I was her brother, who had died over fifty years before. I made no attempt to convince her that I was me. I just sat there and went along with her. Yes, of course I'm your brother who died such a long time ago. Then I deserted her. I never went back. I wasn't even present at her funeral. I left everything in the hands of the undertaker, and paid the bill when it eventually came. Apart from the vicar and the organist, the only other person present in the chapel was a representative of the undertaker's.

I didn't go because nobody could force me to do so. I realised now that I had despised my mother. Somehow or other, I had also despised Harriet.

Perhaps I felt nothing but contempt for everybody. Most of all, though, I despised myself. I was still a small, scared creature who had seen in his father the brutal hell that ageing could bring.

The day passed, just as slowly as the clouds drifted across the sky. When the fire began to die down, I added branches that I had first soaked in petrol. It took time to cremate a human being in the open.

Dusk fell and still the fire burned. I added more wood, raked around in the ashes. Louise came out with a tray of food. We drank what was left of the brandy, and were soon drunk. We cried and laughed with sorrow, but also with relief at the fact that Harriet's pain was at an end. Louise was closer to me now. We sat there in the grass, leaning against each other, watching the smoke from the funeral pyre drifting up into the darkness.

'I'm going to stay on this island for ever,' said Louise.

'Well, stay until tomorrow at least,' I said.

Only when dawn broke did I allow the fire to die down.

Louise had curled up on the grass and gone to sleep. I spread my jacket over her. She woke up when I poured buckets of seawater over the embers. There was nothing left now of Harriet or the old boat. Louise scrutinised the ashes I raked out.

'Nothing,' she said. 'Not long ago she was a living person. Now there is nothing left of her.'

'I thought maybe we could take the rowing boat and scatter the ashes over the water.'

'No,' she said. 'I can't do that. I want her ashes at least to be preserved.'

'I don't have an urn.'

'A jar, a tin can, anything. I want her ashes to remain here. We can bury them next to the dog.'

Louise headed for the boathouse. I felt uneasy about creating a graveyard under the apple tree. I could hear rattling noises coming from the boathouse. Louise appeared, carrying a tin that had once contained grease for the engine of my grandfather's old boat. I had cleaned it up and used it for nails and screws. Now it was empty. She blew out the dust, put it down next to the pile of ashes and started filling it, using her hands. I went to the boathouse and fetched a spade. Then I dug a hole next to the dog. We placed the tin at the bottom of it, and filled it in. Louise went off among the rocks, and after a while returned with a large stone on which sediment had created something that looked like a cross. She placed it on top of the hole.

It had been a tough day. We were both tired. We had dinner in silence. Louise retired to her caravan for the night. I searched around in the bathroom cupboard and found a sleeping pill. I fell asleep almost immediately, and slept for nine hours. I couldn't remember when that had last happened.

Louise was sitting at the kitchen table when I came downstairs the next morning.

'I'm off,' she said. 'Today. The sea's calm. Can you take me to the harbour?'

I sat down at the table. I wasn't at all prepared for her intention of leaving so soon.

'Where are you going?'

'I have several things to see to.'

'But surely Harriet's flat can wait for a few days?'

'That's not where I'm going. Do you remember the cave with the wall paintings that have been attacked by mould?'

'I thought you were going to bombard politicians with letters about that?'

She shook her head.

'Letters don't do any good. I have to take some different action.'

'What?'

'I don't know. Then I shall go and look at some Caravaggio paint-ings. I have money now. Harriet left nearly two hundred thousand kronor. She used to give me some money now and then. And I've always been thrifty anyway. No doubt you wondered about all the money you found when you went snooping around in my caravan. Thrift, nothing more. I haven't only spent my life writing letters. I've occasionally had a paid job like everybody else. And I've never thrown money about.'

'How long are you going to be away? If you're not going to come back, I'd like you to take your caravan with you. This island is no place for it.'

'Why do you get so angry?'

'I'm sad about you clearing off like this, and I don't think you'll come back again.'

'I'm not like you. I'll be back. If you won't allow my caravan to remain here, I suggest you burn that up as well. I'm going to pack now. I'll be ready to leave in an hour. Are you going to take me, or aren't you?'

It was dead calm, and the sea like a millpond, when I took her to the mainland. The outboard motor started coughing soon after we left the jetty, but then recovered and behaved normally for the rest of the trip. Louise sat smiling in the bows. I regretted my outburst.

A taxi was waiting in the harbour. All she had with her was a rucksack.

'I'll phone you,' she said. 'And send cards.'

'How can I get in touch with you?'

'You have my mobile number. I can't promise it will be switched on all the time, though. But I promise to send a card to Andrea.'

'Send one to Jansson as well. He'll be thrilled to bits.'

She squatted down so as to be closer to me.

'Keep my caravan neat and tidy until I get back. Clean it regularly. And keep brushing my red shoes – I've left them behind.'

She caressed my forehead then got into the taxi, which set off up the hill. I took my petrol can to the chandler's to have it topped up. The harbour was almost deserted. All the summer boats had left.

When I got back home I took a walk round the island, looking for the cat again. But I didn't find it. I was now more alone on the island than ever before.

Several weeks passed. Everything went back to the way it had been before. Jansson would arrive in his boat, occasionally bringing a letter from Agnes, but I didn't hear a word from Louise. I phoned her several times, but there was never an answer. The messages I left became like short, breathless diary notes about the weather, the wind and the cat who remained missing.

Presumably the cat must have been taken by a fox, which must have swum away from the island.

I grew increasingly restless. I had the feeling that I wouldn't be able to stick it out for much longer. I would have to leave. But I didn't know where to go.

October arrived with a storm from the north-east. Still no word from Louise. Agnes had also stopped writing. I spent most of the time sitting at the kitchen table, staring out of the window. The landscape out there seemed to be becoming petrified. It felt as if my whole house was slowly being swallowed up by a gigantic anthill that grew silently higher and higher.

Autumn became harsher. I waited.

WINTER SOLSTICE

CHAPTER 1

The first frost came in the early hours of 3 October.

I checked through my old logbooks and found that there had never been minus temperatures as early as this all the years I had lived on the island. I was still waiting to hear from Louise. I hadn't even received a postcard from her.

That evening the telephone rang. A woman asked if I was Fredrik Welin. I thought I recognised both her dialect and her voice, but when she said her name was Anna Ledin, it said nothing to me.

'I'm a police officer,' she said. 'We've met.'

Then the penny dropped. The woman lying dead on her kitchen floor. Anna Ledin was the young police officer with her hair in a ponytail under the cap of her uniform.

'I'm ringing in connection with the dog,' she said. 'Sara Larsson's spaniel. We couldn't find anybody to adopt her, so I took her in. She's a lovely dog. But unfortunately I've met a man who's allergic to dogs, and I don't want to have her put down. Then I thought about you. I had made a note of your name and address, and so I'm phoning to ask if you could possibly consider taking the dog on. You must be fond of animals, otherwise you wouldn't have stopped as you did when you saw her by the roadside.'

I had no doubt when I replied.

'My dog died just a few weeks ago. I can take on the spaniel. How will you get her here?'

'I can bring her in my car. I discovered that Sara Larsson used to call her Ruby. Not exactly a common name for a dog, but I continued using it. She's five years old.'

'When would you come?'

'At the end of next week.'

I didn't dare to try and ferry the dog over in my own boat as it was so small. I made an arrangement with Jansson. He asked me all kinds

213

of questions about what kind of dog it was, but all I told him was that I'd inherited it.

Anna Ledin arrived at the harbour with the dog at three in the afternoon on 12 October. She looked quite different when she wasn't in uniform.

'I live on an island,' I said. 'She'll be the sole ruler.'

She gave me the lead. Ruby sat down beside me.

'I'll leave right away if you don't mind,' she said. 'I'll get upset if I don't. Can I ring now and then to see how she's getting on?'

'Of course you can.'

She got back into her car and drove off. Ruby didn't start pulling at the lead in an attempt to run after the car. Nor did she hesitate to jump down into Jansson's boat.

We sailed back home through the dark waters of the bay. Cold winds were blowing up from the Gulf of Finland.

When we had landed and Jansson had left again, I let the dog loose. She disappeared among the rocks. Half an hour later she returned. Already the loneliness felt less oppressive.

It was now well and truly autumn.

I still wondered what was happening to me. And why I'd heard nothing from Louise.

CHAPTER 2

I didn't like the dog's name.

It didn't seem that she thought much of it either, as she seldom responded when I called her.

No dog can possibly be called Ruby. Why had Sara Larsson given her that name? One day, when Anna Ledin rang to ask about how the dog was doing, I asked her if she knew how the dog had acquired the name.

I was surprised by her answer.

'Rumour has it that when she was a young woman, Sara Larsson had a job as a cleaner on a cargo ship that often visited Antwerp. She was paid off there and got a job as a cleaner in a diamond-cutting workshop. Maybe it was her memories of her time there that inspired her to give the dog that name.'

'Diamond would have been better.'

I suddenly heard lots of banging and clattering in the background. I could hear distant voices yelling and screeching, and somebody apparently banging away at a sheet of metal.

'I'll have to hang up now.'

'Where are you?'

'We're about to arrest a man who's running amok in a scrapyard.'

The line went dead. I tried to conjure up the scene: delicate little Anna Ledin with her pistol drawn, and her ponytail jumping up and down behind her uniform cap. I certainly wouldn't have liked to be on the receiving end of whatever she dealt out in circumstances like that.

I decided to call the dog Carra. Obviously, part of the reason for that name was a reference to my daughter, who never kept in touch, but was interested in Caravaggio. Why does anybody give a pet a particular name? I don't know.

It took several weeks of intensive training to persuade her to forget all about Ruby, and instead become a Carra who would run up somewhat reluctantly when I called for her.

October passed by with changeable weather – some days very hot, a sort of delayed Indian summer, but others characterised by bitterly cold winds from the north-east. Sometimes when I looked out to sea I could make out the flocks of migrating birds gathering, before suddenly setting off on their long journey southwards.

There is a special sort of melancholy that accompanies a flock of migrating birds. Just as we might feel being uplifted when they return. Autumn is closing its books. Winter is approaching.

Every morning when I woke up, I could feel the aches and pains of approaching old age manifesting themselves. I sometimes worried that I could no longer pee as forcefully as I used to be capable of. There was something especially humiliating about the thought of imminent death because I could no longer pee properly. I found it hard to accept that the ancient Greek philosophers or the Roman emperors died of prostate cancer. Even if they did, of course.

I thought about my life and at times made an insignificant entry in my logbook. I stopped making a note of wind directions, or how hot or cold it was. Instead I made up the winds and the temperatures. On 27 October I made a note for future consumption that my island had been hit by a typhoon, and the temperature in the evening was plus thirty-seven degrees.

I sat in my various thinking places. My island was so marvellously formed that it was always possible to find a spot sheltered from the wind. I found such a place, sat down there and wondered why I had chosen to become the person I was. Some of the basic reasons were not difficult to find, of course. I had taken the opportunity to flee the poverty-stricken environment in which I grew up, where the daily reminder of the vulnerable life led by my father gave me sufficient strength to make the effort. But I also realised that I could be grateful for the fact that I had been born into an age in which such flights were possible. A time when the downtrodden children of humble waiters could go to university and even become doctors. But why had I become a person who always looked for hiding places instead of companionship? Why had I never wanted to have children? Why had I lived a life like a fox, with so many alternative exits from its lair?

That confounded amputation that I didn't want to accept responsibility for was just one of those things. I wasn't the only orthopaedic surgeon in the world to whom something like that had happened.

There were moments that autumn when I was struck by panic. It led to endless nights stuck in front of the mind-numbing television, and sleepless nights during which I both regretted and cursed the life I had lived.

In the end a letter from Louise finally arrived as a sort of lifebuoy for a drowning man. She wrote that she had spent many days emptying Harriet's flat. She enclosed several photographs she had found among Harriet's papers, snaps she had known nothing about. I sat staring in astonishment at the pictures of Harriet and me taken almost forty years ago. I recognised her, but was put out, almost shaken by what I looked like. In one of the photographs, taken somewhere in Stockholm in 1966, I had a beard. It was the only time in my life that I'd grown a beard, and I'd forgotten all about it. I didn't know who'd taken the picture, but was intrigued by a man who was standing in the background, swigging vodka straight from the bottle.

I remembered him. But where had Harriet and I been going to? Where were we coming from? Who had taken the picture?

I thumbed through the photographs and was fascinated. I had locked my memories away in a room that I had sealed, and then thrown the keys away.

Louise wrote that she had rediscovered a lot of her childhood during the days and weeks she had spent emptying the flat.

'What struck me most of all was that I had never really known anything about my mother,' she wrote. 'I came across letters, and occasional diaries that she'd never kept going for very long, containing her thoughts and experiences that she had never passed on to me. For instance, she'd dreamt about becoming a pilot. She always used to tell me that she was scared to death whenever she was forced to take a flight. She wanted to create a rose garden on Gotland, and she'd tried to write a book but never been able to finish it. But what affected me most was that I discovered she had told me so many untruths. Memories from my childhood kept cropping up, and over and over again I realised that she had lied to me. Once she told me that one of her friends was ill and she had to visit her. I remember crying and begging her to stay, but she said her friend was so seriously ill that she really had to go and see her. I now realise that, in fact, she went to France with a man she hoped to marry – but he soon disappeared out of her life. I won't bore you with all the details of what I've discovered here, but one lesson I've learned is that it's essential to sort out your belongings and throw away a lot of stuff before you die. I'm surprised that Harriet didn't do that when she'd known for such a long time that she was going to die. She must have known what I would find. The only explanation I can think of is that maybe she wanted me to realise that, in so many ways, she wasn't who I thought she was. Was it important to her that I should know the truth, despite the fact I would see that she had lied to me so often? I still can't make up my mind if I ought to admire her for that, or despise her. Anyway, the flat is now empty. I shall post her key through the letter box and go away. I'm going to visit those caves, and will take Caravaggio with me.'

The last sentence of her letter confused me. How could she take Caravaggio with her? Was there something between the lines that I couldn't detect?

She had not given me an address to which I could send a reply. Nevertheless, I sat down that very same night and started writing. I commented on the photographs, told her about how my own memory had let me down, and also told her about my walks with Carra around the rocks. I tried to explain how I was feeling my way through my past life, a bit like battling through thick, thorny bushes that were almost impassable.

Most of all I wrote that I missed her. I repeated that over and over again in my letter.

I sealed the envelope, stuck a stamp on it and wrote her name. Then I left it on the desk, hoping that she might one day send an address.

I had only just gone to bed that night when the telephone rang. I was frightened, my heart was pounding. Anybody ringing me at that time of night couldn't have good news for me. I went down to the kitchen and picked up the receiver. Carra was lying on the floor, watching me.

'It's Agnes. I hope I didn't wake you.'

'It doesn't matter. I sleep too much anyway.'

'I'm coming now.'

'Are you standing on the quay?'

'Not yet. I'm intending to come out tomorrow, if it's all right with you.'

'Of course it's all right with me.'

'Can you collect me?'

I listened to the wind and the sound of the breakers crashing on to the rocks at Norrudden.

'It's too windy for my little boat. I'll arrange for somebody else to fetch you. What time will you be on the quay?'

'Around midday.'

She ended the call just as abruptly as she'd started it. She sounded worried and evidently wanted to see me urgently.

I started cleaning at five the next morning. I changed the bag in my ancient vacuum cleaner and realised that my house was covered in a layer of dust. It took me three hours to get it anywhere close to clean. After my usual bath, I dried myself, turned up the heating and sat down at the kitchen table to phone Jansson. But I rang the coastguard instead. Hans Lundman was out, doing something with one of the boats, but rang me back a quarter of an hour later. I asked if he could pick somebody up from the harbour and ferry them out to me.

'I know you're not allowed to take passengers,' I said.

'We can always send out a patrol past your island,' he said. 'What's his name?'

'It's a she. You can't miss her. She only has one arm.'

Hans and I were very similar in some ways. Unlike Jansson we were people who concealed their curiosity and didn't ask unnecessary questions. But I doubt if Hans poked around in his assistants' papers and belongings.

I took Carra with me and went for a walk round the island. It was 1 November, the sea was growing greyer and greyer, and the last of the leaves had fallen from the trees. I was really looking forward to Agnes's visit. I realised to my surprise that I was excited at the prospect. I imagined her standing naked on my kitchen floor, with her one arm. I sat down on the bench by the jetty, and dreamt up an impossible love story. I didn't know what Agnes wanted. But I didn't think she was coming here to tell me about her love for me.

I carried Sima's sword and her suitcase from the boathouse to the kitchen. Agnes hadn't said anything about staying overnight, but I made up the bed in the room with the anthill.

I had decided to relocate the anthill to old pasture, which was now overgrown and covered in shrubs. But, like so much else, I'd never got round to it.

At about eleven I shaved but couldn't settle on what to wear. I was as nervous as a teenager at the thought of her visit. I eventually decided on my usual clothes: dark trousers, cut-down wellington boots and a thick jumper that was threadbare in places. Earlier in the morning I'd already taken a chicken out of the freezer.

I went around dusting in places that I'd already dusted. At noon I put on my jacket and walked down to the jetty to wait. It wasn't a post day, so Jansson wouldn't turn up to disturb us. Carra was sitting on the edge of the jetty and seemed to sense that something was in the offing.

Hans Lundman came into sight in the big coastguard patrol boat. I could hear the powerful engine from a long way away. As the boat glided into the inlet I stood up. It was quite shallow by the jetty, so Hans merely nudged against it with the boat's bows. Agnes emerged from the wheelhouse with a rucksack slung over her shoulder. Hans was in uniform. He was leaning over the rail.

'Many thanks for your help,' I said.

'I was passing by anyway. We're heading for Gotland to look for a sailing boat with nobody on board.'

We stood and watched the big patrol boat reverse out of the inlet. Agnes's hair was fluttering in the wind. I had an almost irresistible desire to kiss her.

'It's beautiful here,' she said. 'I've tried to imagine your island. I can see now how wrong I was.'

'What did you imagine?'

'Lots of trees. Not just rocks and the open sea.'

The dog came towards us. Agnes looked at me in surprise.

'I thought you said your dog was dead?'

'I've got another one. From a police officer. It's a long story. The dog's name is Carra.'

We walked up towards the house. I wanted to carry her rucksack, but she shook her head. When we entered the kitchen, the first things she saw were Sima's sword and her suitcase. She sat down on a chair.

'Was it here it happened? I want you to tell me. Right away. Now.'

I gave her all the details that I would never be able to forget. Her eyes glazed over. I was giving a funeral oration, not a clinical description of a suicide that reached its climax in a hospital bed. When I'd finished she said nothing, just went through the contents of the suitcase.

'Why did she do it?' I asked. 'Something must have happened when she came here, surely? I'd never have imagined that she would try to take her own life.'

'Perhaps she found a sense of security here. Something she hadn't expected.'

'Security? But she took her own life.'

'Maybe her situation was so desperate that she needed to feel secure in order to take the final step and commit suicide? Perhaps she found that feeling of security here in your house? She really did try to kill herself. She didn't want to live. She didn't cut herself as a cry for help. She did it because she no longer wanted to hear her own screams echoing inside herself.'

Agnes wondered if she could stay until the following day. I showed her the bed in the room where the ants lived. She burst out laughing. Of course she could sleep there. I said there would be chicken for dinner. Agnes went to the bathroom. When she reappeared she had changed her clothes and put her hair up.

She asked me to show her round the island. Carra came with us. I told her about the time when she had come running after the car, and then led us to Sara Larsson's dead body. Agnes seemed disturbed by my talking. She just wanted to enjoy what she could see. It was a chilly autumn day, the thin covering of heather was crouching down in an attempt to avoid the harsh wind. The sea was blue grey, old seaweed was draped over the rocks, smelling putrid. Occasional birds flew out of rocky crevices as we approached, and soared on the upwinds that always form at the edge of the cliffs. We came to Norrudden where the bare rocks of Sillhällarna can just be seen breaking the surface of the water before the open sea begins. I stood slightly to one side, watching her. She was captivated by the view. She turned to look at me, and then shouted into the wind.

'There's one thing I shall never forgive you for. I can't applaud any more. It's natural to feel jubilation inside and then give expression to it by clapping the palms of your hands together.'

There was nothing I could say, of course. She knew that. She came up to me and turned her back on the wind.

'I used to do that even when I was a child.'

'Do what?'

'Applaud when I went out into the countryside and saw something beautiful. Why should you clap only when you're sitting in a concert hall, or listening to somebody talking? Why can't you stand out here on the cliffs and applaud? I don't think I've ever seen anything more beautiful than this. I envy you, living out here.'

'I can applaud for you,' I said.

She nodded and led me to the highest and outermost rock. She shouted bravo, and I applauded. It was an odd experience.

We continued our walk and came to the caravan behind the boat-house.

'No car,' she said. 'No car, no road, but a caravan. And a pair of beautiful red high-heeled shoes.'

The door was open. I'd placed a piece of wood there to prevent it from closing. The shoes were standing there, shining. We sat down on the bench out of the wind. I told her about my daughter and Harriet's death. I avoided mentioning how I had abandoned her. But Agnes wasn't listening to me, her mind was elsewhere, and I realised that she had come here for a reason. It wasn't only that she wanted to see my kitchen, and collect the sword and the suitcase.

'It's cold,' she said. 'Perhaps one-armed people feel the cold more than others. Their blood is forced to take alternative routes.'

We went back to the house and sat down in the kitchen. I lit a candle and placed it on the table. Dusk had already started to fall.

'They're taking my house away from me,' she said out of the blue. 'I've been renting it, never been able to afford to buy it. Now the owners are taking it away from me. I can't continue with my work without a house. Obviously, I could get a job at another institution; but I don't want to do that.'

'Who owns the house?'

'Two rich sisters who live in Lausanne. They've made a fortune from selling dodgy health products – they're always being forced to withdraw adverts for them because they contain nothing but worthless powder mixed with various vitamins. But no sooner does that happen than they resurface with the same things in different packs and with a different name. The house belonged to their brother who died with no other heirs apart from his sisters. They're going to take it away from me because the local residents have complained about my girls. They'll take the house away, and the girls will be taken away from me as well. We live in a country where people think that anybody who is a bit different from them should be isolated in the depths of the forest or on an island like this one. I needed to get away in order to do some thinking. Perhaps in order to mourn. Perhaps to dream that I had enough money to buy the house. But I haven't.'

'If I had enough money, I'd buy it for you.'

'I haven't come here to ask for that.'

She stood up.

'I'm going out,' she said. 'I'll walk round the island one more time before it gets too dark.'

'Take the dog with you,' I said. 'If you shout for her, she'll follow you. She's good to be with. She never barks. I'll make the dinner while you're out.'

I stood in the front doorway and watched them walk off over the rocks. Carra sometimes looked round to see if I was calling her back. I started to make dinner while imagining that I had kissed Agnes.

It occurred to me that I had stopped daydreaming years ago. I'd had just as few daydreams as I'd had erotic experiences.

Agnes seemed brighter when she came back.

'I have to confess,' she said before she had even taken off her jacket and sat down, 'that I couldn't resist trying on your daughter's shoes. They fitted me perfectly.'

'I can't give you them, even if I'd like to.'

'My girls would beat me up if I appeared wearing high-heeled shoes.'

She curled up on the kitchen sofa and watched me laying the table and serving the meal. I tried talking but she was reluctant to answer. We finished the meal in silence. It was dark outside. We had coffee and I started a fire in the old wood-burning stove that I only ever use in the depths of winter. I was a bit affected by the wine we'd drunk with the dinner. Agnes didn't seem to be a hundred per cent sober either. When I'd filled our coffee cups, she broke her silence. She started talking about her life, and the difficult years.

'I was searching for some kind of consolation,' she said. 'I tried drinking, but it only made me sick. So I started smoking dope. That only made me sleepy and ill and increased my angst about what had happened. I tried to find lovers who could handle the fact that I had only one arm, and I took up sport and became quite a good but increasingly less enthusiastic middle-distance runner. I wrote poetry, and sent letters to various newspapers, and I studied the history of amputation. I applied for jobs as a presenter on all the Swedish television channels, and a few foreign ones as well. But nowhere could I find any consolation, the ability to wake up in the morning without thinking about the intolerable tragedy that had taken place. Obviously I tried using an artificial arm, but I could never make it work properly. The only other possibility open to me was to try God. I searched for consolation on bended knee. I read the Bible, I made an effort to acquaint myself with the Koran, I went to Pentecostal camp meetings and even tried a dangerous sect called the Word of Life. I dabbled in various other sects, and considered taking the veil. I went to Spain that autumn and walked the long route to Santiago de Compostela. I followed the route the pilgrims had taken, and placed a heavy stone in my rucksack as one is supposed to do, ready to throw it away once I had found a solution to my problems. I used a chunk of limestone weighing four kilos, carted it with me the whole way and didn't take it out until I'd reached my destination. All the time I hoped that God would appear to me and speak to me. But He spoke too softly. I never heard His voice. Somebody was always shouting in the background drowning Him out.'

'Who?'

'The Devil. He was yelling at me. I learned that God whispers, but the Devil shouts. There was no place for me in the battle. When I closed the church door behind me, there was nothing else left. But I realised eventually that this emptiness was a sort of consolation in itself. And so I made up my mind to devote myself to those less fortunate than myself. That's how I came into contact with the girls that nobody else wanted to know about.'

We drank what was left of the wine and became even more drunk. I found it hard to concentrate on what she was saying because I wanted to take hold of her, make love to her. We became giggly after all the wine, and she told stories of the reactions caused by her stump of an arm.

'I sometimes pretended it had been gobbled by a shark off the Australian coast. At other times it was a lion that bit it off on the

Botswana savannah. I was always careful to be convincing and people seemed to believe what I told them. When I was talking to people I didn't like for one reason or another, I used to go out of my way to describe really nasty, blood-soaked incidents. I might say that some-body had sawn it off with a power saw, or I might have got my arm caught in a machine that sliced it off inch by inch. I once even managed to make a big, strong man faint! The only thing I've never claimed is that it ended up with cannibals who cut it up and ate it.'

We went outside to look at the stars and listen to the sea. I tried to make sure I was so close to her that I kept rubbing up against her. She didn't seem to notice.

'There's a kind of music you can never hear,' she said.

'Silence sings. You can hear it.'

'That's not what I mean. I'm imagining the existence of music that we can't hear with our ears. At some point a long way into the future, when our hearing has become more refined and new instruments have been invented, we shall be able to appreciate and play that music.'

'It's a beautiful thought.'

'I think I know what it will sound like. Like human voices when they are at their absolute purest. People who sing with no trace of fear.'

We went back inside. I was so drunk by now that I couldn't walk straight. When we were back in the kitchen, I poured out some brandy. Agnes put her hand over her glass and stood up.

'I need to get some sleep,' she said. 'It's been a remarkable evening. I'm not so depressed now as I was when I came.'

'I want you to stay here,' I said. 'I want you to sleep with me in my room.'

I stood up and put my arms round her. She didn't resist when I drew her close to me. It was only when I tried to kiss her that she started struggling. She told me to stop it, but for me there was no stop-ping any longer. We stood there in the middle of the floor, pushing and pulling at each other. She yelled at me to let go of her, but I pushed her against the table and we slid down on to the floor. She managed to work her hand free and scratched my face. She kicked me so hard in the stomach that I lost my breath. I couldn't speak, I searched for a way out that didn't exist, and she was holding one of my kitchen knives as a weapon.

I eventually struggled to my feet and sat down on a chair.

'Why did you do that?'

'I'm sorry. I didn't mean to. The loneliness I have to put up with here is driving me mad.'

'I don't believe you. You may well be lonely, I don't know anything about that. But that's not why you attacked me.'

'I hope you can forget it. Please forgive me. I shouldn't drink alcohol.'

She put the knife down and stood in front of me. I could see her anger and her disappointment. There was nothing I could say. Suddenly I felt truly ashamed.

Agnes sat down in the corner of the kitchen sofa. She had turned her face away and was gazing out of the dark window.

'I know it's unforgivable. I regret what happened, and wish I could undo it.'

'I don't know what you imagine you were doing. If I could, I'd leave here immediately. But it's the middle of the night, it's not possible. I'll stay here until tomorrow.'

She stood up and left the kitchen. I heard her jamming the door handle with a chair. I went outside and tried to look in through the window. She had switched the light off. Perhaps she sensed that I was standing outside, trying to see her. The dog appeared out of the darkness. I kicked her away. I couldn't cope with her just now.

I lay awake all night. At six o'clock I went down to the kitchen and listened outside her door. I couldn't make out if she was asleep or awake. At a quarter to seven she opened the door and stepped out into the kitchen, rucksack in hand.

'How do I get away from here?'

'It's dead calm at the moment. If you wait until it gets light I can take you to the mainland.'

She started to pull on her boots.

'I want to say something about what happened last night.'

She raised her hand immediately.

'There's nothing else to say. You are not the person I thought you were. I want to get away from here as quickly as possible. I'll wait down by the jetty until it gets light.'

'Can't you just hear what I have to say at least?'

226

She didn't answer but hung her rucksack over one shoulder, picked up Sima's suitcase and sword, and vanished into the darkness.

It would soon be light. I could see that she wouldn't listen if I went down to the jetty and tried to talk to her. Instead I sat down at the table and wrote her a letter.

'We could move your girls here. Leave the sisters and the village in peace. I have planning permission to build a house on the stone foundation of the old barn. The boathouse has a room attached that can be insulated and furbished. There are empty rooms here in the main house. If I can accommodate one caravan here, there's no reason why I shouldn't have another. There's plenty of room on the island.'

I walked down to the jetty. She stood up and clambered down into the boat. I handed her the letter without saying anything. She hesitated before accepting it and stuffing it into her rucksack.

The sea was as smooth as a mirror. The sound of my outboard motor ripped open the stillness, scattering a few ducks, which flew out to sea. Agnes sat in the bows with her back towards me.

I hove to by the lowest part of the quay and switched off the engine.

'A bus goes from here,' I said. 'The timetable is over there, on the wall.'

She climbed up on to the quay without saying a word.

I returned home and went to sleep. In the afternoon I dug out my old Rembrandt puzzle and tipped the pieces on to the kitchen table. I started from the beginning, knowing I would never finish it.

A north-easterly gale blew up the day after Agnes had left. I was woken up by a window banging. I got dressed and went to check that the boat was securely moored. It was high tide and waves were breaking over the jetty and slapping against the boathouse wall. I used a spare piece of rope to doubly secure the stern. The wind was howling around the walls. When I was a boy the howling gales used to scare me stiff. Inside the boathouse during a storm the noise is tremendous: like the voices of people screaming and fighting. Nowadays, strong winds make me feel secure. As I stood there I felt beyond the reach of anything and everything.

The storm continued to rage for two more days. On the second day, Jansson managed to reach the island. For once, he was late. When he finally arrived, he told me his engine had cut out between Röholmen and Höga Skärsnäset.

'I've never had any problems before,' he said. 'Typical that the engine should conk out in weather like this. I had to throw out a drag anchor, but even so I very nearly ended up on the rocks at Röholmen. If I hadn't managed to get the engine going again, I'd have been wrecked.'

I'd never seen him so shaken. For once, I asked him to sit down on the bench while I took his blood pressure. It was a bit on the high side, but nothing like what one might have expected, given what he had been through.

He got back into his boat, which was bumping and scraping against the jetty.

'I haven't got any post for you,' he said, 'but Hans Lundman asked me to bring you a newspaper.'

'Why?'

'He didn't say. It's yesterday's.'

He handed me one of the national dailies.

'Didn't he say anything at all?'

'He just asked me to give it to you. He doesn't waste words, as you know.'

I pushed out the bows as Jansson started reversing into the teeth of the gale. As he turned he very nearly ran aground in the shallows. But at the last moment he squeezed enough power from the engine to get out of the inlet.

As I left the jetty I saw something white floating just off the shore where the caravan was standing. I went to investigate and saw that it was a dead swan. Its long neck slithered like a snake through the seaweed. I went back to the boathouse, placed the newspaper on the tool bench and put on a pair of working gloves. Then I picked the swan up. A nylon fishing line had dug deeply into its body and become entangled in its feathers. It had starved to death as it hadn't been able to search for food. I carried it up and laid it on the rocks. It wouldn't be long before the crows and seagulls ate the carcass. Carra came to investigate and sniffed at the bird.

'It's not for you,' I said. 'It's for other hungry creatures.'

I suddenly grew tired at the prospect of the jigsaw puzzle, walked to the boathouse and fetched one of my flat-fish nets, sat down in the kitchen and started to repair it. My grandfather had taught me how to splice ropes and mend nets. The techniques and know-how were still there in my fingers. I sat there working until dusk fell. In my head I conducted a conversation with Agnes about what had happened. Reconciliation is possible in the world of the imagination.

That evening I ate the rest of the chicken. When I'd finished, I lay down on the kitchen sofa and listened to the wind. I was just going to switch the radio on and listen to the news when I remembered the newspaper Jansson had brought with him. I took my torch and walked down to the boathouse to get it.

Hans Lundman rarely did anything without a specific purpose. I sat at the kitchen table and started to scrutinise the newspaper to find what he wanted me to see.

I found it on page four, in the section devoted to foreign news. It was a picture from a top-level meeting for leading European statesmen – presidents and prime ministers. They had lined up to be photographed. In the foreground was a naked woman holding up a placard. Underneath the picture were a few words about the embarrassing incident. A woman wearing a black raincoat had succeeded in entering the press conference, using a forged pass. Once inside, she had taken off the raincoat and lifted up her placard. Several security guards had quickly hustled her away. I looked at the picture, and felt a pain in my stomach. I had a magnifying glass in one of the kitchen drawers. I examined the picture again. I became increasingly worried as my suspicions were slowly confirmed. The woman was Louise. It was her face, even if it was slightly averted. There she was, making a triumphant and challenging gesture.

The text on the placard was about the cave, where the ancient wall paintings were being ruined by mould.

Lundman was a sharp-eyed individual. He had recognised her. Perhaps she had told him at the midsummer party about the cave.

I took a kitchen towel and wiped away the sweat from under my shirt. My hands were shaking.

I went out into the wind, shouted for the dog and sat down on Grandma's bench in the darkness.

I smiled. Louise was out there somewhere, smiling back. I had a daughter I could really be proud of.

CHAPTER 3

One day in the middle of November, the letter I had been waiting for arrived at last. By then the whole of the archipelago knew that I had a daughter who had caused a stir in front of Europe's leading statesmen.

No doubt Jansson had contributed to spreading and exaggerating the rumours: Louise was alleged to have performed a striptease and wiggled back and forth in erotic fashion before being led away. Then she had viciously attacked the security guards, bitten one of them, apparently splashing Tony Blair's shoes with blood. And then she was eventually sentenced to prison.

Louise was in Amsterdam. She wrote that she was staying at a little hotel near the railway station and the city's red-light district. She was resting, and every day visited an exhibition at which the works of Rembrandt and Caravaggio were compared. She had plenty of money. Lots of anonymous people had given her gifts, and the press had paid vast sums for her story. She had not been punished at all for her demonstration. The letter ended with the news that she intended coming back to the island at the beginning of December.

Her letter contained an address. I wrote a reply without further ado, and handed it to Jansson together with the letter I had been unable to send earlier. He was curious when he saw her name, but he said nothing.

The letter from Louise gave me the courage to write to Agnes. There had been no word from her after her visit. I was ashamed. For the first time in my life I was unable to find an excuse for my behaviour. I simply couldn't brush aside what had happened that evening.

I wrote to her and begged for forgiveness. Nothing else, only that. A letter containing nineteen words, each one carefully chosen.

She rang two days later. I had dozed off in front of the television and thought it must be Louise when I picked up the phone.

'I received your letter. My first thought was to throw it away without opening it, but I did read it. I accept your apology. Assuming you really mean what you wrote?'

'Every word.'

'You probably don't realise what I'm referring to. I'm asking about what you wrote regarding your island and my girls.'

'Of course you can all come here.'

I could hear her breathing.

'Come here,' I said.

'Not now. Not yet. I have to think things over.'

I replaced the receiver. I felt the same kind of exhilaration as I'd felt after reading Louise's letter. I went out and looked up at the stars, and thought that it would soon be a year since Harriet had appeared on the ice, and my life had begun to change.

At the end of November the coast was hit by another severe storm. The easterly gales reached a peak on the second evening. I walked down to the jetty and noticed that the caravan was swaying alarmingly in the wind. With the aid of a few rocks normally used for anchoring the nets, and some logs that had been washed ashore, I managed to stabilise it. I had already installed an old electric fire in the caravan, to make sure it was warm and cosy when Louise got back.

When the storm had passed I went for a walk round the island. Easterly gales can sometimes result in a lot of driftwood littering the shore. This time I didn't find any big logs, but an old wheelhouse from a fishing boat had been blown on to the rocks. At first I thought it was the top of a vessel that had been sunk by the storm, but when I investigated more closely I found that it was this battered old wheelhouse. After a moment's thought I went back home and rang Hans Lundman. After all, what I had found might have been the remains of a sunken fishing boat. An hour later, I had the coastguard on my island. We managed to drag it ashore and secure it with a rope. Hans confirmed that it was not a new wreck and that there had been no reports of missing fishing boats.

'It has probably been standing on land somewhere, but the gales have blown it into the sea. It's rotten through and through, and can hardly have been attached to a boat for many years. I should think it's thirty or forty years old.'

'What shall I do with it?' I wondered.

'If you'd had any little children, they could have used it as a play-house. As it is, I don't think it's of much use for anything apart from firewood.'

I told him that Louise was on her way home.

'Incidentally, I've never been able to understand how you noticed her in the newspaper. It was such a poor picture. But even so, you could see that it was her?'

'Who knows how and why we see what we see? Andrea misses her. Not a day passes without her putting on those shoes and asking after Louise. I often think about her.'

'Have you shown Andrea the picture in the newspaper?'

Hans looked at me in surprise.

'Of course I have.'

'It's hardly a suitable picture for children to look at. I mean, she was naked.'

'So what? It's bad for children not to be told the truth. Children suffer from being told lies, just as we adults do.'

He went back to his boat, and engaged reverse gear. I fetched an axe and started chopping up the old wheelhouse I'd been lumbered with. It was quite easy as the wood was so rotten.

I had just finished and straightened up my back when I felt a stinging pain in my chest. Since I had often diagnosed coronary spasms during my life, I realised what the pain indicated. I sat down on a large stone, breathed deeply, unbuttoned my shirt and waited. After about ten minutes the pain went away. I waited for another ten minutes before walking very slowly back to the house. It was eleven in the morning. I phoned Jansson. I was lucky: it was his day off. I said nothing about my pain, simply asked him to come and fetch me.

'This is a very quick decision,' he said.

'What do you mean by that?'

'You normally ask me to pick you up a week in advance.'

'Can you collect me or can't you?'

'I'll be with you in half an hour.'

When we had reached the mainland, I told him I'd probably be returning the same day, but I couldn't say precisely when. Jansson was ready to burst with curiosity, but I said nothing.

When I arrived at the health centre I explained what had happened. After a short wait I underwent the usual examinations and an ECG, and spoke to a doctor. He was probably one of the locums who nowadays move from one surgery to another because they can never manage to attract a doctor on a long-term basis. He gave me the medication and instructions I had expected, as well as a referral to the hospital for a more detailed examination.

I called Jansson from reception and asked him to collect me. Then I bought two bottles of brandy and returned to the harbour.

It was only later, when I was back on the island, that the fear kicked in. Death had taken hold of me and tested my powers of resistance. I drank a glass of brandy. Then I went out and stood on the edge of a cliff and yelled out over the sea. I was shouting out my fear, disguised as anger.

The dog sat some distance away, watching me.

I didn't want to be alone any longer. I didn't want to be like one of the rocks on my island, observing in silence the inevitable passage of days and time.

I had a hospital appointment for 3 December. There was nothing fundamentally wrong with my heart. Medication, exercise and an appropriate diet should keep me going for a few years yet. The doctor was about my own age. I told him the facts, admitted that I had once been a doctor, but had then gone to look after an old fisherman's cottage on an offshore island. He displayed a friendly lack of interest, and as I was about to leave, told me that I had a slight touch of angina.

Louise arrived on 7 December. The temperature had dropped, and at last autumn was giving way to winter. Rainwater in the rock crevices began to freeze at night. She had phoned from Copenhagen and asked me to arrange for Jansson to pick her up from the harbour. The connection was cut before I had time to ask her any more questions. I switched on the electric fire in her caravan, polished her shoes, cleaned up, and remade the bed with fresh sheets.

I hadn't had a recurrence of the heart pains. I wrote a letter to Agnes and asked if she had finished thinking about my suggestion. She sent a picture postcard with her answer. The picture was of a painting by Van Gogh, and the text comprised two words: 'Not yet.'

I wondered what Jansson had thought when he read the card.

Louise stepped on to the jetty carrying nothing but the rucksack she had taken with her in the first place. I had expected her to be struggling with large suitcases containing all the things she'd collected during her expedition. If anything, the rucksack seemed to be emptier now than it was when she set out.

Jansson appeared unwilling to leave. I gave him an envelope containing the fee he'd asked for his ferrying activities, and thanked him for his help. Louise greeted the dog. They seemed to get along like a house on fire. I opened the door to the caravan, which had become nicely warm. She deposited her rucksack there, then accompanied me to the house. Before we went in, she paused for a moment by the little mound marking the grave under the apple tree.

I grilled some cod for dinner. She ate it as if she hadn't eaten in weeks. I thought she looked paler and perhaps even thinner than she was before. She told me that the plan to gatecrash the summit meeting had been hatched before she left the island.

'I sat down on the bench by the boathouse and worked it all out,' she said. 'I didn't feel there was any point in writing the letters any more. It had dawned on me that they might never have been meaningful for anybody apart from myself. So I chose another way.'

'Why didn't you say anything?'

'I don't know you well enough. You might have tried to stop me.'

'Why should I have done that?'

'Harriet always tried to make me do what she wanted. Why should you be any different?'

I tried to ask her more questions about her expedition, but she shook her head. She was tired, needed to get some rest.

At midnight I saw her to the caravan. The thermometer outside the kitchen window was showing plus one degree. She shuddered in the cold and took my arm. That was something she had never done before.

'I miss the forest,' she said. 'I miss my friends. But this is where the caravan is now. It was kind of you to heat it up for me. I shall sleep like a log, and dream about all the paintings I've seen during the past few months.'

'I've brushed your red shoes for you,' I said.

She kissed me on the cheek before vanishing into the caravan.

Louise kept out of the way for the first few days after her return. She came to eat when I shouted for her, but she didn't say much and could become irritated if I asked too many questions. One evening I went down to the caravan and peered in through the window. She was sitting at the table, writing something in a notebook. She suddenly turned to look at the window. I crouched down and held my breath. She didn't open the door. I hoped she hadn't seen me.

While I was waiting for her to become accessible again, I went for long walks with the dog every day, to keep myself in shape. The sea was blue-grey, fewer and fewer seabirds were around. The archipelago was withdrawing into its winter shell.

One evening I wrote what was to be my new will. Everything I owned would go to Louise, of course. What I had promised Agnes kept gnawing away at me, but I did what I've always done in such circumstances: pushed nagging worries to the back of my mind and convinced myself that things would sort themselves out if and when they came to a head.

In the morning of the eighth day after her return Louise was sitting at the kitchen table when I came downstairs at about seven.

'I'm not tired any more,' she said. 'I can face other people now.'

'Agnes,' I said. 'I've invited her to come here. Maybe you can convince her that she ought to move here with her girls.'

Louise looked at me in surprise, as if she hadn't heard properly what I'd said. I had no idea of the danger that was creeping up on me. I told her about Agnes's visit, but needless to say didn't mention what had happened between us.

'I thought I'd let Agnes and her girls come to live here when they no longer have the house where she runs her care home.'

'You mean you're going to give the island away?'

'There's only me and the dog here. Why shouldn't this island start being useful again?'

Louise was furious and slammed her fist down on the coffee cup on the table in front of her. Bits of cup and saucer splattered into the wall.

'So you're going to give away my inheritance? Aren't you going to leave me anything when you've gone? – I haven't had a thing from you so far.'

I found myself stuttering when I replied.

'I'm not giving her anything. I'm just letting her stay here.'

Louise stared at me long and hard. It felt as if I was confronted by a snake. Then she stood up so violently that her chair fell over. She took her jacket and stormed out, leaving the door open. I waited and waited for her to come back.

I closed the door. At last I understood what it had meant to her that day when I turned up outside her caravan. I had given her a possession. She had even given up the forest for the sea, for me and my island. Now she thought I was taking all that away from her.

I had no heirs apart from Louise. I had once entertained the thought of giving the island to some archipelago trust or other. But that would only mean that, at some point in the future, greedy politicians would sit on my jetty and enjoy the sea. Now everything had changed. If I fell down and died that very night, Louise would be my direct heir. What she did with it then would be entirely up to her.

She didn't appear at all the next day. In the evening, I went to the caravan. Louise was lying on the bed. Her eyes were open. I hesitated before knocking on the door.

'Go away!'

Her voice was shrill and tense.

'We must talk this over.'

'I'm getting out of here.'

'Nobody will ever take this island away from you. You don't need to worry.'

'Go away!'

'Open the door!'

I tried the handle. It was unlocked. But before I could move she had flung it open. It smashed into my face. My bottom lip split open, I fell over backwards and hit my head on a stone. Before I could get up she had thrown herself on top of me and was hitting me about the face with what remained of an old cork lifebelt that had been lying nearby.

'Stop it. I'm bleeding.'

'You're not bleeding enough.'

I grabbed hold of the lifebelt and wrenched it from her grasp. Then she started punching me. I eventually managed to wriggle out of her clutches.

We faced each other, panting.

'Come up to the house. We have to talk.'

'You look awful. I didn't mean to hit you so hard.'

I went back to the kitchen, and was shocked when I saw my face covered in blood. I could see that not only my lip but also my right eyebrow had been split open. She knocked me out, I thought. She'd made good use of her boxing skills, even if it was the caravan door that had landed the most telling blow.

I wiped my face and wrapped some ice cubes in a towel which I pressed on my mouth and eyebrow. It was some time before I heard her footsteps approaching the door.

'How bad is it?'

'I might live. But new rumours will spread around the islands. As if it weren't enough that my daughter undresses in front of the men who rule the world, she comes back home and behaves like a violent madwoman towards her ageing father. You're a boxer, you must know what can happen to a face.'

'I didn't mean it.'

'Of course you did. I think what you really wanted to do was to kill me before I could write a will that disinherited you.'

'I got upset.'

'You don't need to explain. But you're wrong. All I want to do is to help Agnes and her girls. Neither she nor I can say how long the arrangement will last. That's all. Nothing else. No promises, no gifts.'

'I thought you were going to abandon me again.'

'I've never abandoned you. I abandoned Harriet. I knew nothing about you. If I had done, everything might have been different.'

I emptied the towel and refilled it with new ice cubes. My eye was by now almost totally closed.

Things had started to calm down. We sat around the kitchen table. My face hurt. I stretched out my hand and placed it on her arm.

'I'm not going to take anything away from you. This island is yours. If you don't want her to come here with her girls while they are looking for another home, then of course I shall tell her that it's not possible.'

'I'm sorry you look like you do. But earlier this evening, that's what I looked like inside.'

'Let's go to bed,' I said. 'We'll go to bed, and tomorrow I'll wake up with a perfect set of bruises.'

I stood up and went to my room. I heard Louise closing the front door behind her.

We had been on the edge of a storm. It had passed by very close to us, but hadn't enveloped us completely.

Something is happening, I thought, almost cheerfully. Nothing earth-shattering, but still. We're on our way to something new and unknown.

The December days were chilly and oppressive. On 12 December I noted down that it snowed for a while in the afternoon – nothing much, and it didn't last long. The clouds were motionless in the sky.

My bruised face was painful and took a long time to heal. Jansson's jaw dropped when I met him on the jetty the morning after the fight. Louise came to say hello. She was smiling. I tried to smile but failed. Jansson couldn't resist asking what had happened.

'A meteor,' I said. 'A falling star.'

Louise was still smiling. Jansson asked no more questions.

I wrote to Agnes and invited her to the island to meet my daughter. She replied after a few days and said it was too soon. Nor had she decided whether or not to accept my offer. She knew that she would have to make her mind up before long, but hadn't done so yet. I could tell that she was still offended, and disappointed. Perhaps I felt relieved that she wasn't going to come. I was still not convinced that Louise wouldn't launch another attack on me.

Every day I walked round the island with the dog. I listened to my heart. I had got into the habit of taking my pulse and my blood pressure once a day. Every other day after resting, every other day without resting. My heart was beating calmly and steadily inside my ribcage. My stead-fast companion on my journey through life, to whom I had not devoted many thoughts. I went round and round the island, tried not to lose my footing on the slippery rocks, and occasionally paused to contemplate the horizon. If I had to leave this island, what I would miss most would be the rocks, the cliffs and the horizon. This inland sea, which was slowly turning into a bog, didn't always produce pleasant smells. It was an unwashed sea that sometimes smelled of a hangover. But the horizon was pure and clean, as were the rocks and the cliffs.

As I made my daily round of the island in my cut-down wellington boots, it was as if I were carrying my heart in my hand. Even if all my readings were good, I sometimes felt panicky. I'm dying, my heart will stop beating a few seconds from now. It's all over, death will strike before I'm prepared for it.

I thought I ought to talk to Louise about my fears. But I said nothing.

The winter solstice was approaching. One day Louise sat down on a chair in the middle of my kitchen and asked me to hold a mirror. Then she used a pair of kitchen scissors to cut off her long hair, dyed what remained red, and laughed contentedly a couple of hours later when she examined the result. Her face became clearer. It was as if a flower bed had been cleared of weeds.

The following day it was my turn. I'd tried to resist, but she was adamant. I sat on a kitchen chair and she cut my hair. Her fingers seemed dainty round the unwieldy scissors. She said my hair was beginning to thin out on top, and also suggested that a moustache would suit me.

'I love having you here,' I said. 'Somehow or other everything has become clearer. Before, when I looked at my face in a mirror, I was never quite sure what I saw. Now I know that it's me, and not just any old face that happenes to be going past.'

She didn't answer. But I could feel a drop on my cheek. She was crying. I started crying too. She continued cutting my hair. We both wept silently, she behind the chair with the scissors, me with a towel round my neck. We never said a word about it afterwards, perhaps becuase we were embarrassed; or because it wasn't necessary.

That is a trait I share with my daughter. We don't speak unnecessarily. People who live on small islands are seldom loud or loquacious. The horizon is far too big for that.

One day Louise tied a red silk ribbon round Carra's neck. Carra didn't seem to think much of it, but didn't try to remove it.

The evening before the winter solstice, I sat up late at the kitchen table and thumbed through my logbook. Then I made a note.

'Calm sea, no wind, minus one degree. Carra is wearing a red ribbon. Louise and I are very close.'

I thought about Harriet. It was as if she were just behind me, reading what I wrote.

CHAPTER 4

Louise and I decided we would celebrate the fact that the days were now going to start getting longer. Louise would do the cooking. In the afternoon I took my medication, then lay down on the kitchen sofa to rest.

It was half a year since we had all sat round in the brief darkness of the midsummer night. This evening, as we marked the winter solstice, Harriet would not be with us. I missed her in a way I had never done before. Even if she was dead, she seemed closer to me than ever.

I remained on the sofa for a long time before forcing myself up to have a shave and get changed. I put on a suit I had hardly ever worn. Despite being badly out of practice, I knotted a tie. The face I saw in the mirror terrified me. I had become old. I grimaced and went back down to the kitchen. It was starting to get dark in preparation for what would be the longest night of the year. The thermometer showed minus two. I took a blanket and sat down on the bench under the apple tree. The air was fresh, chilly, unusually salty. In the distance birds were crying, increasingly fewer of them, and less often.

I must have fallen asleep on the bench. When I woke up it was pitch dark. I was cold. Six o'clock – I had been asleep for nearly two hours. Louise was at the cooker when I came in. She smiled.

'You were sleeping like an old lady,' she said. 'I didn't want to disturb you.'

'I am an old lady,' I said. 'My grandmother used to sit on that bench. She was always freezing cold except when she dreamt of gently soughing birch trees. I think I might be changing into her.'

It was warm in the kitchen. The hob and the oven were on; the windows had misted over.

Strange and wondrous perfumes began to fill the kitchen. Louise held out a spoon with a taster from a steaming casserole.

The taste was somehow reminiscent of old timber warmed by the sun. Sweet but sour, with a touch of bitterness – foreign, enticing.

'I mix different worlds into my stews,' said Louise. 'When we eat, we pay visits to people in parts of the world we have never visited. Smells are our oldest memories. The wood that our forefathers made fires with, when they sheltered in caves and painted all those bloodthirsty animals on the walls – it must have smelled just the same as firewood does today. We don't know what they thought, but we know what their wood smelled like.'

'There's always something constant in things that change,' I said. 'There's always an old lady feeling cold on a bench under an apple tree.'

Louise was humming away as she prepared the meal.

'You travel around the world on your own,' I said. 'But up there in the forest you are surrounded by men.'

'There are lots of nice blokes around. But it's not so easy to find a real man.'

I was going to continue, but she raised her hand in warning.

'Not now, not later, not any time. If I ever have something to tell you, I'll do so. Of course there are men in my life. But they are my business, not yours. I don't think we should share everything. If you dig too deeply into others, you can risk destroying a beautiful friendship.'

I handed Louise some pot-holders. They had always been in the kitchen – I remembered them being there when I was a child. She took a large pot out of the oven and removed the lid. There was a strong smell of pepper and lemon.

'This should burn your throat. No food is properly cooked if it doesn't make you sweat when you eat it. Food lacking in secrets fills your belly with disappointment.'

I watched her stirring the pot and mixing the contents.

'Women stir,' she said. 'Men hit and cut and tear and stab. Women stir and stir and stir.'

I went out for a walk before we started eating. When I got as far as the jetty, I suddenly felt that burning pain in my chest. It hurt so much that I nearly collapsed in a heap.

I shouted for Louise. When she got to me, I thought I would pass out. She squatted down in front of me.

'What's the matter?'

'My heart. Vascular spasms.'

'Are you going to die?'

I roared through my pain: 'No, I'm not going to die. There's a jar of blue tablets at the side of my bed.'

She hurried away. When she came back, she gave me a tablet and a glass of water. I held her hand. Then the pain eased. I was soaked in sweat, and shivering.

'Has it gone?'

'Yes, it's gone. It's not dangerous, But it's painful.'

'Perhaps you ought to go to bed.'

'No way.'

We walked slowly back to the house.

'Fetch a few cushions from the kitchen sofa,' I said. 'We can sit out here on the steps for a while.'

She came back with the cushions. We sat close together, and she laid her head on my shoulder.

'I don't want you to die. I couldn't cope with seeing both my parents dying so soon, one after the other.'

'I'm not going to die.'

'Think of Agnes and her girls.'

'I don't know if that's going to happen.'

'They'll come.'

I squeezed her hand. My heart had calmed down again now. But the pain was lurking in the background. I had received my second warning. I could live for quite a few years yet. But the end would come eventually, even for me.

Our celebratory dinner came to an early close. We ate, but didn't stay on at the table. I went up to my room, and took the telephone with me. There was a socket in my bedroom that I never normally used. My grandfather had installed it towards the end of his life when he and Grandma had started to become ill. He wanted to be able to phone somebody if one or other of them became so frail that the stairs down to the ground floor would be too long and too steep. I wondered if I should ring, but couldn't make up my mind. Eventually, at about one in the morning, I dialled the number – irrespective of the late hour. She answered more or less straight away.

'I apologise for waking you up.'

'You didn't wake me up.'

'I just want to know if you've made up your mind yet.'

'The girls and I have discussed it. They shout no as soon as the word island is mentioned. They can't imagine living without roads or asphalt or cars. They feel scared.'

'They'll have to choose between you and asphalt.'

'I think I'm more important.'

'Does that mean you'll be coming?'

'I'm not going to answer that at this time of night.'

'Can I think what I think I can think?'

'Yes. But we must stop now. It's late.'

There was a click and the line went dead. I stretched out on the bed. She hadn't said as much in so many words, but I was beginning to realise that she would come after all.

I lay awake for a long time. A year ago I used to lie here and think that nothing more was ever going to happen. Now I had a daughter and angina. Life had taken a new direction.

It was seven when I awoke. Louise was already up.

'I need to go to the forest for a while,' she said. 'But can I leave you on your own? Can you promise me that you're not going to die?'

'When will you be back?' I asked. 'If you're not away for too long, I shall keep going.'

'I'll be back in the spring. But I won't be up in the forest all that time. I have somewhere else to go to.'

'Where?'

'I met a man after the police had released me. He wanted to talk about the caves and the mouldy wall paintings. We ended up talking about other things as well.'

I wanted to ask who he was. But she put her finger to her lips.

'Not now.'

The following day Jansson came to fetch her.

'I drink a lot of water,' he shouted as the boat started to reverse away from the jetty. 'But nevertheless I'm always thirsty.'

'We can talk about that later,' I shouted back to him.

I returned to the house and collected my binoculars. I watched them until the boat disappeared in the fog behind Höga Siskäret.

Now it was only the dog and me. My friend Carra.

'It's going to be just as quiet here as it always is,' I said to the dog. 'For the time being, at least. Then we shall build a new house. And girls will play music far too loudly, they'll be shouting and swearing and sometimes they will hate this island. But they're coming here, and we shall have to put up with them, A bunch of wild horses is on its way here.'

Carra was still wearing the red ribbon. I untied it and let it float away on the wind.

Late that evening I sat in front of the television with the sound turned down. I listened to my heart.

I had my logbook in my hand. I noted down that the winter solstice had now passed.

Then I stood up, put the logbook away and took out a new one.

The following day I would write something completely different. Perhaps a letter to Harriet, even though it was far too late to send it now.

CHAPTER 5

The sea in the archipelago didn't freeze over that winter.

Thick ice formed on the mainland, and in sheltered bays and creeks of the islands, but the navigable channels out to the open sea remained open. There was a period of extreme cold and persistent northerly winds at the end of February, but Jansson was never forced to use his hydrocopter and I didn't need to put my hands over my ears on post days.

One day, just after the extreme cold had given way to milder weather, something happened that I shall never forget. I had just removed the thin layer of ice over my bathing hole and was having my bath when I noticed the dog lying on the jetty and chewing away at something that looked like the skeleton of a bird. As dogs can wound their throats on bones, I went over to her and removed it. I threw it into the frozen seaweed, and urged the dog to come back to the house with me.

It was only later, when I had got dressed and warmed up again, that I remembered the bone. I still don't know what made me do it, but I put my boots on, walked down to the jetty and located it. The piece of bone was certainly not from a bird. I sat down on the jetty and examined it closely. Could it be from a mink, or a hare?

Then I realised what it was. It couldn't be anything else. It was a piece of bone from my old cat. I put it on the jetty at my feet, and wondered how the dog had found it. I felt cold and sad inside at the way in which my cat had turned up again in the end.

I took the dog with me for a walk round the island. There was no sign of any more bones, no tracks. Only that little fragment of bone, as if the cat had sent me a greeting in order to assure me that I no longer needed to wonder or to search. She was dead, and had been dead for a long time.

I wrote about the bone in my logbook. A mere three words.

'Dog, bone, sorrow.'

I buried the fragment of bone next to Harriet's and my old dog's graves. It was a post day, so I went to the jetty. Jansson came chugging up on time as usual. He hove to by the jetty and announced that he felt very tired and was permanently thirsty. He had started to get cramp in his calves during the night.

'It could be diabetes,' I told him. 'The symptoms suggest that possibility. I can't examine you here, but you ought to go to the health centre.'

'Is it fatal?' he asked, looking worried.

'Not necessarily. It can be treated.'

I couldn't help feeling a little bit pleased that Jansson, who had always been as fit as a fiddle, had now revealed the first crack in his armour, and was in the same boat as the rest of us.

He thought about what I'd said for a few seconds, then bent down and picked up a large parcel from the deck. He handed it to me.

'But I haven't ordered anything.'

'I know nothing about it. But it's addressed to you. And it's prepaid, so there are no postal charges.'

I took the parcel. My name was clearly written in beautifully formed letters. There were no sender's details.

Jansson backed away from the jetty. Even if he had in fact got diabetes, he would live for many years yet. He would certainly outlive me and my dicky heart.

I sat down in the kitchen and opened the parcel. It contained a pair of black shoes with a hint of violet. Giaconelli had enclosed a card on which he'd written that it had brought him great pleasure to demonstrate his great respect for my feet.

I changed my socks, put on the shoes and walked round the kitchen. They fitted just as well as he had promised they would. The dog was lying on the threshold, watching me with interest. I went into the other room and showed the ants my new shoes.

I couldn't remember the last time I had felt so happy.

Every day for the rest of the winter I would walk around the kitchen several times in Giaconelli's shoes. I never wore them outside the house, and always put them back in their box.

Spring arrived at the beginning of April. There was still a little ice in my inlet, but it wouldn't be long before it thawed.

Early one morning I started to remove the anthill.

It was time to do it now. It couldn't wait any longer.

I used my spade to remove it bit by bit, carefully placing it into the wheelbarrow.

The spade suddenly hit against something solid. When I had cleared away the conifer needles and ants, I saw that it was one of Harriet's empty bottles. There was something inside it. I removed the cork and found a rolled-up photograph of Harriet and me, taken shortly before I abandoned her, when we were young.

There was water in the background. We could have been standing by Riddarfjärden in Stockholm. A breeze was ruffling Harriet's hair. I was smiling straight at the camera. I recalled that we had asked a passing stranger to take the picture.

I turned it over. Harriet had drawn a map. It was of my island. Underneath it she had written: 'We came this far.'

I sat in the kitchen for a long time, gazing at that photograph.

Then I continued transporting the ants to their new life. It was all finished by the evening. The anthill had been moved.

I walked round my island. Flocks of migrating birds were flying over the sea.

It was just as Harriet had written. We had come this far.

No further than that. But this far.

New from

Henning Mankell

THE MAN FROM BEIJING

The internationally acclaimed author of the Kurt Wallander mysteries now gives us an electrifying global thriller, a tale of revenge that stretches from modern-day Sweden to China, Zimbabwe, and 150 years into the American past.

"This is hands down the best thriller I've read in five years. Grade: A" —Tina Jordan, *Entertainment Weekly*

"It cements Mankell's reputation as Sweden's greatest living mystery writer." —*Los Angeles Times*

Available in hardcover from Knopf
$25.95 • 384 pages • 978-0-307-27186-0

Please visit TheManFromBeijing.com